CLUELESS & CO.

CLUELESS & CO.

Pratik Basu

Published 2006 by

Rupa & Co

7/16, Ansari Road, Daryaganj,
New Delhi 110 002

Sales Centres:
Allahabad Bangalore Chandigarh Chennai
Hyderabad Jaipur Kathmandu
Kolkata Mumbai Pune

Typeset in 12 GoudyOldStyle by
Nikita Overseas Pvt. Ltd.
1410 Chiranjiv Tower
43 Nehru Place
New Delhi 110 019

Printed in India by
Rekha Printers Pvt Ltd.
A-102/1 Okhla Industrial Area, Phase-II
New Delhi-110 020

This book, firstly and mostly, is dedicated to Samita, my long-enduring friend, long-suffering wife and part-time therapist who put her own talent and career on almost permanent hold to unearth and nurture mine. If, at the end of it, she has little to show for her endeavour, it isn't because of any lack of effort on her part but because, as usual, I fooled her into believing that I had an aptitude and promise where none, possibly, existed.

This first novel is also dedicated to my wonderful parents— Colonel (Dr) Arun Kumar Basu and Runu Basu—who, if they were alive today, as I sorely wish they were, would have wondered what this new affliction was that had struck their wayward first-born and hoped, probably, that its effects would be less debilitating than the momentary madness that had made him forsake Gray's *Anatomy* for Kotler's *Marketing*.

Finally, to be able to conclude the book without continuously extending self-imposed deadlines, I must acknowledge the invaluable contribution of an MP—Mystery Person, *not* Military Police or Member of Parliament, though both those would have been equally appropriate for the events described in the concluding chapters—who, without the influence of family loyalty or spousal blindness, still held on to the strange conviction that I had a story to write, which some people might, actually, want to read.

Clueless & Co. is an invented tale because if it wasn't, I'd be accused of being short on imagination, which, for a writer, is the most crushing criticism of all. As a declared work of fiction, all the characters in the story are, therefore, of my own creation and any resemblance to persons living or dead, or an indeterminate stage in-between, is purely coincidental although it would be an inconceivable stretch of the truth to say that it is unintentional, too. However, most of the places and institutions mentioned in the story are real: I have the greatest respect for all of them though that might not be immediately apparent from my writing, which is a reflection not of the impurity of my intent but the inadequacy of my authorship.

ONE

Into the Drink

I t's funny how the most portentous days have the most ordinary beginnings.

Rahul Banerjee scrambled out of bed, as he did on most days, with the Calcutta sunshine streaming into his eyes through an inadvertent chink in the curtains. It was 8 a.m. and the heat had already begun to simmer off the streets. The discordant cacophony (is there any other kind?) of impatient air-horns on stunted mini-buses had commenced, as had the temple-throbbing thump of their badly-repaired tyres bouncing over speed breakers constructed, seemingly with demonic purpose, directly under Rahul's bedroom window.

As he had seen being done so many times in movies and advertising commercials, Rahul swept aside the curtains, as if he were breast-stroking through water. And cringed, squeezing shut his sleep-soaked eyes, as the summer sun, unwittingly unfettered, blasted him full in the face with a ferocity that he had not anticipated. In double-speed reverse-motion, he drew the curtains back to their original position and, having temporarily disabled the sun, opened his eyes to survey his surroundings, almost daring them to surprise him.

They didn't. He wasn't.

It was the same bedroom he'd occupied for the last ten years. Things were very much where they'd always been, including Ratna, still cocooned in sleep, wrapped in bedclothes like an Egyptian Mummy, unlikely to surface for at least another hour. The walls were an anxious blue, not the serene shade that the colour charts had promised. The furniture was an unintended smoky-white, despite Ratna's frequent ministrations with water and detergent, the fumes from passing traffic tending to leave a more lasting impression than the International Chemical Company's products ever could. The inverter—a whole new category of consumer durable born out of Calcutta's infamous, and unpredictable, proclivity to shed electrical load at the slightest pretext—had staked an indelible claim to a corner of the room by leaking its hydrochloric acid entrails. The unbranded air conditioner—Rahul's very first, hand-picked nine years ago—had gamely lasted the night—spreading good cheer and cool comfort—but was sputtering to a halt now, in urgent need of rest and resuscitation. The grandfather clock—a family heirloom of sorts—was trapped in a time warp of its own creation, its hands splayed in mock crucifixion, at ten minutes after ten, ante-meridian or post-meridian not known.

But, even in the ordinariness of his surroundings, Rahul could sense—like a half-remembered dream—that this day was, somehow, different. It was the first day of his life as an entrepreneur. After years of working for others, Rahul Banerjee was setting out to launch his own business, albeit in partnership with two others but, nonetheless, his own. Or, if one were determined to nitpick on a momentous occasion such as this, one-third his own.

As the truth of the moment affirmed itself in his mind, Rahul Banerjee panicked. Suddenly, he was fully awake and, like a camera dissolve, the scene changed, in his mind's eye, from the comfort of his ten-year surroundings to the bar of the Ordnance Club where, on impulse, he had committed his future to two relative strangers, one balmy afternoon, a month ago.

The bearer, in his resplendent cummerbund and topee, personified the Club: faded glory. His uniform was the same shade of grey-white as the walls, his complexion the same shade of blotchy. But his manners were impeccably Old World, as he guided Rahul Banerjee across the gravelled driveway and around the open veranda to the bar, which was tucked, somewhat guiltily, behind a large, wooden-floored, wooden-faced, and for that time of day, surprisingly-empty dining room.

In comparison, the bar was teeming, which was equally surprising since it was the middle of a working day, well past the statutory lunch break. As Rahul stepped in from the brash sunlight, he was greeted by blackness, the cool waft of air-conditioned air, and the murmur of voices, all seeming to be speaking at the same decibel level. Disturbed by the slew of light that squeezed unceremoniously past Rahul as he entered the bar, these undefined, indistinct citizens of manufactured night paused in their conversation. The buzz died. But not for much longer than the few moments of silence that one, ordinarily, bestows on some departed soul. In the short time that it took for Rahul to adjust to the relative darkness of the Ordnance Club bar, the conversational drone had resurrected itself, with a purpose that a second chance at life tends to give.

Anoop Chowdhury, self-proclaimed academician and market researcher par excellence, and Chairman of the new venture that he was hoping to persuade Rahul into joining, was at a corner table, shrouded in darkness, but not in anonymity because, even in the few minutes that it took Rahul to get his bearings, he had emitted two inadvertent, whistling snorts of welcome.

'It's not caused by stress, only by the anticipation of it,' he had explained at an earlier meeting, when discussions had been unexpectedly interrupted by a succession of whistles, alternated by snorts, each more vehement than the one preceding it. Even more disconcerting than these involuntary emissions of sound were their unpredictability which, if you did not have prior experience of them, could shock you out of your skin the first time they happened. Not that you could ever quite get used to them.

Sitting beside the whistling and snorting Anoop Chowdhury was Tapas Pan, a hulking, skulking figure that had assumed sinister dimensions in the semi-darkness of the Ordnance Club bar. 'He is our firm's arms and legs,' Anoop Chowdhury had said with the pride of a father for an exceptionally gifted son, although Tapas Pan had given no indication of his talents in earlier meetings, limiting his contributions to monosyllabic grunts, either as punctuation marks in Chowdhury's long-winded discourses, or as a counterpoint to his whistles. Whistle, grunt, whistle, grunt, and whistle, grunt would go the Chowdhury-Pan duo in the middle of every discussion, much like a weary steam engine nearing the end of yet another long, arduous journey.

As Rahul neared them, Pan waved a lugubrious hand in welcome, while Chowdhury's eyebrows did a frenzied form of callisthenics, presumably in welcome, too.

'What will you drink?' asked Chowdhury, by way of greeting, while Pan cast an exploratory eye in search of an accommodating waiter.

'A soft drink will do just fine,' said Rahul, evincing a snort from Chowdhury and a manic giggle from Pan.

'Not permissible,' snorted Chowdhury. 'Not when you are *our* guest.'

'I've had three gin and tonics already,' he continued, as if that were justification enough for Rahul to abandon his unrealistic, albeit quaint, idea of surviving an afternoon with the Chowdhury-Pan combo without partaking of the spirit that, in small doses, is known to calm and, in larger ones, sedate.

'Four,' corrected Pan, with alacrity, suggesting that, in certain in-between dosages, it could also impair your short-term memory and mathematical ability.

Anoop Chowdhury raised a pair of empty eyes, and a limp hand, towards Rahul, signalling him to sit while Pan, in silhouetted profile, a half-empty bottle of Black Label beer clutched proprietarily in his fist, continued his search of the room for a waiter who'd bring Chowdhury his fifth and Rahul his first.

'So, have you thought about our proposal?'

Rahul discovered, to his acute discomfiture, that when Chowdhury asked a question that he thought he might not like the answer to, he looked everywhere but at the person to whom he'd directed his enquiry. Normally accustomed to looking the person he was talking to in the eye, Rahul assessed that catching Anoop Chowdhury's required a sense of purpose and flexibility of neck, that he wasn't capable of. Taking the less-strenuous option of following the approximate direction of Anoop Chowdhury's straying gaze, Rahul also stared at the faded piece of liquor-stained, cigarette-burnt carpet that Chowdhury was appearing to find so fatally fascinating.

While he tried to compose an appropriate response to Chowdhury's question, his peripheral vision sighted a luminescent spray of saliva and beer as Tapas Pan, having finally secured the attention of a waiter, admonished him for the tardiness of his arrival and then briefed him, in somewhat unnecessary detail considering that he had served Chowdhury four drinks already, on how he wished the fifth to be prepared and, in case he had been blinded by Pan's unexpected eloquence, reminded him, in conclusion, that a third person had joined their table and would be in need of similar sustenance. Rahul had never seen Tapas Pan so voluble, nor so decisive. Anoop Chowdhury had done him a grave injustice by referring to him as only the limbs of the firm—he could well be its voice, too.

'A few things still concern me,' said Rahul. 'While my previous job equips me to *appreciate* and *use* market research, I have no experience of, actually, *doing* it. So, I don't see what productive role I can play in a marketing research agency, as a partner.'

Chowdhury snorted, derisively. 'What knowledge of market research does Tapas have?'

Rahul wasn't quite sure what *that* had to do with anything. However, before he could express his confusion, Pan, not understanding that Chowdhury's question might have been rhetorical, launched into an explanation to justify his role in the firm as an executive director and equal partner.

'I ask you,' he asked, 'what use are concepts if they can't be used? What value does theory have if it can't be applied?'

Having made a couple of pronouncements that, he believed, exonerated him from Chowdhury's inferred rebuke, Pan attacked his beer with a disconcertingly loud slurp and, to underscore his perceived triumph, slammed the empty bottle down hard on the table. His emphatic actions were reason enough for Rahul to reach for the drink that an attentive waiter had silently placed before him.

'Yes, yes,' said Chowdhury, impatiently. Rahul noticed with growing concern that his sibilants had begun to develop a marked hiss—like poor quality tape spooling through a much-used tape recorder. 'I conceptualise, Tapas executes, and you get us the business! It's that simple.'

'What is knowledge without...' started Pan again, but was stopped in his tracks by the baleful gaze that Chowdhury threw at him, denying him the opportunity to spout some more of his home-grown philosophy.

'If we'd doubted your reputation in the marketing fraternity, would we have approached you with an offer of a directorship?' asked Anoop Chowdhury, in another burst of rhetoric. 'The combination of our strengths will take us to new heights.'

As the vision of a flourishing enterprise, run by the collective wisdom and expertise of Chowdhury, Pan and Banerjee, flashed past his mind's eye, Anoop Chowdhury half-rose from his seat, his right hand extended, as if some heavenly creature were seeking it for a congratulatory shake. Then, suddenly, the gin hit him and he collapsed into his chair, and oblivion.

An unmistakable slurping sound reminded Rahul Banerjee that a second partner was still available to resume a discussion that had come to a premature halt with Anoop Chowdhury's forced, but not entirely unanticipated, retirement. With some trepidation, Rahul turned to Tapas Pan.

'What is knowledge without implementation?' Triumphantly, Pan completed the philosophical moment that Chowdhury had denied him. His tone of near-evangelical fervour seemed to suggest to Rahul, who had begun to experience the beginnings of a creeping kind of paranoia, that anyone who had the nerve to deny Tapas Pan his minute in the sun, or under a self-directed spotlight, was sure to be rendered hors de combat by forces invisible, but certainly not insubstantial, as exemplified by the comatose figure of Anoop Chowdhury.

'Join us,' said Tapas Pan. It was not an invitation; it was a command that brooked no argument and resounded with an unheard, but ominous, sound of '... or else'; or, so Rahul thought, as he found his sense of equanimity rapidly deserting him.

'What's there to think?' queried Pan, finding sibilants to hiss where none existed.

Rahul sipped his gin and tonic contemplatively while, by his side, Pan drew violent images in the beer spilled on the table, with a podgy forefinger. To Rahul's jaundiced eye, they all resembled skulls grinning toothlessly, like Halloween pumpkins. And, to his confused mind, one of them was his own.

Anoop Chowdhury stirred with the first signs of returning life and, to announce his resurrection, whistled. With eyes still closed, his right hand reached, with intuitive aim, for the half-empty glass of gin and, having reclaimed it, took it unerringly to his mouth, with equally-faultless precision. Pan's artistic gyrations gained momentum and, under the frenzied assault of his moving fingers, the skulls lost their grins and, soon, their form. Within seconds, all that remained on the table was spilled beer and wet cigarette ash.

'You're on, right?' There was the same urgency in Pan's tone that Rahul had recently noticed in his fingers. He wondered if his own face would be erased in quite the same way that the skulls had been, if he refused. The thought of being reduced to water and flaky carbon deposits drove his paranoia to full-blown proportions.

'I suppose...' he started, tentatively.

'So,' completed Tapas Pan, with emphasis and wily timing. Before Rahul could fully realise that his thought had been hijacked and taken in a completely different direction, his hand was separated from the glass of g-and-t and encased in a wet, clammy grasp. Tapas Pan bestowed a smile on him so radiant that it hurt.

It was also the cue for Anoop Chowdhury to re-surface.

'It's done,' said Pan in a tone that, once again, underlined the triumph of execution over theory. 'He's one of us.'

The entire background score of *The Omen*, replete with priests caterwauling in fear, played into Rahul's brain. A kaleidoscope of graphic images—hooded monks, jackal carcasses, ravaged faces, open graves, snarling dogs, hanging nannies, screeching ravens, sinister covens—accompanied it.

'He's one of us,' repeated Anoop Chowdhury, having difficulty with the sibilants and keeping his eyes open.

And, despite every neuron in his brain that hadn't been ruined by gin warning him of the sheer incompatibility of the proposed union, Rahul found himself agreeing to it, not out of any entrepreneurial enthusiasm or, alcohol-induced apathy, but only to escape the numbing ennui of his current occupation, which, he would discover in hindsight, mightn't have been the most reliable way of making a career choice.

As the air conditioners in the Ordnance Club bar were switched off—to inform its patrons that the time for drinking was over, for the next three hours, at least—as the interiors brightened and the shadows coalesced into discernible shapes, as the murmur of whispered voices was replaced by the shuffle of reluctant feet, as the pop of soda water bottles being opened and the swirl of glasses being filled gave way to the clinking of loose change in the pockets of weary waiters, and as Tapas Pan sprayed a last gush of beer and saliva into the air and Anoop Chowdhury whistled and snorted his uncertain way out of a couch that tried to hold him back, like clinging quicksand, Rahul Banerjee realised, with a sinking feeling, that he was, indeed, one of them.

Rahul Banerjee switched his mind off the replay mode. It was time.

Despite the balmy heat of a summer's morning, he found himself clothed in a cold veneer of apprehension. Ratna emerged from the bed sheets, like an awakening Mummy.

'Good morning,' she said, bleary-eyed.

'Is it?' he questioned, philosophically but, as it transpired, rhetorically, because Ratna had already dived back under the sheets to steal a few more moments of shut-eyed bliss.

With his anxiety for company, Rahul Banerjee prepared for the momentous day ahead. Amongst other things, it included the ceremonial opening of the bonnet of his second-hand Ambassador, a name that, sadly, belied the state—and status—of the vehicle. As was his daily custom, he peered at the engine inside, knowledgeably, but completely uselessly. Having ascertained that it was still there and nothing remarkable, or untoward, had happened to it since the last inspection, he persuaded it to growl a response, with some prayer and several persistent turns of the ignition key. Then, he hurried back upstairs to crunch his cereals and say his goodbyes before, like an intrepid traveller, he set forth on the uncharted course that would carry him to a thirty-three-and-one-third percent partnership in a marketing research company, which, according to his associates, was destined to set new standards of professionalism in the city, if not the country.

'Best of luck,' said Ratna, who still had to make the acquaintance of the Chowdhury-Pan duo and could, therefore, be forgiven her optimism.

Temporarily emboldened by her contagious confidence, Rahul traipsed lightly, or, as lightly as the weight of his niggling concerns would permit, out the door and set compass for Bipin Behari Ganguly Street ('landmark, Ruby Bar', Tapas Pan had chortled, somewhat malevolently, Rahul recalled) and a part of Calcutta that turn-of-the-century Bengali litterateurs had written endless paeans about, but one Rahul had visited not more than half-a-dozen times in the ten years that he had been living in the city.

Like some people whose best side you see only when they have their mouths shut, some places also look their best when they have their shutters down. Ruby Bar was one such. Closed, it looked almost innocuous.

As Rahul circled the block searching for an elusive parking slot, he passed the bar at least four times and not once was he given cause to change his first impressions of the place. Shuttered, Ruby Bar looked harmless and not worthy of the malevolence that Tapas Pan had infused it with when he'd given directions to the office. Or, so it seemed to Rahul Banerjee on this bright summer's morning in North Calcutta, as he managed to outthink a rickshaw and manoeuvre his stately Ambassador into a spot recently vacated by a bullock-cart.

'We are on top of Ruby Bar,' Tapas Pan had said.

At the time, in his gin-induced torpor, Rahul had not understood whether Pan had meant that in geographical or competitive terms, as in *a floor above* versus *superior to*. Standing on the sun-soaked pavement in front of the steel-shuttered bar with his mind much clearer, Rahul surmised that it was, most probably, the former since it was unlikely that it would take the collective wizardry of three so-called marketing research experts to out-do a bar on B.B. Ganguly Street, however pedigreed its origins, or exalted its heritage.

Bars in North Calcutta, even closed ones, have side entrances. Side entrances come in handy when you want the premises to remain open even when they are supposed to be officially shut. Or, to conveniently evict high-spirited patrons, who might have become excessively boisterous, without affecting the custom, or mood, of those less so. Or, to quietly extricate supine and comatose clients, whose exit by the main entrance might alarm newer customers into putting an unnecessary brake on their own consumption, lest they should suffer a similar fate. Or, to shake down patrons whose thirst, unknown to them, had outpaced their wallet.

Rahul Banerjee found the entrance and, for none of the reasons cited above, took it.

The first thing that hit him after the abrupt darkness of the antique stairwell was the smell. To be fair, it was not entirely unpleasant. If ever a smell had character, this one did. Overwhelmingly, it was woody, with hints of juniper, malt, spirit, perspiration, musk, barley and dust. For the time that it took for his eyes to adjust to the new ambience, he soaked in the aroma. Then, heavy with it, he climbed the wooden stairs to the level above, and the one after that, his footsteps echoing. By the time he reached the landing of the second floor, the scent of juniper had been insidiously replaced by the smell of urine.

The plaque, in brazen brass, read 'Rexxon Marketing Consultancy Private Limited', though there was very little that was private about it. In the gloom of the stairwell, it shone like a beacon. The door bearing the plaque was, otherwise, stark. It had a large, round knocker, rusty in parts, and a spiral of naked, electrical wire that marked the spot where a bell had once been. To gain entrance, it was clearly advisable to use the knocker. What remained of the bell promised speedy electrocution and a premature end to all entrepreneurial aspirations. Giving the tangle of wire a wide berth, Rahul rattled the knocker, holding his breath, partly in anticipation but, mostly, to ward off the smell of stale urine that had, suddenly, submerged everything that malt, spirit, perspiration, musk, barley and dust could throw at it, singly, or in combination.

'Welcome,' screamed a nasal voice from within, which to Rahul's now-practiced ear could be none other than Tapas Pan's, partner and fellow director in an enterprise that proposed to change the face of marketing research, if not in the world, most certainly, in a slice of Calcutta, atop Ruby Bar, on Bipin Behari Ganguly Street.

TWO

The Red Herring

ahul Banerjee's first, overwhelming impression of the
Rexxon office was that it was a square. It had square
tables, arranged cheek by jowl, and square chairs, on
which sat a dozen square people, their heads buried in square
ledgers. With his hesitant entry, the murmur of low voices died
and twelve square heads turned in his direction, almost in unison,
and twelve pairs of eyes squared him up in their collective sight.

'Good morning, sir,' chorused the square dozen and, having
acknowledged his arrival and performed their dutiful obeisance,
returned to their square ledgers.

'Come in, come in,' bade the disembodied voice of Tapas Pan
from somewhere to Rahul's left. 'We are here.'

'Here' was behind a somewhat vertically-challenged curtain
in a bilious shade of green that separated the Rexxon front office,
clearly meant for lesser mortals, from the inner sanctum, meant
for the more privileged, a category to which Rahul now belonged.
This abode of the gods was a smaller square, with four square

tables, of differing design and height, which indicated to Rahul that they'd been hired from different auction houses. Anoop Chowdhury, as behove his seniority, if not in position, certainly in age, occupied the tallest. Tapas Pan sat at the one to his right, as befitted his position of 'right hand man', both literally and figuratively. The two desks in front were vacant, waiting for Rahul Banerjee to indicate a preference. It was either the devil, or the deep-blue sea or, in the alternative, a rock and a hard place, since one would have placed him with his back to Anoop Chowdhury, the other, to Tapas Pan.

Wisely, Rahul postponed his decision and pulled up a chair, somewhere between the two occupied tables, to the accompaniment of an encore of 'welcome'. As he settled, he noticed that Anoop Chowdhury was sitting astride a pot-bellied cushion, to compensate for the height of his chair, which was substantially shorter than his desk; it left him with his feet inches off the floor, toes pointed like an ungainly ballerina's.

'Paint,' said Anoop Chowdhury.

While Rahul was still debating whether this was a directive demanding some form of creative action on his part, or merely an astute observation from a senior partner that the office needed a coat of it, which it certainly did, Anoop Chowdhury continued, '...is our current priority. The International Chemical Company is launching a new brand of decorative emulsion paint, Satin Feel. They wish to obtain authentic consumer feedback on how existing brands are perceived to develop a focused and effective advertising campaign for its launch.'

'It's all very huss-huss, of course,' cautioned Pan, although the warning tended to lose much of its gravity because of the way he mutilated the consonants. 'Top secret,' he emphasised, just in case Rahul had missed the 'huss-huss' bit.

'Yes, quite,' said Anoop Chowdhury, appearing peeved at having his brief interrupted mid-stream. 'Needless to say, ICC is a very big client for us and if we do this project well, it'll open up endless opportunities for us. Endless.'

'Why *if*,' interjected Tapas Pan, not one to be easily silenced, subtle shows of peevishness notwithstanding. 'When, when.'

The echo syndrome seemed to be wildly contagious.

'We won the business against stiff competition from so-called *established* market research agencies.' A curl of the lower lip, in denigration, emphasised what Anoop Chowdhury thought of *them*. 'Purely on the basis of our past track record for professionalism, integrity and transparency.'

It was as good a time as any for the Rexxon anthem to play in the background; however, Pan diluted the magic of the moment by inappropriately injecting an unnecessary dose of realism: 'At half the cost, too.'

The virtues of integrity and transparency having been savaged at the altar of Mammon, Anoop Chowdhury dissolved into an extended bout of sniffles which, Rahul was now beginning to understand, came to the fore whenever Chowdhury was either denied his say, or contradicted in mid-flow.

'It's all here,' he said, in between sniffs, pushing a sheaf of papers towards the edge of the table, in Rahul's approximate direction. 'We start next week with a group discussion in Bombay. Before that, of course, we have a meeting with Vishal Kaushik, the senior brand manager. This is his first independent project and we need to carry him with us every step of the way.'

'I'm hungry,' announced Tapas. 'It must be lunch-time.' Actually, it wasn't. At least, not for the rest of the country, but within the four walls of that dusty little room in that ancient building, in a dusty by-lane of Calcutta, it was, because Tapas Pan had willed it so.

Lunch was the high point of that first day.

Tapas Pan was a hyperactive dynamo when it came to organising food. As if by sleight of hand, he produced half-a-dozen menu cards and spread them in a fan in front of his animated face. Like a benign genie, he bestowed his attention on Rahul.

'What is the guest of honour in the mood for? Moghlai, Chynij, Continent or Bangla?'

Clearly, it was another of his rhetorical parries because, even before Rahul, as the designated guest, had considered the alternatives, let alone ventured an opinion, Tapas Pan had decided for them all.

'Biryani,' he announced and hollered for 'Partho'.

'Partho' appeared, on cue, from the adjoining room and was cursorily introduced to Rahul as the firm's 'field supervisor'. His immediate function, however, was to supervise lunch, for which he had to take a lengthy brief on what specific kind of biryani would appease Tapas Pan's hunger and discerning palate, and where he had to go to find it.

'Not like the last time,' Pan admonished him. 'Last time', obviously, had been a disaster because the mere thought of it seemed to get Tapas Pan hot under the collar. As memories of that last culinary encounter flooded his mind, the furrows in his forehead deepened and a patina of perspiration glossed his face, droplets of it beading at the end of his nose and pausing, like championship divers, before plunging towards the doodle pad on his desk to splatter the ink-scribbles he had spent most of the morning doing.

There was a mathematical precision to Tapas Pan's brief on how he wanted his biryani (given that the other participants had very little say in the matter, the biryani could, indeed, be termed his). As he waxed eloquent on basmati rice, firm yet succulent mutton pieces, where the flesh slid easily off the bone at the gentle nudge of a finger, the mandatory potato, cooked till it wore a light-gold sheen, and the lightness of dum pokht cooking, Rahul turned to Anoop Chowdhury, curious to know whether he was equally involved in the proceedings because if he was, then, lunch would be a protracted affair every day, not just today because it was his first, and deserving of some kind of celebration.

Thankfully, Chowdhury wasn't. While Tapas prattled on, he busied himself with the day's crossword which, if the rapidly-changing mosaic of expressions on his face was anything to go by, seemed to be giving him greater stress than the thought of having to carry the senior brand manager of ICC 'every step of the way' on what was, by his own admission, Rexxon's most important journey yet.

With his two business partners engaged in pursuits that demanded their undivided attention, Rahul had a little time to himself, although the loudness of Tapas Pan's endless instructions and Anoop Chowdhury's frequent sniffs, perhaps because a four-letter word (*slang*) starting with 'f' danced tantalisingly beyond the reach of his mental grasp, were not particularly conducive to even the mildest form of introspection. But, on that first day, as the lunch break punctuated proceedings with a degree of semi-permanence, Rahul Banerjee could not help but feel the sharp taste of unease that a tumbling flash-flood of recent images left behind—something that not even the exceptional quality of 'Tapas Pan's biryani' could quite erase.

'Vishal Kaushik has to be handled,' pronounced Anoop Chowdhury, in a tone that suggested he'd given the matter a great deal of thought. To underline the importance of the issue, he meticulously folded his newspaper and kept it aside, even though he still had some way to go to finish the daily crossword.

The paper packets, plates, tumblers and plastic cutlery had been removed, but grains of basmati rice still lay scattered on the tables, like forgotten debris, mute testimony to the frenetic activity that had consumed the last hour. Tapas Pan allowed himself the satisfaction of a prolonged belch and wiped his mouth with a page from his doodle pad, leaving on it the indelible marks of his recent excesses. He gave his trademark gurgle, which Rahul had begun to recognise as an expression of amusement, usually of the perverse variety.

'Rahul's job,' said Tapas Pan, the gurgle threatening to explode into a guffaw, his recently-fed face, still shining from the cooking oil that a non-absorbent page of his doodle pad had failed to remove completely, reddening in its effort to suppress the pleasure of some private joke.

Rahul Banerjee felt his practiced composure slipping, the sliver of unease he'd experienced at lunch replaced by a fingernail-scratch of irritation. It must have shown on his face because Anoop Chowdhury was quick to intervene.

'It's no big deal,' he said. 'As I mentioned, Kaushik's new to the job and doesn't want anything to go wrong with what is, effectively, his first, independent assignment, lest his future growth in ICC be compromised.'

'In what way does he have to be *handled*?' asked Rahul, not easily waylaid by Anoop Chowdhury's attempted diversionary tactic.

'He plans to accompany us to all the focus groups. Says it'll be a learning experience for him, getting consumer feedback directly, like it is. Straight, undiluted.'

'But, in what way does he have to be *handled?*' repeated Rahul obdurately, while, behind him, Tapas Pan suffered a prolonged bout of coughing, as guffaw stole a march over gurgle.

'It can get uncomfortable and stifling to have a client peering over your shoulder constantly,' explained Anoop Chowdhury. 'Certainly cramps *my* style. When I've got a job to do, I don't want to be worrying about social niceties and whether my client is gainfully occupied or not.'

'Nor do we want the client to know all our trade secrets, now, do we?' interposed Pan, mischievously. 'Certainly wouldn't want him to be peering at our profit margins!'

'Can't have interference if we have to get the job done properly,' said Anoop Chowdhury, hastening to overrule Tapas Pan's implication that clients had to be kept at bay or, at the very least, distracted, only to protect the conspiracy of the bottom-line. It was still too soon for him to yield the position that he'd taken with Rahul Banerjee that Rexxon was meant, if not destined, to scale new heights of professionalism in the world of marketing research, despite his right-hand man showing no particular discretion in expressing an embarrassingly contrary view.

'That's where you come in. To keep Vishal Kaushik busy while we get the focus groups out of the way quickly. The faster we finish, the faster we bill,' said Tapas Pan, making it amply clear, if clarity was still required, that he harboured no misconceptions about what the firm of Chowdhury, Pan and Banerjee was meant to do and it was, certainly, *not* to get case studies published in the Harvard Business Review, for successive generations of management students to mull over and wonder at.

And so it transpired, on that first day, that Rahul Banerjee was offered his first significant role as an entrepreneur—that of the Red Herring—a responsibility that he accepted, not without trepidation and not without a deepening of the foreboding that was already threatening to become his constant companion.

The rest of the afternoon raced by, with his partners unfolding, for his consumption, a dossier on Vishal Kaushik, complete with personal observations, analytical interpretations and dollops of unsolicited gossip. What were, for instance, his interests (wall paint and cricket), his ambitions (to be the youngest marketing director that ICC had seen and, on the side, a cricket commentator, in preparation for which he'd developed the unnerving practice of deepening his voice at unexpected moments in a conversation), his hobbies (golf at Tolly, amateur dramatics and practicing cricket commentating in front of any conveniently-located mirror, with an appropriate implement in hand: fountain pen, toothbrush or telephone handset), his pet peeve (that management graduates were an overrated lot and didn't deserve the higher starting salaries that they got over ordinary graduates like him; Rahul was strongly advised to downplay his own business school origins, if not distort them altogether), his anxieties (that an overrated and overpaid management graduate would pip him to the marketing director's post, or he'd lose his cultivated baritone on his first commentating assignment) and his aspirations (which were no different from his ambitions, only a little less forceful in intent)?

'Any good at golf?' asked Anoop Chowdhury, pausing in the profiling of their client.

'Not really,' said Rahul, remembering that the only time he'd been persuaded to have a swing, he'd nearly got black-balled for having propelled the ball on a trajectory that was at ninety degrees to the one he'd intended for it and perilously close to the venerable head of Tolly's managing member who, on that refreshingly-chilly winter's morning, had been lingering over his bacon-and-eggs at a table that anyone with the most rudimentary knowledge of golf swings, and their consequences, would have considered one hundred percent safe.

'So much the better,' said Tapas Pan, with irrefutable logic. 'Then, you'll have less difficulty losing to him.'

'It's unlikely that he will accept an invitation to golf if he wishes to actually participate in the groups. Or, as you seem to think, look over our shoulder,' said Rahul, peeved with the diversionary strategy being proposed. 'Maybe his presence will be all for the better! Might get us to tighten up our act.'

A fresh bout of sniffing indicated that Anoop Chowdhury was displeased that anyone should think that his act was not tight enough already. 'I just thought that golf might be a good way for the two of you to get acquainted.'

'How come you don't play golf?' Tapas Pan persisted, with the curiosity of a cat that still had all its nine lives. 'Everyone in Calcutta, who is anyone in the private sector, does,' he continued, happy with this new toy he had between his teeth. 'I'm told that the successful ones spend more time on the greens than they do behind their desks.'

'Not in my experience,' said Rahul, with mild irritation. 'You seem to have a very early Sixties image of the Calcutta executive. That lifestyle died with Firpo's, the decline of the tea industry and the ascent to power of the Communists.'

'Couldn't have,' said Tapas Pan, unfazed. 'Doing business in this city is all about networking, either on the golf course or at the club, over gin-and-tonic.'

'We concluded our business at a club over gin-and-tonic,' reminded Anoop Chowdhury, as if he'd uncovered the final, conclusive piece of empirical evidence to prove his fellow-director's hypothesis beyond any reasonable doubt.

'Possibly for its price advantage rather than its networking potential,' offered Rahul, in riposte. 'I don't see the medical fraternity that predominantly frequents Ordnance Club, to have much need for our kind of research.'

'Membership was closed everywhere else,' said Anoop Chowdhury, defensively, deliberately missing the point and hurrying to make amends, in case Rahul were to belabour the point about clubs, and who was better qualified to join which. 'Personally, I don't think networking can do much more than open a window of opportunity. To be able to capitalise on it requires merit.'

'Merit's an overrated virtue. It's all about networking, really. And when it isn't that, it's about pay-offs.' Tapas Pan still had the toy firmly in his jaws and he wasn't going to surrender it till he'd gnawed all the skin off. 'Take our bread-and-butter urine project, for example.'

Trying to ignore the contrary images that Pan's statement conjured, Rahul asked, in some alarm, 'What urine project?'

'Yes, yes. We can discuss that later. Mustn't overload Rahul on his first day,' intervened Anoop Chowdhury, hurriedly. 'Otherwise, we'll lose sight of our priorities.'

And with that, the subject of bread, butter and things less palatable was deemed closed, till the matter of Vishal Kaushik and the New Wall Paint had been satisfactorily disposed of.

However, as he was about to return to the papers on his desk, Rahul couldn't help but notice the quick, sly glances that Anoop Chowdhury and Tapas Pan exchanged: one of admonition, the other, of apology. Or, it could just have been his hyperventilating imagination, fuelled by the rich biryani and his collaborators' convoluted philosophy. But, by the end of that first day, the sense of unease that he had hoped was only a temporary guest, had started making preparations for a more permanent residency.

THREE

Dirty Harry

About the time that Rahul Banerjee had fingers of foreboding, and the such-like, traipsing along the nether regions of his spine (though I was to know that only much later), I was climbing my own mountain, caught as I was in the hypnotic stare of one Police Sergeant Harold Mann, who bestrode his World War Two-surplus (possibly, -discard) motorcycle, like a Colossus, his belly resting on a conveniently-located fuel tank, and a gloved hand imperiously extended, like a dictator acknowledging the tumultuous applause of loyal subjects. Within moments, the said gloved hand had insinuated itself through the car window and was clenching and unclenching in front of my face, in disconcerting fashion. Around this half-frozen tableau, traffic stopped, started and stumbled in a manner that was, and, I believe, still is, typically Calcutta.

'Papers,' hollered Police Sergeant H. Mann. From his apoplectic demeanour, I could safely surmise that it was not the creased copy of *The Statesman*, lying on the unoccupied seat next to me, that he desired.

Considering that I, in a moment of irresponsible impetuosity, had beaten a red light and, more to the point, been caught, red-handed, as it were, beating it, it was not an altogether unfair demand. The simple response it required of me was to reach across my seat, click open the dashboard compartment, delve into its recesses, pull out a plastic-sheathed bunch that contained what, in popular vehicular parlance, was called the Blue Book (although it was definitely green in colour) and a red, hardcover driving license, resembling the little book with which Chairman Mao had gained immense popularity among Calcutta students, and, accompanied by a suitably-ingratiating smile, hand the lot over to the authority figure, who stood in my way, like an immovable and intractable burden, astride his beast of a two-wheeled machine. Admittedly, the driving licence was a little risky because it contained, among other things, a passport-sized photo identification that seldom served the purpose that it was intended for; instead, it usually convinced officialdom that the owner was not only capable of committing, but also pathologically inclined to commit, greater misdemeanours than the one for which his driving licence had been demanded.

But, the circumstances were far from normal.

In an act of premeditation, whose consequences were turning out to be no different from those of my current impetuosity, I, in a private rebellion against the insufferable condition of Calcutta's roads, had refrained from paying the statutory road tax that was the bane of all vehicle owners. My protest had remained private for two years and would have continued in that same, silent, unnoticed vein, if I had just adhered to traffic rules for the rest of my life. I hadn't, because I couldn't, and now the cat was preparing to leap out of the bag in what would be an unsavoury display of public hi-jinks, if permitted to do so.

In fact, all told, it had been a day that had seen more displays of public hi-jinks than I really cared for, and I was still only halfway through it.

My job with a multinational company that produced and sold pipes—not the kind that you blew on to make music, which might have been interesting, but the kind that conveyed industrial fluids and gases over long distances, which was not—had sent me in the morning to Writers' Building, the place from where the State Government functioned, or did not, depending upon your state of mind and your political leaning. My task—relatively simple, one would have thought—was to collect a set of Tender documents for supply of pipes to the Public Health Department which, I imagined, differed from the Public Works Department only in that it, presumably, cared slightly more for the wellbeing of its public than did the other, if the desperate condition of Calcutta's roads—for which the PWD was responsible—was taken as a yardstick, although it must be said that yardsticks, particularly those measuring the lowest levels of uselessness to which public utility services could stoop in Calcutta, were always in a state of flux. There was more competition among them to see who could do the greater disservice to the public than there was to provide the better benefit. If, one day, the crown belonged to the PWD, the next day, it would be usurped by the Electric Supply Corporation, for surpassing its own record, set less than a week earlier, for the longest period that a city could be kept in total darkness, without permanently unhinging its citizens. Sometimes, I thought, they might have gone quietly insane already, for it was hard to explain how the same people who, in a highly inflammable, albeit extremely irrational, expression of protest, could take to the streets and torch vehicles when bus fares rose by less than the amount it took to buy a single bidi (if you were inclined that way, or a sliver of bubblegum, if you were not), could exhibit a submissive patience that even a Job would have envied, and suffer, in stoical silence, when lights, fans and everything else that it took to run their lives, went into increasingly-long, and increasingly-frequent, periods of coma.

The simple task of collecting the Tender documents hadn't been quite that simple, after all.

First, it took me three circuitous rounds of Dalhousie Square—if a square, at all, can be rounded—to park my aging Standard Herald. Then, I had to stand for nearly an hour in a queue that was distinguished more by its inertness than its length, though, that too, was not inconsiderable. To give the impression of motion, a police constable would appear, from time to time, to bark confusing commands at us which, from the perfunctory actions of my queue-colleagues, I surmised to mean that he wished us to shuffle ourselves into a straighter and neater line. Clearly, this was meant to distract us from the fact that, for reasons beyond our control and still unknown to me, the queue wasn't getting anywhere, or any shorter, however much we rearranged it. Someone more versed in the practices of the local bureaucracy guessed that the staff who handled visit requests was, as usual, at half-strength, which was why it would take twice as long to reach the door of the Visitors' Room assuming, of course, that the employees, who *had* deigned to turn up, would work at their customary level of inefficiency.

As it turned out, it took thrice as long, which meant that either the staff was at one-third its normal strength or, for purely perverse reasons, they had chosen to work at an even lower level of inefficiency than the one we'd grudgingly come to accept from them.

So, I wasn't in the most amiable of moods when, after traversing several labyrinthine corridors and avoiding countless touts offering to ease my task with a persistence that bordered on the pestilential, I found myself at the end of yet another line, in a room where, presumably, the documents I sought were being distributed. Harnessing my impatience at the unhurried pace of our progress, I consoled myself that it wouldn't be very much longer since deliverance lay, if not quite around the corner, at the end of this line.

The man behind the counter had his head buried in a steaming cup of tea and his hand in a paper cone of what smelled like exceptionally spicy jhaal mudhi, when I finally reached him. I stood before him, hoping to catch his attention with my deep breathing. I was breathing deeply, partly because I thought that might alert him to my presence, without my having to say anything that he might construe as the wrong thing to have said, partly because my patience was fraying at the edges, and partly because I had begun to wonder what special skills my business school education had imparted to me to handle an assignment such as this.

My stentorian breathing was ignored, as the man continued to slurp his tea and chomp his jhaal mudhi, carrying on a conversation with a colleague next to him about, if I'd heard it right, his morning ablutions, more particularly, his most recent bowel movement.

'Excuse me,' I ventured, daring, out of desperation, to interrupt him in the middle of his scatological discourse. 'I've come for the Public Health Tender document.'

He continued sipping his tea, nibbling his jhaal mudhi and apprising his neighbour of the kind of regimen that, in his opinion, ensured trouble-free mornings and an easy disposition, although going by his current behaviour, I didn't think whatever it was had helped him any.

'Can I have the Tender documents, please?' I attempted again, at my most ingratiating, extending a cheque from the company for something called Earnest Money, although there was nothing particularly earnest about it, except for the fact that you'd, probably, never see it again nor know where it had disappeared, or for what purpose.

Nothing changed in the behaviour of the man behind the counter, except for a finger to be raised out of the paper cone and extended, with bits of puffed rice adhering to its end, in the general direction of a small notice that was stuck to a glass window. Given the importance of the communication, it said that lunch was between one and two-thirty, in as many as three languages. Reading it, I had the distinct impression that the end-time had been expertly tampered with and an additional half-hour found where none had existed. By my watch, it was still ten minutes to the hour, enough time, I thought, to conclude our business.

The tea-sipping, jhaal mudhi-chomping man behind the glass window thought otherwise. Despite my pointing out to him, with a lot more assertiveness than I had shown so far, that it was only 12:50, he still refused to bestow his attention on me, so insignificant was I in his scheme of things. Instead, with the cup of tea stuck to his mouth to suck out the last drops, he waved his left wrist at me, where a stainless-steel HMT watch said, in big Roman numerals, that it was one o'clock already, and so it had to be. When I turned to gather support for my cause, and the correct time, from my fellow-sufferers, I discovered that I was the last man standing, the others having peeled off for rest and recuperation, quite unknown to me.

It was the longest ninety minutes I've ever spent. Despite my throat crying out for a chilled Double Seven, I wasn't prepared to give up my place in front of the counter, lest I find myself at the tail-end of another queue. Nor was I willing to take the risk of starting all over again with the man behind the counter, with whom, I thought, I'd established a rudimentary relationship at least, even though I had still to catch his eye and his attention.

So, I stood there, counting the minutes, and my bad luck, and thinking how different life really was from the boardrooms and executive chambers and all-night strategy sessions that textbooks and case studies in business school would have you believe are the playgrounds of the management graduate. Reality, often, is a cluttered Government office, with high, cobwebbed ceilings; slow, antique fans that manage only to raise the dust that years of neglect have settled on the room and everything in it; poor lighting that throws gloomy shadows and makes ominous corners out of walls and cupboards, where none were meant to be; mismatched, unstable furniture that spew cotton and plastic like vomit, and bulge at all the wrong places for all the wrong reasons; skyscraper stacks of dirty files where rodents, and all creatures crawly, seek refuge, and find it, and paan-chewing, clock-watching, excreta-obsessed clerks who find reprieve from the stagnancy of their own lives by baiting those whom they believe to be more fortunate than them which, in the end, is everybody else. So, they keep you waiting for hours while they parade their lives in front of anyone who cares to watch, and you quietly lose your own.

To be fair to the man behind the counter, he was back at his position on the dot of 2:30. Lunch must have been to his liking for he wore a satisfied demeanour and actually acknowledged my presence with a nod of recognition, although, considering that he'd never set eyes on me, I was left to wonder whether he'd confused me with someone else. I decided to correct that by giving him my visiting card.

He looked at it and sighed, exaggeratedly.

'Hopeless,' he said.

Before I could ask what was, and how he'd read my future off a small piece of board, he repeated, with added conviction, 'Completely hopeless.'

'Pardon?' I asked, uncertainly.

He wiggled my visiting card at me, with great vehemence.

'Your company, there's no point in it getting our order. Waste of your Earnest Money and our Tender documents.'

Relieved as I was that the cause of his despair wasn't me and that my future wasn't already in my past, I was still quite confused about where his source of anxiety lay. I asked.

In response, the man behind the counter got up from his chair. He leaned towards me, above the glass partition and, like an expert tracker dog, sniffed the air around me in short intakes of breath and, then, long, chest-expanding draws.

'Nothing,' he announced, much to my relief that neither my future nor my personal hygiene were causes for any immediate concern.

'I don't smell hilsa,' said the man.

'I don't understand,' I confessed.

'When any other pipe company gets our order, we have reason to celebrate. We smell hilsa, not any old hilsa but

Bangladeshi hilsa, from the Padma river, the best there is,' he said. 'But with your company, there's nothing.'

As I exchanged the Earnest Money cheque for a bulky set of Tender documents, I finally understood what he was despairing about. And ever since, whenever there is hilsa cooking in the house, its distinctive aroma filling every room, I also catch an underlying smell of the grease that, when applied liberally to some palms, makes a difficult job easy or, as in the vernacular, mushkil aasaan. Although over the years I've forgotten what that grease actually smells like, in my mind, hilsa will always remain strongly associated with enticement which, to the inveterate Bengali, that fish most certainly stands for, although not quite in the same way that the man behind the counter in an untidy room in Writers' Building may have meant it.

'Papers,' hollered P S Harold Mann once again, in a voice whose over-riding flavour was menace. 'I haven't got till Christmas, you know.'

That was, certainly, something that I knew and did not need to be reminded of, at least not in early summer.

'Sir,' I ventured, hoping that obeisance might gain me some respite, if not win me the day altogether. 'I'm terribly sorry but I was rushing to an important appointment that I am already very late for.' Somewhat weak under the circumstances, I admit, but the best I could muster, ensnared as I was in the penetrative, all-seeing glare of Calcutta's own Dirty Harry.

'The only appointment you're late for is your own funeral and rushing to it mightn't be the brightest of ideas,' said the police sergeant, in a display of dark humour that, I thought, was quite misplaced and untimely. It also left me confused about what might be the appropriate response to ease me off the hook: a short, carefree laugh to acknowledge the police sergeant's mordant wit, or a self-deprecatory, suitably-apologetic smile, to confirm that his low assessment of my mental faculties was spot-on?

I chose the short, carefree laugh; wrongly, as it turned out. 'You think this is funny?' queried P S Mann. I held my peace, assuming that the question was rhetorical. Again, I was mistaken.

The gloved hand clenched, ominously. 'Park the vehicle at the side of the road. Please.' Seldom had a word of entreaty sounded so venomous, or been accompanied by gestures so contrary.

Calcutta has always had this enormous reserve of people who, individually, seem to be gainfully employed in some seemingly-productive pursuit or another but, at the slightest hint of a diversion, readily surrender their occupation to congregate, in ever-increasing numbers, at the scene of an event, however inconsequential it might be. Then, they stand around, for hours if need be, waiting, and willing, for the plot to unfold, showering shards of twisted humour at the dramatis personae, by way of encouragement. And nothing attracts them in larger numbers than the age-old concept of Crime and Punishment.

By the time I had obeyed P S Harry Mann's commandment, relayed from Mount Royal Enfield, a sizeable crowd had gathered around us, keenly interested to know when, not whether, because the final outcome of these street operas was seldom in doubt, I would get my comeuppance, and what gloriously-devious form it would take.

Clutching my driving licence, I climbed out of the relatively-safe confines of my second-hand Standard Herald and approached the sergeant, who still sat astride his sturdy steed, a jackbooted foot tapping his impatience on the dusty tarmac.

'Where's your Blue Book?'

I thought I would be pushing my luck—such as it was—if I were to claim *not* to have any knowledge of the book in question, by virtue of its colour actually being green, and not blue, as the honourable P S Mann seemed to think. It was not a good time to be literal, or liberal, with the truth.

'At home,' I admitted, hoping that confession would get me absolution, as it is known to do for sins more serious than mere traffic violations.

'And why aren't you, too? Instead of being a menace to yourself and everyone on the road? Call yourself educated? If this is the fruit of your so-called education, what chance does this city have?' P S Mann wasn't in the mood for forgiveness, it seemed, nor for turning to priest from policeman.

In the face of his blistering rhetoric, I decided that silence was the best defence—better berated than sorry—and hoped that, without the stimulation of any worthwhile opposition, Dirty Harry would run out of steam soon.

I couldn't have been more wrong.

No doubt encouraged by the audience, gathered in rapt attention around him, P S Mann let loose a monologue that would have done a Shakespearean actor proud, though the iambic pentameter received scant respect, replete as his speech was with words of very few syllables. Having trashed my education, he proceeded, with escalating sarcasm, to maul my 'apology of an upbringing' and to provide a lengthy and insightful interpretation of my world as he saw it. He suggested, in conclusion, in a tone that brooked no argument, that I should accompany him to the Park Street P.S., where he would personally deify me, as the finest example of, and the last beacon of hope for, a generation rapidly losing its way, sarcasm pungent and intended.

Then, he grabbed the driving licence from my hand, cursorily glanced through its pages, scribbled a receipt for it, pocketed the document, kicked his motorcycle into growling wakefulness and, with a peremptory wave that signalled that I should follow, set off in the direction of Park Street P.S. The crowd dispersed, disappointed that the performance had stopped well short of bloodshed.

We were still some distance from the police station when my pilot and escort took a sudden right into Middleton Street. Police Sergeant Harold Mann stopped, parked his motorcycle, dismounted and strode in my direction. He peered through the car window.

'We can do this the hard way or we can do it the easy way,' he said, in a voice shorn of its earlier malevolence. In case I didn't know what the hard way was, he drew it for me in quick brush-strokes: being booked for driving without proper documents; violating traffic rules; waiting (indefinitely) for a call to a magistrate's Court; wasting two days (at least) for one's case to be announced and heard (hopelessly); pleading guilty (the only option); paying a penalty (an amount to be decided by the good magistrate on the basis, most likely, of the condition of his digestion on the day, rather than any tenets of law) and, last but not least, suffering the indelible ignominy of having the misdemeanour recorded in one's driving licence for all posterity to frown upon.

P S Mann paused; clearly, the easy way did not need elucidation.

'And what's the easy way?' I asked, just to be perverse, still smarting from the prolonged public humiliation he had subjected me to, particularly that cutting bit about being the last hope for a generation that had muddled its directions.

P S Harold Mann's face began to turn the mottled red of a Calcutta sky at sunset, on a monsoon day. Before he slammed the escape hatch shut on me, I quickly reached into my wallet and extricated a crisp one hundred-rupee note. Not having transacted business with someone of the seniority of a sergeant before, I did not know if it was too much, or too little. Apparently, it was adequate, because, in a sleight of hand that would have had that great magician, P.C. Sarkar, applauding he plucked it from my fingers, smoothly substituting the driving licence in its place.

'Keep your wits—and your papers—about you when you drive,' advised Dirty Harry, withdrawing one long arm of the law from the scruff of my neck and the other, from my wallet. Then, in a complete reversal of conventional behaviour, he whisked a voucher-book out of a capacious rear pocket, scribbled industriously in it, tore off a sheet and handed it to me through the driver's window. I looked at it in surprise.

It was a formal, printed, sequentially-numbered receipt from the Charity for Retired Constables, C/o Police Club, made out for One Hundred rupees, favouring a name that he had lifted off my license.

As he puttered away on his behemoth of a motorcycle, I felt a flood of contradictory emotions course through me. One was a feeling of loss, for the money, certainly, but more for my innocence, or whatever little was still left of it; the second, of satisfaction, for having disentangled myself from a knotty situation that might have got prolonged unnecessarily, if I'd played by a more respected book; a third, of bewilderment that there were so many things—the man behind the counter and Dirty Harry Mann, for example—that my business school had done little to prepare me for and, a fourth, of soaring ambition, in the realisation that just about anything that you set your mind to could be attained, through artifice and subornment which, in a way, made for a level playing field, where background, education and skills, intrinsic or acquired, mattered little, if at all.

In those early days of my executive career, it was a lesson well worth the learning.

FOUR

The Inverted M

The contretemps with P S Mann, and the morality play that had ensued thereafter, had diverted me from my itinerary by close to ninety minutes. The sun had called it a day by then and the colours in the sky that its passing had left behind were fast fading into oblivion. The fingers of night were spreading, as I guessed was Surjo Sengupta's panic.

Surjo Sengupta was a writer, or so I had been informed some days ago over the static of a telephone line from Moscow, where my in-laws were temporarily stationed.

'Eighteen years ago, he left the country, with a French exchange student he took a fancy to, married her and settled in Paris. Been there ever since. This is his first trip back in nearly two decades—a return to his roots, as it were,' my father-in-law summarised for me.

'A reconnaissance for a more permanent homecoming?' I offered, by way of a possible explanation for Mr Sengupta's sudden urge to return to the home of his birth, after doing quite well without it for nearly twenty years.

'Perhaps, though it is unlikely that his French wife will see Calcutta in quite the same romantic light that she did in her youth.'

'Any great expectations that he has of his stay with us?' The fact that he would be our guest had been established quite early in the conversation, before the static could really kick in and distort what one heard, or cared to hear.

'Wouldn't imagine so; he'll be too busy retracing old haunts and rediscovering old friends. Says that all he needs is a comfortable bed to come back to.' From the hint of apology in my father-in-law's voice, although it might just have been the static acting up, I had the impression that he was underplaying the role expected of us in case, in a sudden relapse to the contrariness I was especially vulnerable to when people I didn't know were foisted on me, I should slam the door shut on the expatriate's return, scuttling the belated search for his roots.

And so, it came to pass that our one spare bedroom was made ready for Surjo Sengupta, unknown poet and unpublished essayist, to seek comfort in, for the seven days that we thought it would take him to voyage to the ports of his past. (As it turned out, it was more like seventy; but then, I go ahead of myself.)

My itinerary for the evening—that an unplanned confabulation with Dirty Harry had delayed by nearly two hours—had been decided by a telephone call the previous day. The voice on the telephone had been strained. Beyond the basic necessity of identifying who the caller was, it had had little time for introductory niceties and had dispensed with them, rather abruptly.

'This is Surjo Sengupta from Paris. I've reached Delhi. Traumatised.'

'Oh! Not been in some kind of accident, I hope?'

'No, no, no. It's the crowds, the heat, the dust, the din!'

'Bit of a change from Paris, what?' It was, on consideration, a poorly-timed attempt at levity. It did nothing to dampen the flames of alarm that were shredding the edges of the disembodied voice.

'I'm reaching Calcutta tomorrow, by the Rajdhani Express. I'll take a taxi from Howrah Station to the YMCA. Perhaps you could pick me up from there at seven p.m.? Please don't be late.'

With that cautionary advice and before I had had a chance to ascertain which YMCA he would find his way to, considering that there were at least half-a-dozen, I had heard the click of the receiver being replaced at the other end, terminating our conversation and any chance of my getting a clarification, since, in the throes of his trauma, he'd neglected to leave a call-back number.

It was 6:30 p.m. when I entered the lobby of the YMCA on S.N. Banerjee Road. It was cavernous, done predominantly in wood, of a texture that had been scuffed beyond recognition through years of use. My footsteps made a hollow, echoing sound as they traversed the parquet floor towards the reception desk. It was bare, except for a thick, scratched ledger and an old-fashioned bell that called out for tinkling. I tinkled it and waited. Five minutes dragged by on tired feet. I tinkled some more.

A young man, sheathed in perspiration, wearing shorts and a sleeveless vest, poked his head out of an adjoining room where, presumably, he had been working out till my repeated tinkles interrupted his exertions.

'Yes?'

'I was wondering if a gentleman by the name of Surjo Sengupta has arrived.'

'If he's staying here, his name will be in the ledger. Have a look.'

I did. It wasn't.

'There you are, then. If he isn't in the ledger, he'll be somewhere in the lobby and if he isn't in the lobby, he isn't here.'

No doubt the callisthenics the young man had been doing were sharpening his grasp of logic as much as they were toning his body.

'Is there another YMCA in the vicinity?'

'How many do you want? They're cheaper by the dozen.' The young man decided to give his sense of humour a workout, for a change. The look on my face discouraged him from travelling further down that path. Having recently survived Dirty Harry, I was high on an adrenaline flow that feeble attempts at irony, by a guy in ill-fitting shorts, who had yet to develop the kind of musculature that I'd consider even remotely threatening, were unlikely to stem.

'Off-hand, I can think of one on Dharamtala Street, another on Lower Circular Road and a third in Sealdah. I'm sure there are at least a couple more.'

I looked at my watch. It was 6:45. I had barely fifteen minutes to scour the city for a YMCA, out of at least five serious contenders, that temporarily sheltered a returnee Bengali poet, recently arrived from Paris via New Delhi, by his own admission, traumatised.

It is an urban legend that, when you are in the greatest hurry, circumstances conspire to throw the most obstacles in your path to slow you down. Calcutta traffic, which isn't the smoothest in the best of circumstances, was never as excruciatingly tangled, or as agonisingly slow, as it was that evening. To add to my misery, parking was, predictably, almost impossible to find. Each time I located a YMCA, after a nerve-jangling ride through a muddle of dodgy directions, I had to circle it for several minutes, like an aeroplane in holding pattern, till I found somewhere to park, which was, generally, streets away, in a spot that was always a little ambiguous about whether it allowed parking or not. So, when I left my Herald and trudged my way through an unholy mess of men, beasts and machines to the YMCA in question, I was never really sure whether it would still be there when I got back, or whether another round of lopsided jollity awaited me with a certain P S Harold Mann holding centre-stage, and all the aces.

My experiences at the three YMCAs that I trawled that evening were as similar as to be replays. I would, invariably, be greeted by a gloomy, unmanned reception area, always with a desolate desk at its centre, where an ubiquitous bell would sit, its frenzied ringing bringing forth someone, of impatient temperament and distracted disposition, from some unknown and undisclosed recess, after a wait of at least ten minutes. The responses I would get to my searching queries would be, as usual, far from edifying.

'Anyone arrived from Delhi this evening? No, I don't think so.'

'Why don't I think so? Because there aren't too many places for him to hide in here, are there? And, even if there were, why would he be hiding if he really wants you to find him?'

'He might be traumatised and not thinking clearly, you say? Shouldn't you, then, be looking for him at a hospital rather than a YMCA?'

'How would I know which hospital? Wouldn't that depend on what caused the trauma, and where? By the way, what *did* cause it?'

'You don't know? You don't think he has a trauma? Then why did you suggest that he did? Well then, do you know what he looks like? You don't? Funny, there doesn't seem to be very much that you *do* know. Are you sure he isn't a figment of your imagination?'

By the time I exited YMCA, Sealdah, after the fourth such predominantly one-sided and uninformative exchange, I'd begun to believe that he was.

I had lost the adrenaline buzz that my encounter with Dirty Harry had left me with and, instead, had the sense of numbness that comes from receiving so many knocks on the same spot that you, finally, stop feeling. I was also starting to think that the previous day's telephone conversation had not happened, at all, and was another fabrication of a fevered imagination, although why my imagination should be fevered, I couldn't even begin to guess.

It was nine. Claiming a medical emergency which, from my disturbed appearance, they had no difficulty believing, I cajoled an open pharmacy to allow me use of their telephone. I called home.

'What's keeping you?' demanded Rita, my wife who, if her tone was any indication, was shedding her usual equanimity, very rapidly. 'He's called four times already asking for you. I think he's lost it completely.'

'Haven't we all?' I proceeded to give her a pithy version of events, ending with an entreaty that she must try and extract from him, on pain of death, if necessary, the address of the YMCA he was hiding himself in, if he were to call a fifth time.

My stressed nerves craved liquid healing. The bright lights and watering holes of Park Street beckoned. I nosed the Standard Herald into a vacant parking slot. With images of chilled beer frothing in my head, I noticed, purely by chance, that the building opposite the bar I was headed for had a sign that announced, in dazzling neon that was hard to miss, that it was a 'YWCA'. Accident, happenstance, quirk, coincidence, fluke, twist of fate—call it what you will—but something quite inexplicable made me forego the inviting glass-door of the bar for the relatively less hospitable entrance of the premises opposite. I entered a lobby decidedly smaller than the ones I had visited for the better part of three hours and considerably less gloomy. Or, maybe, it just felt like that to me because it was different.

Walking the wooden floor, at a pace as regular as a metronome's—left to right, right to left—was a middle-aged, fair-complexioned, bald-headed gentleman carrying, on his back, a bulky rucksack and, on his face, an expression of complete disorientation. Watching his frenetic pacing was a young female receptionist wearing spectacles, nervousness and too much make-up. As I stood uncertainly at the door, the pacer reached the end of his delineated parade-ground and turned on his heel for the return march. His eyes found mine. Exasperation, bordering on outrage, replaced the bewilderment.

'Mr Surjo Sengupta, I presume?' I ventured tentatively, doing a Stanley to his Dr Livingstone.

'This is really too much,' Dr Livingstone exploded, clearly disinterested in literary reconstructions. It might have been my fevered imagination, but I thought I saw wisps of steam leave his dilated nostrils and turn opaque in the white of the overhead neon light, before dissipating in the dark of the high ceiling.

'I've been waiting here for three hours! And that's on top of a twenty-four-hour train journey!' A gush of what I surmised was frustrated French followed. The actual words may have been unintelligible to me, but the essence certainly wasn't. A few recognisable sounds, like driftwood in a flood of rounded vowels and nasal consonants, left me with the impression that my intelligence was under serious scrutiny, as it had been earlier, in more recognisable terms, by Police Sergeant Harold Mann.

'I'm sorry, but you *do* know where you are, of course,' I retaliated, flinching under the tirade, although an inner voice whispered, as inner voices are prone to do, that I had no reason to be apologetic.

'What, what!' exclaimed Surjo Sengupta in duplicate, clutching his brow in an exaggerated show of exasperation and turning to the receptionist for intervention believing, presumably, that the divine variety would be slower in coming.

'I did tell him that he couldn't stay on the premises, certainly not for as long as he's been here, but he wouldn't listen,' said the receptionist to no one in particular. In execution of its rapidly-eroding role of moral guardian, the YWCA had somewhat archaic rules about who could visit its wards and who could not. Men, particularly the middle-aged, bald-headed variety, with manic gleams to their eyes and a tendency to resort to French under stress, certainly didn't qualify.

'I was just about to call the Police,' ended the receptionist.

'Not Police Sergeant Mann, I hope,' I muttered under my breath.

Our collective misery had congealed into a low-flying pall of gloom. It was almost four hours since I had extricated myself from the clutches of P S Harold Mann and started the hunt for this elusive poet from Paris; it was nearly thirty, since Surjo Sengupta had started his, for reprieve from the heat, dust and din of Delhi.

'You said that you'd be at a YMCA, not even *which* YMCA, which was bad enough,' I said, somewhat heatedly. 'Now, after hunting for you high and low, I find you at a YWCA. For the hours that you've been pounding the floor here, I've been pounding the streets of Calcutta, not to mention avoiding the ire of a certain Police Sergeant Mann!'

'Who's Police Sergeant Mann?' asked my guest, his irascible demeanour beginning to dissolve into a less aggressive mien at the mention of the gendarme. In fact, I thought I caught a hint of concern, for his own self-preservation, no doubt, in his tone.

'Never mind,' I said, lifting the large suitcase that stood next to the reception desk. 'Let's take you home.'

Thus, in circumstances that were a strange brew of deliberation, unexpectedness, accident and error, Surjo Sengupta landed in my life. As I was to find out in the days and weeks ahead, it was a combustible concoction.

FIVE

Kick-off

The meeting with Vishal Kaushik, senior brand manager, ICC, was in the first hour of the day, which saved Rahul Banerjee a trip to B.B. Ganguly Street and the cramped office above Ruby Bar. In striking contrast, ICC occupied the uppermost floors of an imposing, spanking-new structure of aluminium, glass and granite, on Chowringhee Road, its floor-to-ceiling windows affording a panoramic view of the Calcutta Maidan, all the way up to the Hooghly river.

Anoop Chowdhury was waiting for him at the bank of elevators that took up one end of a spacious lobby, all marble and stainless steel.

'The agenda is to introduce you and confirm the focus groups for Bombay,' said Anoop Chowdhury watching, with the concentration of a die-hard punter, a bank of light-emitting diodes industriously tracking the ascent and descent of half-a-dozen elevators, on a wall-mounted display. At the moment, it was anybody's guess which one would reach the ground floor first, No. 1 or No. 3, though No. 6, if it managed to maintain the speed that it had unexpectedly picked-up since quitting the fifteenth floor, could well pip them both at the post.

Anoop Chowdhury grimaced, as he mentally lost a month's income, with No. 6 purring to the finish-line a floor, or two, ahead of the favourites. They stepped into its stainless steel cocoon and were transported to the twenty-second floor, with an uninterrupted, hydraulic whoosh. Rahul Banerjee noticed that his senior partner had his eyes tightly shut during the few minutes that it took them to reach their destination.

The reception area was all granite and mahogany. So was the receptionist.

From her tough-as-nails demeanour and world-weary visage, Rahul Banerjee surmised that she had been minding the ICC store for decades and, by now, looked upon the entire staff on the twenty-second floor as *hers*, to be protected unto death or destruction, if need be, from the unwanted intrusion of outsiders, particularly those who sniffed noisily and walked into glass doors, as Anoop Chowdhury had almost done, in his haste to leave the elevators before its doors closed on him and he was transported to heights that he had no desire to attain just yet.

'Do you have an appointment?' asked the Keeper at the Gate in a voice that was like glaciers slowly shifting, rubble and all.

She paid scant regard, or respect, to the visiting card that Anoop Chowdhury whisked out of a pocket and dangled under her nose, or to his somewhat incoherent deposition that their meeting was pre-arranged and, certainly, had the consent of Vishal Kaushik, senior brand manager. After a cursory glance, which if it had stayed longer on Chowdhury may have burnt him to cinder, she dialled a number on her intercom.

'Alice, dear,' she said, in a tone that was a distant cry from the enormous block of ice it had resembled just moments ago, 'how are you?'

From the prolonged squawking that emanated from the other end, Alice seemed to have a lot to say about her general health and disposition, her peroration extended by the empathetic sounds that the Keeper at the Gate made, each time Alice showed the slightest signs of winding down. From her timely punctuations in what was, essentially, a one-sided conversation, Rahul Banerjee surmised that (a) Alice had had a terrible weekend with Tony, presumably an errant boyfriend, having stood her up at the eleventh hour, despite having promised, earlier in the week, that he'd definitely escort her to the Merchant's Navy Ball (b) insult had been added to injury when she'd been informed, by an unnamed well-wisher, that not only had the unreliable Tony gone to the Ball, after all, but had been observed dancing, and unashamedly canoodling, with a certain Tessa until the wee hours of the morning (c) Alice was justifiably devastated, since she'd believed, on the evidence of the three months that they'd been together, that this was, indeed, the real thing, quite unlike the two-week fling she'd had with Derek previously which, if one were to confess in the strictest confidence, had been a physical thing altogether, never expected to last the course (d) all men were cads and she was tempted to go off them for a while, although that wasn't such a good idea really, as she tended to put on weight that was tough to get rid off when she wasn't dating, and (e) with Secretaries' Night around the corner she'd better get herself a new boyfriend, and a new dress, quickly, although not necessarily in that order.

After nearly twenty minutes, the Guardian of the Citadel may have felt that she'd sympathised with Alice long enough, or established sufficient superiority over her waiting, visitors for, with an imperious glance in Rahul and Chowdhury's direction to let them know that she was doing them a favour, which they should be eternally beholden to her for, she interrupted Alice's broken-hearted soliloquy to impart the information that there were some people waiting to see her boss. Rahul guessed that this act of apparent generosity came not from any sudden feeling of sympathy for them but, possibly, from a realisation that there was nothing more of consequence to be extracted from Alice who had, presumably, provided enough grist for the gossip mill to run for the rest of the week, at full efficiency.

'Down the corridor, last door on the left.' The Dragon who, Rahul noticed, went by the name of Agnes, returned to her igloo, her words hanging like stalactites in the space that she'd occupied moments earlier.

The corridor was a long, neon-lit strip of marble flooring, with dark panelling and mahogany doors on either side. Shining brass plaques identified the species that resided within. The door opposite the one that said *V. Kaushik, Sr. Brand Manager* bore another unmistakable and universally-understood legend: *Gentlemen*. With barely-concealed relief, Anoop Chowdhury flung it open, the twenty-minute wait in the Dragon's lair having, no doubt, put his internal plumbing under severe stress.

Ablutions completed and composure restored, they entered the domain of V. Kaushik. A secretary's cubicle served to protect the privacy of the primary inmate. Alice, of the broken heart, rose from behind an overloaded desk to bid them 'good morning', smiling bravely to obfuscate the fact of the terrible one she'd been having herself. She peeped around another door to announce their arrival.

'You're late,' said a condemnatory baritone, even before they'd entered the inner sanctum. 'Not a good way to start our association, is it?'

The first impression that Rahul had of Vishal Kaushik was that his parents had been ill-advised to give him the name that they had. But then, at age three months, they could have scarcely known to what height the apple of their eye would, finally, grow. Contrary to its meaning (*large*), Vishal Kaushik was a small man, which meant that there was little of him to see when he was seated behind an executive desk. (This also explained why, as Rahul would discover subsequently, he preferred to conduct most of his meetings standing up.)

Vishal Kaushik stood up.

Anoop Chowdhury mumbled profuse apologies and, as an obvious ploy to divert Kaushik from the uncomfortable subject of punctuality, waved a proprietary hand in Rahul's direction.

'Rahul Banerjee, the marketing chap I spoke to you about. Just joined us. Will personally oversee the paint project,' he gushed by way of an introduction. 'Business school, class of '75.'

Rahul realised that Anoop Chowdhury, seasoned campaigner, had casually inserted that last bit to try and recapture the psychological advantage that had been temporarily lost because of their tardiness, albeit through no fault of theirs, the Dragon's delaying tactics being too convolute to explain.

'Hi,' said Vishal Kaushik, his voice growing deeper in an attempt to compensate for the slight unease he felt at being in the presence of a business management graduate, which he was not. 'Good to see that Anoop is finally taking our business seriously. Ha, ha. Good to meet you, Rahul. Call me Veekay.'

Rahul surmised that 'Veekay' was another way for him to obliterate the contradiction of his name, like his soon-to-be revealed propensity for conducting all his meetings standing up. Chowdhury and Rahul seated themselves in leather-cushioned swivel chairs, while Veekay peered down at them from about five feet two inches above sea level.

'Okay, then,' said Kaushik, assuming the reins of the meeting, which as a client was his prerogative. 'Take me through the research design and schedule, please.'

Finally in familiar waters, Anoop Chowdhury plunged in with enthusiasm, although, to make the project weightier and more complex than it actually was and therefore more deserving of the high price that was being charged for it, his dissertation was overly peppered with jargon that had Rahul silently wincing and Veekay blatantly dumbstruck, or so it seemed, unless the glazed look in his eyes was from the pain of standing still.

Anoop Chowdhury held forth, twisting and turning like a paper sailboat caught in high wind, on the merits of random selection, right-hand sampling methods, probability theory, confidence levels, questionnaire formatting, transactional behaviour, group dynamics and so on, reasserting that the market research for Vishal Kaushik's New Paint was in the safest and most capable of hands, in case there was even the remotest doubt remaining.

'The quality of the moderator is critical,' Chowdhury concluded, awarding himself a self-congratulatory pat. 'He must be able to make the participants comfortable so that they can air their views freely. Without leading them or biasing them, he must be able to pick-up key consumer insights that can impact your brand's marketing, and help it steal a march over competition.'

'Quite so,' acknowledged Veekay, cringing a bit, either from having to maintain an erect posture in the thin sliver of space between his executive desk and his high-backed executive chair, or from Anoop Chowdhury's continuing onslaught of research jargon.

Encouraged by the approbation, Anoop Chowdhury dived back into the waters, energetically.

'Of course, as important as the quality of the moderator, is his ability to attract the right kind of people to the focus groups,' he said. 'They've got to represent your target audience: you know, house owners who have a discerning lifestyle and a definite point of view on things that concern their home, including the actual paint that goes up on their walls; not like the majority who, at best, only choose the shades they want and leave all the rest, including the choice of brand, to their painting contractor.'

Veekay's wearying back won over his need to maintain a psychological advantage; he sat down and almost sank below the vision of his visitors. He compensated by introducing a deeper timbre to his voice.

'Precisely,' he boomed, the word banging around the small room like a ball in a squash-court.

'Tea?' asked Alice, poking her head in. She must have received the word in misshapen condition after all the demented bouncing it had done.

'Pardon?'

'You called for tea?'

Though Vishal Kaushik hadn't, he must have decided that it was too much trouble to argue the point, more so, because of the dry and brittle expression he saw on his secretary's face, for, without further Q & A, he agreed that tea did, indeed, sound like a sterling idea.

Rahul Banerjee was to learn later, as his education in the mores of Calcutta's corporate life reached a higher level, that often, the quality of the tea-service separated the men from the boys, the stars from the dogs and the favoured from the less so, in the hallways and cabins of the city's commercial establishments. He was to learn that, at the bottom of the pecking order, were those who got their tea in ordinary cups from a common, stainless-steel tea trolley that was wheeled in twice a day, usually at 11 a.m. and 3 p.m., by a uniformed peon who, when he was not doing duty as a tea-server, carried files from one floor to another and, often, went missing in-between. Babus and probationary officers still green around the gills, seated in open work areas, were the recipients of this dispensation.

A notch or two up the totem pole were those who got their tea *on trays*. The quality of tea was the same, coming as it did off the same common, stainless-steel tea dispenser, wheeled around by the same peon, except that, in this case, it travelled the last distance on a tray. The trays were aluminium, bruised and battle-scarred, as they also did duty in the staff canteen when they weren't being used to serve tea. The beneficiaries of this service were, generally, junior officers who shared cabins—two or three to a cubicle—and utilised the services of a male stenographers' pool, usually located on a different floor.

Then, there were those, like Vishal Kaushik, who occupied individual cabins and had female secretaries exclusively to themselves, not only on the same floor but, actually in the same suite! They were considered to have a future, or so the company would have them believe; whether the potential was finally realised depended on the individual and his karma and, among other things, his golf handicap. In recognition of their more exalted status, they were not circumscribed by the 11 a.m. and 3 p.m. routine and had the flexibility to call for tea whenever they wanted, whether it was to get their own batteries recharged, extend hospitality to a visitor, or keep the insidious hand of Morpheus at bay after an indiscreetly-prolonged lunch. The tea was Leaf, a mix of Darjeeling and Assam, one for aroma, the other for colour and strength. It was brewed in pots in the officers' canteen and delivered to the door of one's office, complete with serviettes, separate milk and sugar containers and a plateful of biscuits, usually chocolate cream. Thereafter, your secretary picked up the baton, as it were, carrying the tray into your cabin and proceeding to play Mum.

Those in the rarefied atmosphere of the uppermost floors had their tea service divorced from the officers' canteen, or any other outside interference. Tea for them and their guests was prepared by the secretary herself, *in situ*, using the finest china and tea blends, all stored in a locked cupboard next to her file cabinet, the easier for her to access when the call for the cup that cheered came from the room adjoining. Of course, on these floors, too, like everywhere else, there were firsts amongst equals, the china becoming finer, the tea blends more customised and the trays graduating to silver, as the square footage of one's room increased and the view it commanded, of the resplendent Calcutta Maidan and the Hooghly river beyond, expanded.

But all this and more, Rahul Banerjee was to discover much later. For the moment, the tea ceremony that Alice presided over afforded welcome respite from Chowdhury's prolonged and impassioned diatribe, which had driven their prospective client to seek refuge behind his baritone and the expanse of his executive desk.

'The trip to Bombay has to be planned meticulously,' announced Anoop Chowdhury, on the way back to their office on B.B.

Ganguly Street. 'Right down to the last detail, so that nothing goes wrong when Veekay arrives.'

Vishal Kaushik had decided earlier that, rather than travel with the Rexxon directors, he would arrive on the day of the first group discussion.

'I think I can let you guys get on with the business of deciding the venue and the participants,' he'd said after Anoop Chowdhury had pinned him to the vertical position again, for another forty minutes, post-the tea break, with a monologue on how to spot dominating personalities early in the game and discourage them from hijacking a discussion, overwhelming the meeker, but, possibly, more relevant, views of others who were considerably less aggressive in airing their opinions.

'We'll send Partho a few days ahead of us to do the preparatory groundwork. Identify the right participants, get them to agree, fix the venue,' said Anoop Chowdhury, as they bumped uncomfortably along the tramlines on Bentinck Street, hemmed-in by crazily-leaning, overloaded, smoke-spewing buses, which bullied for right of way on a road that had been sheared to less than half its original width, which hadn't been much to start with, by the ongoing construction work for the city's much-vaunted, but much-delayed, underground metro railway.

Rahul was relieved to learn that Partho had a role more substantial than just procuring biryani for Tapas Pan's exacting palate. His further participation in Chowdhury's musings was discouraged by the need to concentrate on threading his car through the temporary, and all-too-brief, breaks that opened in the sluggish flow of traffic, more by happenstance than by any individual or collective intention.

'We'll *have* to find ourselves a new office soon,' said Anoop Chowdhury, squirming uneasily as a tempo swerved drunkenly into the path of their car, missing its front fender by a whisker. 'Another project or two like ICC's and we should be able to move to somewhere nicer.'

Through the stress of manoeuvring his vehicle out of the tangle of unruly cars, boisterously-undisciplined buses and suicidal pedestrians, Rahul had the realisation that this was a shared moment, an expression from his senior partner of both aspiration and apology. Chowdhury, in a flash of intuition, or guilt, had grasped that the plush, air-conditioned offices of ICC were too recent a memory, and too stark a contrast with the bewildering confusion of their current location, for Rahul *not* to doubt his purchase of the entrepreneurial dream. However, the shared moment passed as quickly as it had appeared.

They managed to enter B.B. Ganguly Street despite mystifying and contradictory signals from a home guard perched, like an urban scarecrow, on top of an overturned oil drum, in the centre of a crossroads. Home guards, a breed peculiar to Calcutta, were pressed into service when a large number of traffic lights failed simultaneously (which, in those days of inadequate power supply, was often), or *real* traffic policemen had been commandeered to manage the crowds at a Mohun Bagan-East Bengal football match, or had gone to answer a call of nature from which they were seldom in any tearing hurry to return. Untrained as they were in any form of traffic control, and tending towards the diminutive in physical construction, home guards were, usually, more a hindrance than a help. Some speculated that the breed had been conceived by the local government, with the specific purpose of providing employment to rural sons of the soil since all the *real* policemen's jobs had been usurped by immigrants from neighbouring States who were, physically, closer to the minimum height and weight parameters that the job laid down.

Therefore, it usually came as no surprise to anyone when, in the middle of a particularly puzzling hand signal, a home guard would climb off his perch and vanish into the crowd, struck by the realisation that his incomprehensible, public contortions had mangled the traffic into such a state of anarchy that not even all the king's horses and all the king's men could put it back in order again.

Thankfully, B.B. Ganguly Street was too close to Lal Bazaar (Red Market—a somewhat unfortunate choice of name for Police Headquarters) for a home guard to enjoy complete independence; the chaos was controlled. Rahul was fortunate to find a parking slot on only his fifth circling of the block, although that was long enough for Chowdhury to have convinced himself that the good meeting that they'd had with Veekay deserved a small celebration, preferably a long lunch of the wet kind.

Tapas Pan, sulking from having been excluded from the morning's meeting and denied the opportunity to air more of his homespun wisdom, had other ideas.

'We must hit while the still is steel hot,' he propounded, mixing metaphors and alloys and mauling a vowel or two. 'If Vishal is impressed with our speed, we will get more business out of him.'

The logic was irrefutable, though Anoop Chowdhury winced exaggeratedly at this unbecoming show of avarice, possibly for the benefit of their new partner. 'More than speed of action, we must do a good job.'

'Quickly,' reiterated Tapas Pan, in obstinate support of his hypothesis that swiftness of execution was the surest way to ensure repeated purchase of their service and good could only get better, if it was on time.

As the morning progressed, Rahul Banerjee was able to learn a little more about his two partners who, if you were to look at it dispassionately, were complete strangers to him. Other than that one gin-soaked afternoon in Ordnance Club, and a half-dozen occasions when he had been mined—unsuccessfully—for business, they had always travelled on different roads. Sure, they had met, even exchanged a word or two, at some advertising agency get-together or the other, but that had been due more to the limited width of Calcutta's marketing fraternity, where the same people got invited to the same parties, than any predisposition, on his part, to further their acquaintance. So, in retrospect, Rahul's decision to hitch his wagon to their train was not because the sight of Messrs Chowdhury and Pan unleashed an uncontrollable tidal wave of entrepreneurial zeal within him, but because, at the time that they happened to blunder into his path, he was in the throes of extreme ennui with his existing occupation. And still too young in the ways of the world to realise, let alone fear, the consequences of impulsive action.

Anoop Chowdhury had positioned himself, through no small effort on his part, as the knowledgeable, greying, head-in-the-clouds academic, whose sole purpose in life, single-handedly if it came down to it, was to raise the standards of marketing research in the country: how imaginatively it was conceived and with what level of integrity, and transparency, it was executed. Tapas Pan had elected to play his able foil, not that any other role of consequence was available to him, given his intrinsic nature—practical, blunt and outspoken, usually to the point of incomprehensibility and embarrassment, due to a rather tenuous grasp of spoken English.

In consonance with his self-defined role, Tapas Pan took charge of organising the imminent field trip to Bombay. Partho was summoned; he arrived carrying an array of menu cards, which he was berated to lose promptly. This was not a matter of just today's lunch but *all* future lunches, Tapas Pan informed him. In a Bengali that was significantly more lucid than his English, Pan spoke of the grave responsibility that was being bestowed upon him by the directors—one that he had to fulfil with no regard to mind, body or soul. Realising that this passionate call to the trenches might greatly alarm someone whose defining role, so far, had been to locate the right biryani, he hastened to declare, with a broad wink in the general direction of Anoop Chowdhury and Rahul, that the company would certainly not be found wanting, when it came to distributing largesse for a job well done.

'Do you understand?' asked Tapas Pan, though the vividness and flamboyance of his peroration should not have left the slightest doubt, in even the most limited of intelligences, about what he meant.

Partho admitted that he did, whereupon Pan launched into a monologue on costs, which concluded with his observation that ten thousand rupees should adequately cover Partho's travel, board and lodging, local conveyance and any advance that he might have to pay to secure a suitable venue for the first group discussion.

When Partho, harangued into submission, returned to the staff enclosure, Tapas Pan, in an act of great intimacy, dug out a steel box from the innards of his desk and opened it with a key and a four-digit combination. Under Rahul's bemused gaze, he extricated a roll of notes tied with a rubber-band, and, with the same concentration that had marked his detailing of the biryani he'd wanted for lunch the previous afternoon, counted out ten thousand rupees. Then, he locked the box and returned it to concealment.

'Four days should be enough for you to set things up nicely,' said Anoop Chowdhury, when Partho was recalled to be handed his tour advance. 'We will schedule the group discussion for next Monday, and book our flight tickets accordingly.'

Then, through a mist of smoke rising from a cigarette that drooped insolently from the corner of his mouth, in the manner of an unshaven hero from a spaghetti Western after he has despatched the guys in black to their respective graves in several imaginative ways, Tapas Pan relented to give his senior partner the celebration that he'd proposed a while back, suggesting that this might be as good a time as any to inaugurate Ruby Bar. It must have been a thought uppermost in Anoop Chowdhury's mind too, for, with the same nimble-footedness that he'd shown earlier in the day leaping out of an elevator before it closed on him, he led the charge to the front door.

In the days and weeks to follow, Rahul was to discover that Messrs Chowdhury and Pan possessed an irrepressible streak of optimism that ensured that no occasion was too small to merit a celebration.

It was 1 p.m. when they entered Ruby Bar, but it was the darkness of night that greeted them. After the brittle brightness of the streets, it was like blind men walking that they groped their way to a vacant table. The unmistakable, cloying smell of spilled spirit and leaked urine hung, invisibly, over everything, like a diaphanous blanket. Rahul recognised it from his first visit to the building, except that it was stronger, sharper and more immediate inside.

A silhouette, its features indistinguishable from the surrounding blackness, took their order of Black Label beer. Before the beer was served, a bill was inserted into an empty glass and placed on their table. The phantom waited, hand extended. Anoop Chowdhury looked at him, quizzically. They formed a dark, silent tableau, as the seconds stretched into minutes and then, reluctantly, dragged themselves away into a deeper darkness.

'What's up?' Chowdhury's puzzlement was replaced by angry impatience at being denied the bottle that is known to cheer significantly more than the proverbial cup can ever do.

'I think the policy here is that you pay before you get served,' Rahul ventured an explanation. The wraith with the extended hand nodded vigorously in agreement.

'We aren't your regular drunks, you know,' muttered Tapas Pan, peeling off the required number of notes from an untidy bundle that he scavenged from his back-pocket. The spectre vanished, bestowing on them a parting look that seemed to suggest that not yet they weren't, but only a fool would stake his life on such an eventuality not happening soon.

The Black Label was just a few degrees above room temperature. Clearly, Ruby Bar's regular clientele comprised those who were entirely dedicated to the pursuit of value-for-money and gave potions of the lesser kind, beer, for instance, a wide berth; not for them the long wait, punctuated by frequent visits to the toilet, before the arrival of the Heady Buzz; not for them the unwanted interval of coherence before the delightful oblivion of the Great Leveller and not for them the insidious, creeping onset of Sensory Numbness, when a couple of stiff shots could do the trick in less than half the time.

But that did not deter Anoop Chowdhury from consuming large amounts of it and rationalising, in anticipation of any misguided criticism, that warm beer was, in fact, preferable in the circumstances as it would prevent a sore throat, a condition that he could ill-afford only a few days away from the most important assignment in Rexxon's short history, when his voice needed to be in fine fettle, if not, actually, on song.

'Did you know that this place converts to a dance bar in the night?' asked Tapas Pan of nobody in particular. He was proving to be an adequate foil to Anoop Chowdhury, matching him glass for glass, cigarette for cigarette.

'How do you know?' The bleary camouflage of Black Label couldn't quite mask the gleam that developed at the corner of Anoop Chowdhury's eyes.

'Even *my* market research can be relied upon sometimes,' gurgled Tapas Pan, spraying beer in all directions, his humour threatening to unshackle itself further, having already elicited a measure of prurient interest from his senior.

'Nonsense. Can't be true,' said Chowdhury, his tone betraying the hope that it was just the opposite. 'Not next to Lal Bazaar.'

'More so, *because* of it. Protection, you know.'

'Where do you come up with such ideas?'

'Even law enforcers need recreation! You can't deny them that!'

'Should be worth a visit, then,' said Anoop Chowdhury, easily convinced that any place that had the blessing and patronage of the law acquired a gloss of respectability that even the omnipresent smell of stale urine could not erase.

'Imagine: no closing-time deadline, booj always on tap and no sudden raids to spoil your party!' Tapas Pan presented his concluding argument with a flair that would have swayed even the most hardened and sceptical of juries. In comparison, Chowdhury was a soft target.

He closed his eyes. Rahul wasn't sure whether it was because he'd taken Tapas Pan's argument to heart and was seeing, in his mind's eye, a bevy of scantily-clad women sinuously shaking their hips at him, or whether the excess of warm beer had, finally, so overwhelmed him that sleep offered the only respite. In an uncanny replication of his senior partner's actions, Tapas Pan also leaned back in his chair and promptly went to sleep, the burbling snores emanating from the darkness indisputable confirmation of his condition.

Looking at his business partners in various stages of unconsciousness, Rahul Banerjee decided that not much was likely to be achieved in the rest of the afternoon. He also surmised, from what little he could see of the expression on the waiters' faces, that comatose customers were not an uncommon sight in Ruby Bar. No doubt having learnt its lessons the hard way, the Management made sure that payment was collected in advance of serving the stuff that salved parched throats and turbulent consciences and, as long as customers had paid for their sleep, Ruby Bar was never in any hurry to evict them.

Leaving his fellow directors to the ministrations of a smiling spectre, whose palms Tapas Pan had greased heavily, and frequently, to ensure an uninterrupted flow of Black Label beer, Rahul stepped back onto the pavement of B.B. Ganguly Street. Coming suddenly out of the darkness of the bar into the glare of a late afternoon sun, hurt. But, it also cleared away the cloying dankness that had escaped the confines of Ruby Bar and insinuated itself into his clothes and psyche. However, it could do little to separate him from the sense of foreboding that, in such a short time, had become his close companion.

'It's not going to work out,' confessed Rahul Banerjee that evening as he fumigated his mind from the lingering after-effects of fermented oats and barley with a glass of chilled nimbu pani.

'Isn't it a little too early in the day to come to that conclusion?' asked Ratna, ever the practical one.

'Isn't there a saying about the dawn heralding the day?'

'Isn't there one about the darkest hour preceding the light, too?'

'What worries me about *that* is that I'm not sure whether spending a couple of hours guzzling warm beer in not the most salubrious of environs, when most people of any repute are more productively employed, *is* the darkest hour. Because if it isn't, my mind boggles at what else could be in store for me before I catch even the remotest glimmer of light!'

'Guzzling warm beer in not the most salubrious of environs with dancing girls cavorting before you and the echo of police sirens in your ears?' posed Ratna, teasingly. Having endured Rahul Banerjee's refrain—constant for the last six months—that working for others was a mug's game, she was not about to let him reverse his opinion in a hurry.

'Very amusing,' said Rahul, not the least bit amused. 'I have a market research specialist who's always searching for a reason to drink himself silly and, surprisingly, always finding it, too, like some hyper-efficient divining rod. The guy, who's supposed to look after our finances, doesn't really care to as he's mostly busy consuming large amounts of beer, as well. And biryani. If that isn't scary enough, there is whispered talk behind my back about something called 'the urine project', which I'm kept totally in the dark about!'

'You're over-reacting,' said Ratna.

Rahul knew that she was right. But the sight of two founder directors of an enterprise tipped to change the face of marketing research in the country, in a state of supine immobility in the middle of a summer afternoon, in a bar not known for the savoury reputation of its clientele, had been disconcerting, to say the least.

'I guess so,' he admitted. 'It's early days yet though these frequent detours for biryani and beer, on the flimsiest of excuses, do take some getting used to.'

But from the unease that lingered, despite several attempts to drown it with chilled nimbu pani, Rahul Banerjee had a feeling that it was only a matter of time before the fragile relationship that he shared with his fellow directors collapsed like a house of cards, although, admittedly, forty-eight hours was too short a period to test the hypothesis.

'You guys only need this Bombay trip to succeed for everything to be hunky-dory again,' said Ratna, with convincing sanguinity.

Rahul searched his most recent memories for a reason to share her optimism. Unfortunately, he couldn't find one.

SIX

The Unfocused Focus Group

Five days later they were in Bombay. It was still called that.

The flight had been uneventful except for Anoop Chowdhury picking the exact time that the Airbus was juddering its way through a pocket of exceptionally bad turbulence to divulge his fear of flying. This untimely disclosure was followed by a desperate clutching of the arm-rests, a spasmodic opening-and-clenching of the jaw and the emission of a low, undulating whine, all of which contributed to transfer a large part of his paranoia to Rahul Banerjee sitting next to him. However, a problem shared did not a problem halve. At the end of the flight, two equally-miserable people boarded a yellow-and-black at Santa Cruz airport for the long drive to Shalimar Hotel at Kemp's Corner

In those days, everything about Bombay intimidated the inadequately-travelled Calcuttan: that it stretched longitudinally where Calcutta was comfortingly circular; that its main arterial roads permitted motorists to clock more than sixty kilometres per hour when the clearest stretch of Red Road in Calcutta allowed only half that; that there *were* so many cars on the road, in the first place; that the city had such an imposing skyline when most of Calcutta seemed to be lying flat on its back; that the people of Bombay seemed to be in a perpetual state of motion when, in comparison, Calcutta was a city frozen in time; that Calcutta boasted of only a handful of buildings that gave you a view of anything more than your neighbour's washing when, in Bombay, towering edifices, climbing imperiously to the sky, giving you a limitless view of the sea and places beyond, were the rule rather than the exception.

They checked into Shalimar Hotel in the late afternoon and retired to their respective rooms: Anoop Chowdhury to trace Partho, who was supposed to have spread the good word, plentifully, in advance of their arrival and Rahul, to recover from the shared fright of their inward flight. Thankfully, Tapas Pan, acknowledging the importance of the trip, had extended himself—and Rexxon's resources—to provide them the privacy of single rooms. It was another matter that the only thing that Rahul could stretch in a room of the size that he was allotted was his imagination. But, at least, the air-conditioning was adequate.

It must have been more than adequate, or Rahul was more fatigued by Anoop Chowdhury's antics on board the incoming flight than he'd imagined, because he dropped off to sleep almost as soon as his head hit the pillow. When he awoke the LED display on the bedside clock read a bright 16:32 and the furniture in the room had turned to shadows. The temperature outside must have dropped a long way too, because the room was very cold, colder than what a Voltas air-conditioner of advanced years could manage on its own.

Glancing at the telephone, he noticed that the red 'Messages' light was blinking with an urgency that almost bordered on desperation. He pressed the button wondering who in Bombay could have known of his arrival to have tracked him down so soon.

'Oh, God,' groaned the telephone with more despair in its tone than devotion before it returned to an impenetrable, grave-like silence.

Message 2 was a medley of strange background noises prominent among which was the recognisable sound of heavy things falling.

Message 3 commenced with a melancholic groan before it veered, somewhat aimlessly, towards a mid-tempo crescendo: 'Rahul, where are you? We are finished.'

Message 4, the last, had been left some fifteen minutes earlier. The noise of falling things, so prominent in Message No. 2, had returned, except that this time, it was one, loud, definitive thump, not a series of muffled ones. It sounded as if an article of considerable weight had descended to the floor from a considerable height in somewhat ungainly haste.

His senses alert, the alarm bells in his head jangling a discordant tune, Rahul Banerjee raced out of his room. The door to Anoop Chowdhury's was a few strides along the narrow, carpeted corridor. It was ajar. Gently, Rahul nudged it wide open.

The room was a replica of his own—a single bed with bed linen in similar disarray; the same, shadowy furniture, curtains drawn the same way his were; the same table-lamps except that these lay on the carpeted floor when they should have been standing on the bedside tables; the same breathless air-conditioner, gasping from its perch above the window. The only *real* difference was Anoop Chowdhury who lay on the floor in the narrow space between the bed and the wall, his head caught in a penumbra of light spilling from the duo of table-lamps that lolled beside him. Standing on the bedside table, like guilty suspects at a police line-up, was a couple of tall glasses, an almost fully-drained bottle of Blue Riband gin, a half-dozen empty bottles of tonic water and a capacious ice pail. The faux-silver bucket had leaked its condensation onto the scarred table in a rivulet that meandered unsteadily past squeezed lemon wedges and squashed cigarette butts. Amidst the detritus lay Anoop Chowdhury, a low, whistling snore assuring Rahul that he hadn't quite departed the corporeal world yet, though he was certainly dead to his immediate surroundings.

The digital clock said 17:00, in a virulent shade of green. Veekay was expected, in a little over three hours, to attend a focus group that would determine the future of ICC's new decorative paint. And, possibly, Rexxon's, as well. With the minutes ticking away, there was no time for ceremony. All the ice in the bucket had melted but the water was still cold; without further ado, Rahul overturned it on Anoop Chowdhury's head.

He surfaced, spluttering, cleaving his way out of the depths of gin-induced unconsciousness. He shivered to full wakefulness as the ice-cold water trickled down his neck and found its way past the open collar of his shirt. He shook his head to clear it but the sudden movement must have set off a pain reaction because he cringed and abruptly went very still.

'We've had it,' he predicted like a doomsday soothsayer having a particularly bad day. 'Partho is untraceable. He isn't at the New Bengal Lodge in Crawford Market where he was booked to stay. Nor has he called to tell us where the venue of this evening's group discussion is. I think he's absconded with our money.'

Given his tendency to slur and lose his way in the middle of a thought, it took Anoop Chowdhury twice the time to impart this information than it would have if he hadn't ingested 375 millilitres of 45%-proof gin. But the cold water appeared to have done the trick: he was rapidly regaining full consciousness although the reality that he was returning to seemed to offer him little comfort. The horrible, indisputable, bare-bones fact was that Rexxon was a few hours away from disaster: its most important client was arriving to attend a group discussion that wasn't even there.

'You've got to do something.' The desperation was like a neon-lit billboard on Anoop Chowdhury's face. 'You've been to this city more times than I have. You know people. Call in some favours.'

It was 17:30. So said the digital clock, gobbling up the minutes hungrily, without a sound, not even the faintest of clicks.

'Have a cold shower. It'll clear your head. Get yourself ready. I'll see what I can do.' Rahul was already rifling his memory for half-remembered names and telephone numbers. 'How many do you need for a group that'll pass muster with Veekay and also be productive?'

'At least twelve.'

'What if I find it easier to make up the number with couples instead of individuals?'

'I'll make do. Get the partners to sit separately, if need be. Get them to pretend that they don't know each other. The wives can introduce themselves to Veekay by their maiden names.' For someone who'd just come out of an alcoholic haze, Anoop Chowdhury was thinking pretty clearly. Rahul guessed that when one's back is to the wall, it frees the imagination. Desperation and alcohol have a thing or two in common: both make the imagination fertile. Both also make it easier to discard the concepts of principles, ethics and fair play that one may have propounded, with evangelical conviction, in some previous lifetime.

Leaving Anoop Chowdhury to recover his senses, and his balance, under a stinging shower, Rahul Banerjee returned to his room to work the telephone and his charm. This was as good a time as any to test whether the widely-flaunted, much-revered and oft-worshipped 'old school' network actually existed, let alone worked. In the next thirty minutes, Rahul Banerjee busied himself retrieving telephone numbers and getting the hotel operator to call people he remembered from his business school days, sometimes through the mistiest of hazes. With most, a connection had been maintained through the device of the ubiquitous greeting card (usually, Birthday and New Year salutations) or the occasional appearance at an alumni association dinner. However, with those who had left the cloisters of academia to pursue a profession similar to his, the link was somewhat more tangible—a quarterly telephone call to compare notes and bosses or even an actual sighting, on the occasions when one took a business trip to the other's city of residence. It was the second category that yielded the first hint of a solution.

Sanjay Sood was a senior executive in a music company, which was a bit of a paradox because from what Rahul remembered of him he had been tone deaf in business school. Not for him the twang of guitars, the heartbeat of a drum-set, the swelling luminosity of strings or the warble of a mellifluous voice; he'd rather be kicking a leather ball, and any shins that came in his way, across a field of mud, or wielding a cricket bat, with unshackled ferocity if somewhat dubious talent. However, even in those days of relative innocence, Sanjay Sood had exhibited the fluidity of tongue, readiness of wit and quickness of mind that, in later life, would help him to disgorge large quantities of the proverbial snow to an overawed, under-thawed Eskimo population or, as was more relevant in his case, stacks of Hindi film song records to the Great Unwashed, who, possibly, had a more advanced ear for music than he did or would ever have.

'This is rich,' laughed Sood. 'An absolute corker. One for the records.' Obviously, he did not mean the vinyl kind.

'Can you help?' With time running out, like water through a sieve, Rahul was not in the mood for jocular jousting.

'What are friends for? Though we *are* cutting it a bit fine. It's a weekday. Can't guarantee a full house at such short notice. This is Bombay, you know.'

Rahul confessed that he did know it was Bombay, which was why he was seeking Sanjay's assistance; if it had been Calcutta, he could have fended for himself, quite adequately.

'Look, if you guys are volunteering to bring in some heavy-duty snacks, we could do this at my place,' said Sood. 'It's on Napeansea Road, a stone's throw from your hotel. I'll try and get some of my office chaps over. Call in some neighbours, too. What time does the show get on the road?'

'Eight p.m. give or take. I need to give your address to the car hire firm that's meeting our client off his flight. We should be twenty, twenty-five minutes into the discussions by the time he gets in.'

'Okay, see you in a while.' Sanjay Sood rattled off his address and gave precise directions to his apartment. It was a brisk ten-minute walk from Shalimar Hotel, on the fifteenth floor of a building called Apsara. Rahul relayed the information to Orbit Travels who were about to send a car to Santa Cruz airport to await the arrival of one Vishal Kaushik.

At the risk of being prematurely self-congratulatory, Rahul Banerjee told himself that he might have just pulled it off and saved the young firm of Messrs Chowdhury, Pan and Banerjee its blushes. The occasion demanded a quiet, meditative cigarette.

He was denied it. There was a perfunctory knock on his door and in walked Anoop Chowdhury, freshly bathed and laundered, a sheepish, shamefaced Partho in tow.

'Arrived a few minutes ago,' said Anoop Chowdhury, pointing to Partho, like a butcher brandishing a fresh cut of meat. 'Apparently, he was too ashamed to meet us having achieved very little in the five days he's been here. Says he was denied entry wherever he went—couldn't get past either the boss's secretary if it was an office, or the security guard, if it was a residential building.'

Partho mumbled something about the impotence of his Rexxon visiting card. It had failed to gain him access to the sanctum of people who, conceivably, were potential users of expensive decorative wall paints and, therefore, targets for his persuasion; except that his rehearsed sales pitch had failed to reach their ears, having suffered a premature demise either in a secretary's cabin or at the security gates of a multi-storied apartment block.

'So, what stopped you from letting us know?' snapped Anoop Chowdhury taking umbrage at the implied diminution of the might of his enterprise.

'I'm sure we can get to the bottom of it later,' intervened Rahul. 'Right now, we have a group discussion to manage.'

He brought them up-to-date on his pact with Sanjay Sood. Anoop Chowdhury regained his colour—and humour—visibly. Even Partho showed some animation. With renewed urgency, directions were given, counsel exchanged and responsibilities assumed; the Rexxon train, which had been on the verge of derailment, appeared to have retrieved its balance and bearings and was, once again, chugging along nicely.

Despite a convoluted argument with an obstreperous security guard at the entrance of Apsara to convince him that they had no mala fide intentions, they were at Sanjay Sood's apartment on the dot of 7:30. At the press of a button, the doorbell burst into prolonged birdsong, which, in combination with the muted rumble of the sea that wafted above the scream of horns and the throaty growl of a thousand cars on Napeansea Road, made for a soothing balm. A curious maid, no doubt surprised by instructions to prepare for a party at short order, bade them enter.

By Bombay standards, it was a spacious apartment. A corridor opened onto a large sitting-cum-dining hall with bay windows that gave an unimpeded view of the lights of Warden Road and the sea beyond, on one side, and the luxuriant plumage of Malabar Hill, on the other. In the hall, which was tastefully appointed and mutedly lit, sat two couples, cursorily nibbling nuts, sipping drinks and exchanging words. They paused in their dangling conversation to acknowledge their entry.

'Are you one of us?' asked a bespectacled gentleman with a well-manicured beard and a head of hair decidedly less so. 'Are you victims or perpetrators?'

Rahul confessed that they belonged to the latter category and made the introductions, while Anoop Chowdhury twitched nervously by his side, taking in his surroundings with short, abrupt swivels of his neck. Partho went in search of a kitchen to store the boxes of snacks that had been procured from Shalimar Hotel's patisserie.

Sanjay Sood ambled in from an adjoining room, greeted Rahul cheerily and clasped him in a hug that would not have been out of place at a reunion of long-lost bears. For that matter, neither would Sood himself have been—Rahul observed that in the intervening years since their last sighting, he had acquired a low-slung belly and a ponderous gait. And some height, too, if that were at all possible.

'Have the introductions been made?' he asked and then, assuming that they hadn't, launched into them with gusto. 'These are the Chopras, Pankaj and Anita,' he said, taking in the bespectacled gentleman with the beard and a petite lady, with short hair, by his side, in an exaggerated sweep of one arm while, with the other, in a fair imitation of a windmill slightly out of control, he introduced the Rahas, Ajit and Anu. 'Pankaj is with a bank, Anita's in advertising, Ajit's with me in the music business and Anu teaches. And they are all here to bail out an old friend who seems to have got himself into a bit of a bother. Ha, ha.'

While Rahul Banerjee thanked them, collectively and individually, for heeding his SOS, Sood placed a proprietary arm around his neck and suggested, in a resounding stage whisper, that it would be nice if they were to get on with it because he might pass out unless permitted immediate access to the 'heavy duty' snacks that were going cold in his kitchen.

Anoop Chowdhury drew Rahul and Sood aside for a quick consultation.

'Are these all the people we're going to get?' he asked, crestfallen.

'Afraid so, old chap,' replied Sanjay Sood somewhat peeved. 'My wife, Rekha, will join us at some point. That gives us six. Treated as strangers, that's six individual participants.'

'Not enough,' said Anoop Chowdhury, his disposition gloomy and hopeless once more. 'Certainly not enough to pass muster with our friend Veekay.'

It was five minutes to eight. The Chopras and Rahas had run out of nuts, drinks and conversation. Sanjay Sood hastened to replenish bowls and glasses and, he hoped, their reservoirs of patience. As additional insurance, he recommended that the heavy-duty snacks be served, his theory being that if mouths were busy masticating they'd be less likely to be complaining.

Asking Rahul to lay out the seating arrangements and brief the participants on what the subject of the focus group was and what was expected of them (exceptionally animated interaction when the client made his appearance, for one thing), Anoop Chowdhury drew Partho into a private huddle. From the corner of his eye, Rahul saw them in protracted discussion with Chowdhury doing most of the talking and Partho, as was his custom, all the listening. A peremptory gesture of dismissal saw Partho leave the room, and the apartment, to perform whatever task Anoop Chowdhury had assigned to him.

Within ten minutes of the scheduled time of 8 p.m., which, in the circumstances, wasn't a bad recovery from an almost hopeless start, the focus group commenced. With commendable realism, Anoop Chowdhury began moderating the staged utterances of five people professing undying devotion to wall-paints while pretending to be complete strangers to each other. However, because of the artificial and unrehearsed nature of the focus group, interactions were desultory for the most part, with participants finding greater stimulation in sampling the wares of Shalimar Hotel's patisserie, and responding to Sanjay Sood's attempts at levity, than in following Chowdhury in his quest for key insights about prospective paint customers. As a result, the discussions tended to blunder into a dead-end more often than not.

At 8:20 p.m., the doorbell warbled.

Anoop Chowdhury paused in the middle of a particularly obfuscating observation, his features tightening with tension. The room went quiet in anticipation of Veekay's entry. Instead, a lady of indeterminate age and uncertain demeanour followed Sanjay Sood's maid into the room. She was dressed in a grey pant-suit and carried a leather brief-case. She wore high heels and little make-up, her hair tied in a business-like knot. Nodding her head in tentative greeting to the silent assemblage, she found herself a vacant seat.

'One of yours?' asked Sanjay Sood in a whisper, rushing to Rahul's side.

'No. Yours?'

'Never mind,' said Anoop Chowdhury. 'Let's continue.'

The doorbell didn't allow him to. At 8:23, it trilled again.

This time it was a man in his early-thirties wearing a beige jacket, black trousers, an unloosened tie and an anxious expression. Momentarily, he stood at the entrance to the hall. Then, he spotted the snack-laden table and, his priority decided, made a beeline for it. Plate filled to the brim, he found himself an empty chair and, quite oblivious to the several pairs of eyes gazing enquiringly in his direction, went about the task of emptying the platter of its plentiful bounty in double-quick time.

With rising apprehension, Sanjay Sood accosted Rahul, again. 'Yours?'

'No. I thought this one was definitely yours.'

'Let's continue,' said Anoop Chowdhury benignly. He returned to the discussions, hitting his stride, Rahul noticed, with increasing confidence.

And so it transpired that within the space of the next twenty minutes, the apartment's doorbell erupted in song at least five more times. Each performance was followed by the entry of a man, or a woman, belonging neither to Rahul's nor Chowdhury's nor, to his increasing befuddlement, Sanjay Sood's list of invitees. The strangers were in their early- to late- thirties and reasonably well-dressed, though not in the latest of trends. From the accessories they carried and the expressions they wore, it could be surmised that they held mid-level executive positions. What could *not* was whether they had the slightest interest in wall-paints. However, a trait that they definitely had in common was an astute eye—and an insatiable appetite—for the products of Shalimar Hotel's patisserie, which they attacked and demolished with single-minded focus.

'Who *are* these guys?' Sanjay Sood would ask, nonplussed, each time his query of 'yours?' was met with a negative shake of the head from Rahul. Nor could Rahul ignore his own deepening unease each time an empty plate was filled or an empty chair taken. What was inexplicable was the equanimity with which Anoop Chowdhury accepted these arrivals. In fact, at one point, he actually rejoiced.

'Full house,' he exclaimed, as the count went to thirteen, with Sanjay Sood's wife Rekha having joined the party.

The magic number crossed, it hardly seemed to matter whether this motley group was capable of throwing any light at all on the way consumers perceived wall paints; or, whether Anoop Chowdhury would ever unearth *the* crucial consumer insight that ICC needed to mount the mother of all advertising campaigns. Comfortable in the belief that their bacon had been saved, Anoop Chowdhury leaped confidently from role of moderator to role of raconteur, although the climax of his long-winded story eluded the comprehension of his audience, his train of thought having derailed somewhere along the way after a promising start.

The derailment coincided with all hell suddenly breaking loose.

It was 8:55 p.m. when the doorbell screamed, its sweet birdsong mutilated into an ear-deafening clangour. This was accompanied by insistent knocking and the heavy thud of boots kicking door.

'Open up!' This authoritative bellow was followed by further thumping, impatient and belligerent.

The maid rushed into the room, her eyes dilated in fright. The room assumed the stillness of a tomb, its inmates transfixed in a frozen tableau.

'What's happening?' asked Sanjay Sood plaintively, no doubt deeply regretting having extended a hand of cooperation to an old colleague. Perhaps, unknown to him, his friend, Rahul Banerjee, had gone irredeemably bad in the company of people like this Anoop Chowdhury fellow who, certainly, had something very strange about him, if his nervous tics and inane anecdotes were anything to go by.

While Sood was raising rhetorical questions, like little red flags of alarm, his wife, Rekha, was taking charge. Exasperated by the assault on her ears, and her home, she strode purposefully down the corridor and yanked open the front door.

Outside, stood three bulky policemen, in billowing half-pants, bulging shirts, rakishly-aligned caps and aggressive postures. In their upraised fists were the batons they'd been pounding the door with. Their faces wore dark, menacing scowls. Behind them was a gaggle of gaping neighbours, in different forms of attire and stages of awe. At the epicentre of this human montage were Vishal Kaushik and Partho, the former red and apoplectic, the latter, blue and morose, their hands tied with hemp in front of them.

Rahul rushed to Rekha's side while Sanjay Sood tried to manage the sensitivities of his guests—known and unknown—

although they appeared to be more curious than alarmed by this unexpected and rather noisy invasion of privacy by the Bombay constabulary.

'What do you want?' demanded Rekha stridently.

She was greeted by a loud burst of rapid-fire Marathi from which she was able to decipher that she—if she, indeed, was the owner of this apartment—was under suspicion of managing a house of ill-repute; that her employee (the word by which Partho was identified was infinitely more derogatory) had been nabbed red-handed in the act of propositioning, and that their client (again, the word used to describe Vishal Kaushik, senior brand manager, ICC, was substantially more descriptive) was also being charged along with them for having easily submitted to sexual solicitation, although it wasn't clear what, exactly, they had an objection to—his having succumbed at all, or for having succumbed *easily*.

Not understanding a word of an exchange that might have been sealing his fate, Vishal Kaushik grew even more agitated. Rahul's being the only face he readily recognised in these unfamiliar and intimidating surroundings, he screamed at him, his usual baritone conspicuous by its absence.

'What the fuck's going on?' he demanded, flailing his tied wrists. 'I get out of my car and this guy approaches me. He asks me whether I'm game to attend a party in the opposite building. Says there's great food going. Good company, too. All I need to do is sit around and gaff for an hour or so, no strings attached. Before I can ask what the hell he's talking about, I'm surrounded by these goons threatening me in a language I don't understand. I give them my business card, which they laugh at; I protest my innocence though I don't know what I'm being accused of and they laugh some more. Then they tie my wrists, as if I'm some fucking criminal. Small mercy they didn't put a hood over my head, too! They do the same to this guy and ask him something, repeatedly. Knock him around a bit till he gives them an address. The next thing I know is we've been hauled up here where my focus group is taking place, for which your guy, presumably, has been picking participants off the damn street. Including me, although I just happen to be the damn client— a fact that this moron isn't aware of, obviously!'

While this emotional soliloquy was centre stage, an equally-absorbing sideshow was being enacted by the three policemen and Rekha, who'd by now been joined by Sanjay Sood, Ajit Raha and Pankaj Chopra, thereby tilting the balance a considerable way towards equilibrium. Dismissing the allegations as complete nonsense and threatening legal action against what was tantamount to libel, slander and harassment, Rekha invited the trio into her apartment, reminding them to wipe their dirty boots before daring to enter her pristine premises. Tripped-up by the open invitation and the sight of normal-looking people in normal-seeming surroundings—not the smoky, dimly-lit sordidness that they'd been expecting—the three policemen hesitated, craning their necks to catch a glimpse of sleaze in action. Then, deciding that discretion was the better part of foolhardiness, they hastened to untie Veekay and Partho, attempting to pass it all off as a regrettable misunderstanding deserving of profuse apologies. These they proceeded to offer, unendingly, until Rekha had to insist that they desist and depart before she was encouraged, by their continuing presence, to report the matter to a higher authority which, she claimed, she knew quite well.

Replicating the Keystone Cops in their customary disorder, the three policemen, batons sheathed under sweaty armpits, clattered down the stairs, too embarrassed to wait for the elevator.

With their hurried departure, the curious neighbours returned to their respective flats, adequately sated by the unexpected dose of improvised entertainment.

Then, high on adrenaline, Rekha returned to the sitting room to clear it of guests who, she believed, had greatly overstayed their welcome. The seven people whom Partho had lured into the apartment with the promise of good food and company, took their leave, quite voluntarily, complimenting Rekha on her table, thanking Partho for the invitation and hoping to do it all over again some day. They, certainly, had no cause for complaint: investing an hour of free time had given them, in return, a free meal of sufficient fullness to sustain them on the long train-ride home to distant suburbs.

'I say, old chap,' said Sanjay Sood sheepishly. 'This shindig's got the old girl a little on edge, as you can see. Don't you think we should wrap it up?'

The blistering glare that Rekha directed at Anoop Chowdhury, as he sat crumpled like a ball of discarded wastepaper, was enough to dispel even the remotest hope of there being an option *not* to.

Meanwhile, distancing themselves from the contretemps, the Chopras and Rahas were engaged in a conversation that was designed to keep the perpetrators of the disaster out of it. Back to nibbling nuts and sipping drinks, they had assumed the role of victims which, they believed, would go down well with the lady of the house and ensure continuance of her hospitality and, possibly, their stay.

Sanjay Sood, his loyalty to Rahul Banerjee not entirely forsaken, flitted between the two groups like an overweight bumblebee. And, in a far corner, an apoplectic Veekay vented his spleen, which he had plenty of, on a hapless Partho.

'I've never been so insulted in my life,' fumed Vishal Kaushik as they stood, uncomfortably, at the gates of Apsara. Anoop Chowdhury, his brilliant initiative transformed into an unmitigated disaster, had retreated into a shell and no amount of persuasion was going to get him out of it in a hurry. Partho had retired hurt to a dark corner behind the guardhouse, not wishing to be an obvious witness to his bosses' public humiliation.

'I'm appalled at the way you guys conduct your business! Bloody, bungling amateurs,' Veekay continued, picking up the tempo—and his baritone—again. 'You know it's over, don't you? Not only are you chaps *not* going to be doing any business with me but, when I'm done with you, not too many other companies in Calcutta will, either.'

A strange calmness came over Rahul Banerjee as Veekay stomped and shouted in front of him. After a time, the uncontrolled outburst stopped reaching him, or having any kind of meaning at all. The heated words seemed to blunt by the time they got to him, ebbing and flowing all around him but not quite entering. To his surprise, he discovered that he was no longer affected by them. Vishal Kaushik's rants and threats had become a dull, not entirely unpleasant, echo, his tirade, a pointless pantomime. Rahul Banerjee, suddenly, was very tired of his role of red herring.

'It's not over till the fat lady sings the Blues,' he said, beginning to change, at least, the colour, if not the role.

'What?' Vishal Kaushik screeched to a stop, mid-rant.

'You're not done with us, till *we're* done with you!'

'What the hell are you talking about? Have you lost it completely?' The look on Kaushik's face was the kind that an early bird would have if the worm it had been chasing turned suddenly around and faced it.

'My friend, you *are* going to complete this project with us. You mightn't know it yet but you *are*. And you aren't going to be talking about this to anyone, either, not to a soul. Our motives were well-intentioned. Maybe a trifle misguided, but well-intentioned all the same. Mistakes can happen to anyone. All we have to do is make sure that they don't happen again.'

'What the hell are you threatening me with?'

'Exposure, if you want to see it that way,' said Rahul Banerjee coldly. 'With a few embellishments, this makes one hell of a story! Senior marketing executive of a multinational company lands in Bombay, comfortable in his anonymity, naughtiness on his mind. The first thing he does, even before he's checked into a hotel, is to go looking for some illicit, night-time action. It's just his bad luck that the Vice Squad has chosen this particular night to lay a honey-trap for the wicked, pun intended. Our man from Cal lands plumb in the centre of it. Gets arrested, dragged to the nearest police station, like a common criminal, dumped in the cooler overnight with drunks, dregs, druggies, pickpockets and the like, and hauled to Court the next day. Things are looking really bleak for him, till enters one Rahul B who, pulling innumerable rabbits out of innumerable hats, and all the right strings, saves him from greater ignominy and gets him off with just a warning and a bruised ego.

'I can see the guys at Tolly lapping it all up and asking for second helpings. Not to mention the regulars at The Saturday Club. You know how these stories are. They have a life of their own, growing with each re-telling and creative embellishment. Of course, for maximum impact and credibility, it's important who gets in his story first, where, in all fairness, you have as much of a chance as I do.'

The silence that followed Rahul's delineation of a probable future scenario was deafening.

Vishal Kaushik looked at Rahul Banerjee, his mouth open. As did Anoop Chowdhury, yanked out of the cosy comfort of his retreat by the kind of brazen, combative behaviour that, as a North Calcutta bhadralok, he was seldom, if ever, exposed to except, perhaps, at a Mohun Bagan–East Bengal football match. Rahul looked at himself, too; at the hidden depths he'd plumbed and the buried truths about himself he'd uncovered. In a moment, he'd changed. Irrevocably.

'This is blackmail,' spluttered Vishal Kaushik finally, his affected baritone packed off on an indefinite holiday.

'Blackmail, survival,' Rahul shrugged, with chilling indifference. 'Different circumstances, different meanings.'

'You needn't worry, the remaining groups will be conducted impeccably,' assured Anoop Chowdhury, stepping in to dissipate the palpable tension that bridged the two central characters in this intense street-play. 'I'm sure we'll have enough material for you to launch a winning advertising campaign.'

'Yeah. Sure,' said Veekay bitterly. 'I suppose you expect me to stake my life on that?'

'What choice do you have?' With the subtlety of a bludgeon on an unprotected head, Rahul Banerjee reminded him that he didn't. 'I think that's your car waiting.'

Then, with two recent acolytes in harness, Rahul Banerjee started his walk back to Shalimar Hotel while Vishal Kaushik climbed into the gloom of his rented car to try and begin his own solitary journey out of it.

SEVEN

Storm Clouds Gathering

By the fifth day of Surjo Sengupta's visit, Rita and I were walking time-bombs waiting to explode. It might have been even earlier, if he hadn't taken a couple of days to recover from the trauma of his arrival. But once he'd managed to put behind him the heat and dust of Delhi and the disorientation of being lost for four hours in an unknown place not knowing whether he'd ever be found again, he bounced back with commendable alacrity.

I soon discovered, to my disadvantage, that, amongst his many talents, one was the uncanny knack that he had to bring you to the brink of detonation without, apparently, meaning to. On the surface, he was politeness personified, always seeming to demur to your point of view and accommodate your every wish; but, if you really thought about it, he, somehow, always managed to have it his own way, often at great inconvenience to everyone else around him which, in most instances, was me. Such was the curious genius of the man.

For example, he had the exasperating penchant for introducing unfamiliar names into conversations when I least expected them, ambushing and throwing into complete disarray any cogent train of thought that I might have had. Equally infuriating was his perverse sense of timing to launch conversational initiatives.

Like, when I would be choking on food that I might've distractedly inserted into my mouth because my mind, to which Surjo Sengupta was persistently trying to stake a claim, had alerted me to the fact that I was going to be an hour late to office and no last-minute, death-defying urgency was going to change that. Serenely oblivious to my predicament, Sengupta would start on a fresh subject, as irrelevant to me as all his earlier ones, while I tried to survive assassination by bread and asphyxiation by tie and, simultaneously, propel myself out of the house at a speed that would have got me a ticket from even the most somnolent of traffic cops, let alone the ever-vigilant P S Harold Mann.

Or, when I'd just returned home, in the middle of the night, from a particularly exhausting visit to a factory that was a hundred miles away from where any self-respecting factory should have been and was fondly contemplating the paradise offered by a rejuvenating shower and a revivifying drink, Surjo Sengupta would storm into my reverie, with a purpose that was almost demonic, demanding to know how someone called Manoj was, these days.

'How's Manoj these days?' he'd ask, with complete disregard for my state of being, or the time of night.

Suddenly, my mind would go blank as I would realise that paradise was about to be lost yet again, unlikely to be regained any time soon. The names, thrown at me, like confetti, would never have the slightest meaning for me, though each time one was thrown, it would be accompanied by such a look of expectancy that I'd feel hugely guilty about why it had no significance for me, at all, like all the ones that had preceded it and, probably, all the ones that would follow. Seeking deliverance, I'd turn to Rita but she'd choose that precise moment to assume an air of invincible stoicism and turn to matters more mundane, like taking the dog for a walk, even though he may have just returned from one. Usually, I'd be left to do battle on my own.

'Manoj?'

'Manoj Bose,' he'd clarify, fond father to idiot child.

'Of course!'

'Well, what kind of stuff is he doing these days?'

'Stuff?'

'You know...writing. After all, he *is* one of the founding fathers of modern Bengali literature!'

'Is he?! Oh, *that* Manoj Bose,' I'd say lamely, completely clueless about modern Bengali literature and who, if anyone, had fathered it, singly or in collective collusion.

'Is he maintaining the standards he set some years ago?'

'Can't say,' I'd admit, finally, afraid to let the conversation drift into uncharted waters that I would find it impossible to navigate out of. 'Haven't read him. Recently, that is.' The postscript would be a weak attempt to dilute the humiliation of another technical knockout.

'Pity. I was hoping you'd help me select the books that I should be carrying back with me to Paris.'

'I guess not,' I'd confess, willing to concede defeat, unequivocally, if it meant a respite from further inquisition on the state of contemporary Bengali literature. In the silence that would inevitably follow, I'd pray that Surjo Sengupta, disappointed by my abject performance, would fling me to some dark corner, like an old shoe that was beyond repair, where, in blissful solitude, I could resurrect my dream of cold showers and iced drinks. Just about when I'd begun to believe that I might have actually escaped, Surjo Sengupta would light one of his colourful French cigarettes, take a long, satisfying draw and pose his next conundrum:

'Any news of Arun?

And battle would be rejoined in right earnest. Having learnt some lessons from the previous ones, this time I'd be more circumspect, and less willing, to commit to any specific course of action, lest it be the wrong one.

'Hmmm?' I'd murmur, hoping that he'd reveal his hand some more.

'Haven't seen him in years. Wonder how he's getting along,' he'd ruminate, continuing to hold his cards firmly to his chest.

'Yes,' I'd say, remaining warily non-committal.

'Know anything about his recent work?'

'Not much,' I'd admit truthfully, having a sudden premonition that I might be walking into a trap if I revealed any more than I was doing already, although, on the face of it, Surjo Sengupta's queries seemed innocent enough.

'I believe he got an award for the last one,' he'd inform me. 'Read about it somewhere.'

'Yes. Quite,' I'd mumble, ambiguously, still hesitant to commit, although, from the sequential logic of his queries, I'd be coming around to the conclusion that Arun was one of the other fathers, who, in tandem with the previously-mentioned Manoj, had laid the foundations of Bengali literature's modern edifice. Emboldened by my reasoning, I'd initiate a tentative, conciliatory move: 'I guess you'll get all his recent books at the Book Fair that starts in a few days.'

At this juncture, Surjo Sengupta would give me a strange look, a mix of disbelief, condescension and commiseration.

'Unlikely,' he'd say, shaking his head, a father reconciled to living with the limitations of a retarded son. 'Arun Chatterjee? The last I knew, he made avant-garde films.'

Checkmate. Or, for greater finality, Game, Set and Match.

On the seventh night of Surjo Sengupta's stay, after extricating myself from a convoluted discussion, a monologue really, since Rita and I had almost nothing to contribute, on why Buddha, the Enlightened One, had Mongoloid features and where he might have acquired them (Mongolia, I would have thought), I did some serious introspection, over a double-peg of Indian-made Foreign Liquor, as everything that wasn't beer, or backyard-distilled hooch, was called, in those days.

For some inexplicable reason, Surjo Sengupta had convinced himself, with no assistance at all from my side, that I was a mine of information on contemporary Bengali culture. Starved of it during his eighteen-year, self-imposed exile in Paris, he was in a mad hurry to catch up on all that he believed he'd missed. He thought, quite mistakenly, that I would be his guide—his short-cut—to a postmodern, literary world where, I was beginning to suspect, he fancied he could be a player, too, thereby recovering the prominence that might have been his if he'd never left the city eighteen years ago. Unfortunately for him, his chosen short-cut was turning out to be the longest way around and, unfortunately for us, the longer it took him to get to where he wanted to go, the more prolonged would be his occupation of our spare bedroom. That thought was sufficient to galvanise me into contemplating a change of strategy.

'I feel an absolute fool each time he trips me up,' I complained to Rita when she surfaced from her meditation, a discipline that I found her to be pursuing a great deal more since the arrival of our overseas guest.

'You tend to lead with your chin,' she said bluntly, using terminology from a sport that I never knew she had any interest in. 'Actually, *you* trip *yourself* up. I don't think *he* starts out wanting to do that to you.'

'Thank you very much,' I said with what I hoped was cutting sarcasm, but came out sounding like petulance. 'I guess I can do one of two things: either I tell him, once and for all, that he's digging in the wrong place, or I bone up on everything that one should know about the Bengali cultural renaissance. Which?'

'I don't think you have the time, patience, inclination or aptitude for the second,' Rita said, with sharp acuity. Then, she assumed an intricate yoga posture that discouraged further conversation on the subject.

I was left to work things out for myself, which I did, convincing myself, with an argument that was more insubstantial bluster than cold reasoning, that strange problems demanded strange remedies and if artifice offered an escape from my dilemma, then artifice it had to be. In retrospect, I think I was quite easily convinced.

The next morning, I had little time to fine-tune my new strategy to navigate Surjo Sengupta's unexpected conversational detours. An early telephone call put the subject quite out of my mind. It was an office colleague, Chaks (abbreviated from a somewhat long-winded Suryanarayan Chakravarti), sounding breathlessly anxious.

'Have you heard?'

'No, but I'm sure you're about to tell me.'

'A conference has been called, at short notice, to discuss the unresolved differences between Sales and Production. All the bigwigs from Works are descending on us later this morning. We are scheduled to start at noon.'

'It's a great start-time; it means that we can break for an extended lunch even before we've discussed the full agenda!'

In those days of The Great Eastern Pipe Company (TGEPC), pipes that conveyed liquids and gases over long distances were, like most things, in short supply, which meant that Sales had the happy providence to sit in air-conditioned offices all year round, not really needing to break a sweat to make any, while their less fortunate Works brothers toiled in the furnace-heat of a factory, in some arid and barren location, to desperately churn out pipes to feed an over-filled order-book. Work made the people of Works very unhappy and desirous of frequent conferences in Calcutta, where they could complain about the unfairness of life, and the futility of their expensive engineering educations, in air-conditioned comfort. Sales, in turn, could grumble about how unenviable their job *really* was—blowing-up bulky expense accounts to pacify irate, disgruntled and intemperate customers, who'd seen neither hide nor hair of orders placed and paid for months ago, wasn't the barrel of monkeys it was made out to be and, *really*, how much golf could you play? Usually, the mention of the game would attenuate frayed tempers and arguments would end amicably, at least till the next conference, on an assurance from the Chief of Sales to his counterpart in Production of a lavish dinner that night at Bengal Club and a leisurely swing around the Tolly course the next morning. For greenhorns, like Chaks and me, the price to be paid, for lunches and dinners at protected sanctuaries, like Bengal Club, where you were, normally, denied membership till you had either grown enough grey hair or lost it completely, was to keep ourselves awake, particularly during the languor of a post-lunch session, and take copious notes of the proceedings sans the frequent outbursts of vitriol. Subsequently, these notes would be circulated to the powers-that-be, after the due diligence of our Sales and Production chiefs, as incontrovertible proof that a meeting had actually taken place and the expenses on travel, lodging and expansive, bonding gestures at the Bengal Club bar and the Tolly golf course were, therefore, fully justified.

'See you soon,' said Chaks, cutting short the telephone call, no doubt rushing off to sharpen his pencils, and his mind, for the meeting to follow.

The Great Eastern Pipe Company was housed, like many prestigious and profit-making firms of the time, on Chowringhee Road, in the top five floors of a twenty-storey, steel-glass-granite-and-aluminium structure. The building, like most others in the area, had an enormous lobby, with a bank of elevators at one end and one, single, high-speed lift at the other. This had the rather obvious name of 'Executive Lift', slyly implying that those at the other end of the lobby might not be, and was meant for use by senior TGEPC executives only. It serviced the sixteenth floor and beyond, by-passing all intervening floors, which meant it got you to where you wanted to go in less than half the time it took on the mass-transit elevators. For us to avail of it, required that we convince ourselves, which wasn't too difficult, that seniority was just a state of mind, not some imposed or, as in our case, absent designation. Of course, it strengthened our resolve if we knew that our bosses had already arrived and been installed in their respective lairs, unlikely, therefore, to be witnesses to our illegal use of their facility.

This invaluable information, whether your bosses where *in situ* or not, was the preserve of the receptionist who, like the

'Executive Lift', was equally superfluously identified as the 'Receptionist' by a plaque on her desk. Inclusive of her desk and a chair that did not swivel, because some sharp administrative mind had brilliantly surmised that she had nothing important to swivel towards, she occupied less than one percent of the lobby space, which made her a comforting buoy in a choppy sea, when there was human traffic around and a lonely dot, on a bleak horizon, when there was not. She was a lonely dot most of the time. As a consequence, she was usually occupied fixing her hair, or her fingernails, or both, and flicking through an endless array of magazines that flaunted the indiscretions, imagined or real, of cinema stars, established and aspiring. Or, the off-the-wall excesses of the newest fashion designers. Or, pop quizzes that probed you on everything from your culinary skills to your sexual predilections. Since her location kept her in solitude for the most part of her working day, she welcomed the company of others, whenever it was offered, with embarrassing gratefulness. For Chaks and me, her gratitude was expressed by way of her maintaining a mental log of our bosses' movements, particularly recent sightings in and around the vicinity of the 'Executive Lift'.

'They've all arrived,' she informed me in response to my cheery greeting. 'Believe there's some big meeting on.'

'Yup,' I confirmed, implying that I enjoyed the confidence of my seniors on matters of such import and that she would, therefore, be doing the right thing by continuing to provide me with information on their movements.

'So, you guys will be tied-up all through the day,' she said, a trifle wistfully, realising that neither Chaks, nor I, would be able to slip away to share with her our usual cup of tea and slice of conversation.

'Unless I decide to skip the ceremonial lunch.' It was practical to keep the idea of such a contingency afloat in case the elders decided, in their collective wisdom, to go into a private huddle over lunch sans our company.

'Where's it today?' she asked, innocently.

I thought that that was as opportune a moment as any to enter the 'Executive Lift'. I pressed sixteen.

I surfaced on a floor above the Sales floor and nipped down a flight to my desk, before my illegitimate use of the 'Executive Lift' was spotted by unsympathetic and envious eyes. Like a homing pigeon, Chaks was at my table even before I had sat down. He had a bulky file under one arm.

'I have summarised the issues that might come up for discussion,' he said. 'A reading of the top few pages should suffice. We have an hour before we're summoned.'

Though our lowly status in the Sales hierarchy militated against any active, or productive, participation in such meetings, Chaks, being the meticulous sort that he was, believed in the old Boy Scout adage of always being prepared, just in case the conventions were to be changed, unexpectedly. I harboured no such expectation, not as long as the elders and betters of TGEPC continued to seat us in an open office, in the company of the non-management staff or, as they were loosely termed, babus. It was only when you were transferred to the relative privacy of a cabin that you knew that your career had begun to shake off its somnolence.

The open space took up more than half the entire fifteenth floor. Like a Line of Control, to be crossed only with proper identification, a long, neon-lit strip of corridor separated the vast, open space from a row of same-looking, wood-panelled cabins, and two undying symbols of corporate India inherited from the

British (who, if one were to really think about it, were no less class-conscious, in certain matters, than the Indian caste system that they held in such disdain): the 'Executive Lift' and the 'Executive Toilet'.

The door of the latter opened to two more: one carried a brass plaque that loudly shouted 'Management' and the other, a simple wooden tablet that said, more self-deprecatingly, 'Executives', suggesting that the two were different, which they might well have been, although I was never quite able to fathom how. If the two weren't considered a breed apart, they were, certainly, assumed to want to conduct their ablutions differently, 'Management', theirs in the privacy of toilets designed for individual use, with the additional luxury of doors that actually locked, and 'Executives'—lesser mortals, they—in public view, albeit partial, of others of their ilk. Of course, community cleansing had its advantages, among which was the licence it gave you to not only purge your body but, also, your soul, particularly if you'd had an exceptionally trying session with someone from the category that used the toilet next door to yours.

The open seating space was divided into sections by cleverly-positioned furniture—mainly steel filing cabinets painted a bilious shade of green—that delineated the different Sales groups. Within the territory of each such delineation were arrayed the babus, row upon row of them, sitting cheek-by-jowl, all facing the same direction. At the apex of each babu cluster were two larger desks, usually occupied by corporate greenhorns, like Chaks and me, facing in the *opposite* direction, suggesting that, in some way, we were the babus' keepers when the truth was quite the opposite.

The wheels of commerce were greased by the babus, and the babus alone, and would not only come to a grinding halt, but actually unhinge, if they were to cease their labour. Their toil entailed the fastidious maintenance of daily records—in fat, dusty ledgers that went back at least two decades and which, in certain companies, merited a separate 'ledger carrying allowance'—the mind-numbing preparation of order requisitions, material purchases and delivery challans—usually, in quadruplicate—the endless writing of memos—to each other, the factory, the customer, the management and a confusing assortment of Government regulatory bodies—and the chronological, and careful, archiving of reams of correspondence that they generated every day. All this kept the façade of productivity, and the pretence of industriousness, intact, and gave time to senior executives to pursue more invigorating challenges, like improving their golf handicap or their capacity for vodka-tonics.

Most babus, despite their vital cog-in-the-wheel status, did not have enough to occupy them a full eight-hour day. So, other than frequent visits to, and unnaturally-long periods in, the staff toilet, and extended lunch and tea breaks, until the two, often, merged, they had to, constantly, think of ingenious ways to fill their time. Sleep was a popular choice, except that it had to be resorted to cleverly, so that some spoilsport in Management, eager to gain the approbation of his boss, did not disturb it when it was at its deepest. A gentleman in my babu cluster, who had the unenviable task of updating ledgers, had developed a unique method: after lunch, he would grab a pen in his right hand, poise it over an open page of his ledger, rest his head in the palm of his left hand, as if in deep concentration, and promptly fall asleep; the beauty of his talent was that, even in slumber, not only would he continue to move his pen across the page, as if he were alertly checking entries but also, in a crowning touch of realism, turn a page of the ledger every twenty minutes! He had me fooled for months till, one day, an undisciplined snore let him down while he was turning a page in his sleep. But I let it pass, in silent appreciation of his technique.

Another babu would suddenly start a search for a non-existent piece of correspondence, his exploration timed to commence at around noon so that he had the hour, before lunch, to rifle all the cabinets in our section of the fifteenth floor. That left the common filing section, on the floor below, to be searched after lunch. This cavernous barn of a room was the final resting place for old files before their cremation and, if one did not mind the musty smell of aging paper, it provided a near-private sanctuary for the sleepy, or for those in search of a memo that no one had ever written. On the off-chance that you visited the common filing section post-lunch, either out of mischief or curiosity, you were likely to be greeted by a chorus of snores, of varying pitch and performance, emanating from its four corners.

As long as they found innocent ways to occupy themselves, I had little to complain about but, when they turned their attention on me to relieve their postprandial lethargy, it was time to take evasive action. Romen-babu, one of four people who occupied the first row opposite my desk, was given to striking up conversation in the midst of his preparations for lunch, which were, usually, half-an-hour ahead of the actual event and, therefore, too early for me to make my own legitimate escape. On such occasions, which were far too many for comfort, I was thankful for the four feet of space that separated us.

'Not having lunch?' he'd ask, raising his lantern jaw and giving me a gaze that was meant to be friendly but, because of the unfortunate placement of his eyes and the beetle-ness of his brow, came across as distinctly menacing. It didn't help that Romen-babu, possibly to economise on razor-blades, shaved only once a week, despite the propensity that his facial hair had of growing in abundance and riotous abandon.

'Soon,' I'd mutter, embarrassed that the short exchange had already drawn the attention of the other front-benchers, who seldom needed very much to divert them from their ponderous pursuit of industry.

'You don't use the *officers'* lunch-room much, do you?' Had there been a tinge of irony in the way he'd stressed the word 'officers' or was it just my overheated imagination?

I'd admit that I usually brought a light repast from home, which I preferred to the heavy meal served in the canteen on the second floor.

'Dieting!' he'd announce, in a stage whisper that would carry to the extreme corners of the open seating area, without the benefit of microphones.

'Not really,' I'd demur, weakly.

'Then what?' he'd challenge, belligerently. 'A couple of sandwiches can't satisfy the appetite of a young, growing body!'

Fearing that the conversation might tread even more personal waters, I'd hesitate to argue that *this* body had done all the growing that it was meant to do and wasn't ever going to be as young as it had once been, in case it prolonged the discussion about my diet. And while I purpled in embarrassment and attempted to find cover in a letter from a frustrated customer complaining bitterly about overdue deliveries that I had read many times already, he'd whisk one container after another out of his jute carrier-bag and arrange them on his desk lovingly.

'Here,' he'd command, when the bag had surrendered all its contents. 'This is what a real lunch is all about. How can you carry your enormous responsibilities on the back of two sandwiches?'

I'd look up sharply, convinced that there'd been a definite undercurrent of sarcasm in his tone. But I would find Romen-babu happily engaged in the task of emptying food-containers, virtuousness and unblemished innocence writ large on his face, if ever an unshaven, lantern-jawed, beetle-browed countenance could have anything, other than menace, written on it.

'It's time,' said Chaks. I broke out of my reverie to accompany him to the conference room on the eighteenth floor, which was as high as we lesser creatures were normally permitted to go, the two floors beyond being the sacred preserve of the executive directors and their secretariat.

The conference room had been designed with comfort foremost in mind, on the premise, no doubt, that long hours would be spent in it by the captains, and cadets, of the flourishing firm of TGEPC. It had a long, oval-shaped table at its centre, with two rows of high-backed, deeply-upholstered chairs around it. The first row was for senior executives who, befitting their hierarchical positions and designations, were expected to do all the speaking and table-thumping which, therefore, justified their proximity to it. The second row was for the supporting cast, people who fed their bosses the cues they needed to lift their performance from mere pantomime to the level of theatre.

Bay windows, overlooking the ubiquitous Calcutta Maidan, stretched across one side of the room. On the opposite wall hung huge ornate-framed photographs of the founding fathers of TGEPC, and their favourite sons, most of whom were still alive and active, although that was not always apparent from the funereal grimness of their black-and-white portraits.

At one end, was an expansive blackboard and the facility of a drop-down screen, which operated by a wired remote located on the underside of the table. On one past occasion, in the middle of a particularly-heated debate, with excited participants vigorously hurling multi-coloured chalk arrows, and accusations, at each other, someone, either accidentally or mischievously, had pulled the remote switch to bring the curtain down over the blackboard. So carried away had one gentleman been by the force of his own argument that he'd continued with his presentation, undeterred, covering the pristine-white screen with hieroglyphic doodles, in luminescent red, an act for which he was still paying the price by having to occupy a second row seat from where the blackboard and screen were out of his reach. Despite the well-intentioned motive behind it, his reckless act had led to his temporary exile from the arc-lights. There could be no greater punishment for an elder, attending a meeting in the conference room on the eighteenth floor, than to be relegated to the second row.

For those, like us, unfamiliar with the rarefied air that elders breathed, the arc-lights held little fascination. For us, it was more important to find a seat that gave easy access to the tea service before it went cold, or the supply of cookies, before it ran dry. The closeness of an exit also helped us to escape, usually on the pretext of locating evidence that would seal the opposition's fate, to some cosy corner, where we could light up and relieve the tension of keeping ourselves awake, as the same questions were raised, the same arguments made and the same excuses given, over and over.

However, today was different.

For one, the elders, irrespective of caste, creed or function, appeared more united. Outside the conference room, the Works' bigwigs were huddled together with their Sales counterparts in small, intimate clusters, speaking in hushed tones, as if at a funeral wake. Even the Chief of Sales, normally, a loud, cheerful, extroverted sort, famous for his malapropisms, was lacking his customary bonhomie. He beckoned to me.

'We'll call for lunch from the officers' canteen,' he said. That a decision had been taken to forego the usual, leisurely lunch at Bengal Club which such occasions merited, was an ominous sign. 'Keep Mrs Dalal informed. She should have the food sent up and served at 1:30 sharp.'

I did a quick head count of the clusters in the corridor and those who'd already wandered into the conference room in search of advantageous seats. It made a round dozen, substantially fewer than the number that normally congregated at these conferences, another sign that this one was out of the ordinary. In the midst of reading and interpreting these clues, another thought, somewhat self-congratulatory, registered at the back of my mind: that Chaks and I had been invited to attend could only mean that our careers were, finally, awakening from their slumber.

Raj Singh, Chief of Sales, took a position at the head of the table, with S.K. Gupta, Head of Production, by his side. Their new-found camaraderie indicated that they had decided to bury their differences, temporarily, and take a united stand against what seemed to be a threat from outside, not within.

'Gentlemen, we have a crisis,' said Raj Singh, grimly.

'A crisis,' confirmed S.K. Gupta, who, I was to discover, had the disconcerting habit of repeating the last words of whatever anyone said, unless it was a question.

'The Board has decided to let loose some management consultants in our midst.'

'In our midst.'

'Pardon? Did you say something?'

'No.'

'I thought you did.'

'You did.'

Raj Singh, in his newly-assumed role of colleague, collaborator and cohort, decided to give his patience some additional rein and ignore the echo chamber seated beside him.

'In its collective wisdom, the Board believes that the differences between Sales and Works cannot be resolved without professional . help from outside.'

'From outside.'

'Isn't that what I said?' Raj Singh's patience and self-inflicted mood of camaraderie were showing signs of cracking.

'Yes. Quite right.'

With a visible effort of will, Raj Singh returned to his theme. In the face of a crisis of such magnitude, it did not do to return to the confrontational behaviour that usually typified Sales and Works interactions, although the provocation was intense.

'It is also believed—wrongly, in my humble opinion—that the Sales organisation is *not* geared to meet the competitive challenges of the future, both in structure and in practice. This team of so-called experts has been asked to study the Sales–Production interface and suggest changes, including any re-structuring that may be required, to improve our combined response to the needs of the emerging marketplace.'

'Needs of the emerging marketplace,' parroted S.K. Gupta.

'Is there anything that you would like to add before we discuss the matter?' asked Raj Singh of his Works counterpart, with deliberate politeness.

'We must have a combined response for the consultants before we have one for the marketplace!' said S.K. Gupta, with a laugh, the self-conscious, booming kind that characterised Production people. In my experience, they all spoke and laughed louder than they needed to, probably because they spent most of their time trying to be heard over the noise of metals and machines. I suspected that Gupta had timed his attempt at humour not only to ease the tension that had been created by Raj Singh's opening salvo but also to steal a bit of his thunder.

A murmur of relieved laughter rippled through the conference room, much to Raj Singh's annoyance.

'That's what this day-long conference is about,' he said, clambering to regain his position in the pulpit. 'To discuss alternative approaches, agree on what we can reveal to these outsiders and what we must necessarily protect. We have got to find a mia vidia.'

I received a chit of paper from Chaks bearing the numeral 1 and a question, 'Via media, perhaps?' indicating that he was volunteering to keep the score and interpret, Raj Singh's malapropisms, the first of which had just been released.

'Find a mia vidia?' repeated S.K. Gupta faithfully, except that he attached a tentative question-mark to the echo.

'My VD is cured-a, how about yours-a?' whispered Rajesh Mehra, a year my senior in the firm and known as much for his impersonations of bosses, whom he disliked, as his irreverence for the conventional. Though he sometimes skirted the edge of impertinence, if not outright insubordination, he got away with it because, despite all his affectations to the contrary, he was a staunch Sales loyalist—a potent weapon in the constant battle against the forces of evil—and extremely competent in his job.

Thankfully, his aside went unnoticed by Raj Singh, who continued, 'I know these consultant types. They first find out what the top brass wants to hear and then write a report that delivers those expectations.'

'Delivers those expectations.'

'So, it's crucial for us to find out what those expectations are; otherwise, spending time with the lot of them will be an exercise in fertility.'

'Infertility,' resonated S.K. Gupta, while Chaks scribbled 2 on his scorecard and Rajesh Mehra mumbled something about the futility of a sterile meeting like this when our time could be so much better utilised downing vodka-tonics at the Saturday Club bar.

'Yes, Rajesh? Any ideas?'

'Many, Mr Singh. But none that are immediately relevant.'

'Which consulting firm is it?' I asked. If we had to resort to cloak-and-dagger tactics, it certainly helped to know who we had to insert a sharp instrument into, to cause grave, if not permanent, damage.

'Big Brother Consultancy,' said Raj Singh. 'Heard of them?'

'Haven't we!' said Rajesh Mehra, joined in his lament by most of us from the Sales side of the assembly.

'Well? Have you or haven't you?' persisted Raj Singh, not in the mood for imprecision, or ambiguity.

'We have. And it isn't good news,' I said. 'Basically, BBC is a firm of old-fashioned head-hunters, something they are, reportedly, pretty good at. What they are not, are experts in organisational restructuring. The trouble starts when they pretend that they are.'

'What kind of trouble?' asked Raj Singh, intrigued.

'Well.'

I hesitated because what I had to say about Big Brother Consultancy was based entirely on hearsay and conjecture. It wouldn't stand up in a Court of Law, not that I was testifying at a trial where my testimony, if it wasn't as pure as the driven snow, might put a hangman's noose around some innocent neck.

'Well? Well? Well?' Raj Singh's curiosity had turned to impatience.

'They are known to do Management's bidding, a commercial approach that earns them big, fat fees and plenty of future business, if the same, friendly Management prevails, that is. So, when some senior people have an adverse opinion about some other people in the organisation that they can't quite validate, they call in BBC to do an "impartial" study, which, by some strange coincidence, ends up confirming Management's preconceived notions every time!'

There was a moment's silence while Raj Singh, and the rest of the congregation, digested the cunning piece of business strategy that some people planned and plotted in the privacy of corporate boardrooms.

'So,' concluded Raj Singh, funereally, 'what you are saying is that Big Brother is quite capable of putting a scope in the wheel.'

'Scope in the wheel,' resonated S.K. Gupta, returning to the fray from the echo-less wilderness that Raj Singh had relegated him to with his series of questions.

'Three,' scored Chaks in a hoarse whisper.

'Whose wheel?' asked Rajesh Mehra, innocently.

Heated discussions, sometimes focused but, mostly, wayward, ensued: the extent of the threat that BBC posed and whether it was real or imagined; if it was imagined, what was causing the paranoia that made it seem real and, if it was real, what needed to be done to neutralise it. And, while taking out a contract on the owner of BBC, as proposed by Rajesh Mehra only half in jest, was a tempting option, it was not thought to be practical by the majority.

Thankfully, Mehra was dissuaded from prolonging his anarchic argument by the entry of a cavalcade of food trolleys, expertly manoeuvred into the conference room by a phalanx of uniformed waiters, signalling that lunch was served and reiterating that an army, however disorderly, marched best on its stomach.

'Lunch,' said Raj Singh, superfluously. 'Gentlemen, let's attend to it quickly and get back to our deliberations in forty-five minutes. We still have a lot of ground to uncover.'

'Lot of ground to uncover,' echoed S.K. Gupta, like a well-trained but ill-educated parrot.

'Four,' said Chaks, triumphantly, swinging his arms in imitation of an explosive golf stroke, which, if it had been real, would have sent the ball into permanent orbit. By my side, Rajesh Mehra intoned, in a lascivious whisper, that, neither being a gardener nor a gravedigger, he'd rather be spending his time uncovering things a lot more stimulating than ground, if I caught his general drift.

I assured him that I did and that his exaggerated wink was quite redundant. Nonetheless, he gave me another.

EIGHT

Requiem for a Poet

It was past seven-thirty when the meeting came to a close, not because a viable plan had emerged to combat the unwanted incursions of Big Brother Consultancy, but because discussions were tending to tread the same weary ground and wander, time and again, into dead-ends from where there were no clear exits. Also, it was well past sundown; by this time, any God-fearing, self-respecting senior executive worth his salt should have been at his club propping up the bar and calling for the second round, at least. From a whispered aside that Raj Singh shared with S.K. Gupta before bringing the curtain down on the day's proceedings, I imagined that they were planning to do just that—drown their collective sorrows in a bottle of Scotland's finest. Crisis made for strange bedfellows.

'We'll reconvene at 9 a.m. tomorrow. Sharp,' announced Raj Singh by way of farewell.

'Sharp,' echoed S.K. Gupta as we reconciled ourselves to the fact that not only had we been deprived of the lavish lunch that was, customarily, an integral part of such occasions, but were going to be denied dinner, too. When revered traditions, such as these, fell by the wayside, it meant that someone, in this instance, BBC, had really put an enormous spanner in the works or, as Raj Singh was prone to say, a very large 'scope' in the wheel, indeed.

Driving homewards, I must have been distracted by thoughts of cloak-and-dagger machinations, corporate back-stabbings and hostile takeovers because it was a while before I noticed a familiar backside bobbing in front of me, astride a monster of a motorcycle. From the manner in which the two-wheeler was weaving in and out of my path, I surmised that the owner of the big butt wanted me to stop. Since he also wore a helmet of authority, which I had no difficulty in recognising, I did, easing my Standard Herald to the side of the road opposite Calcutta Maidan. It was 8 p.m.

The motorcycle turned and came towards me, the big backside replaced by an even bigger belly. As its owner drew closer, my headlights caught his face. It was my good friend of some days ago, Police Sergeant Harold Mann, again.

He jack-booted his way to my side of the car and peered through the window, shining a torch in my face.

'Good evening,' he said, not meaning it. 'Haven't I seen you before?' Dirty Harry played the light over me and the interior of the car, as if searching for contraband, or guilt, or both.

'I don't think so,' I ventured, tentatively, hoping that P S Harold Mann accosted more errant drivers in the course of his daily peregrinations than his memory could store.

'I'm sure I have. On Park Street, the other day,' he said, dashing my hopes and establishing that he had a better recall than I'd given him credit for.

'What have I done this time?' I asked, unable to bear the suspense any longer and knowing that whatever it was, it was going to make me lighter in the wallet again.

'Oh! Don't you know?' The sarcasm that had been so all-pervasive in our last encounter was returning, with escalating sharpness.

Before I could admit that I, seriously, did not, he answered his own question: 'You beat the red light at that last crossing. Turning out to be quite the serial traffic offender, aren't you?'

'I'm sorry. I didn't notice it.' I thought confession might bring forth forgiveness.

'That's worse,' said Dirty Harry, obviously not in a forgiving mood. 'If you'd intentionally beaten the light, at least I'd know that you had your wits about you. Beating it unknowingly, means that you were absent-minded, which isn't the best way to be, when you're on the road.'

'I had a lot of things on my mind,' I confessed, still believing him to be a priest when he was quite obviously a policeman, and an irate one at that.

As with most things, practice makes perfect. Despite only a single performance to back it, I was impressed with the fluidity with which I managed to free a hundred-rupee note from the confines of my wallet to the halfway house of my palm. The darkness of our environs made me braver than the previous occasion; possibly, it also had something to do with my having been so successful in my very first attempt. I could understand now what serial murderers meant when they claimed that the subsequent killing was always easier than the one that had preceded it. I proffered the hundred-rupee note, like the currency of compromise and harbinger of conciliation that it was meant to be.

P S Harry Mann continued to splay the light over me. It crept lingeringly up my right arm to the note fluttering at the end of it; then, it returned to my face. A tram clattered by next to us.

'You're going to do yourself some serious damage if you continue to ride your road luck the way you've been doing,' cautioned Dirty Harry, switching off his torch and turning on his jack-booted heel to take the few strides that separated him from his loyal Royal.

'You forgot something,' I said to his retreating back.

'I don't charge for the same lesson twice. And you've already made your contribution to the retired policemen's fund this week,' said PS Harold Mann airily over his shoulder, as he walked away. He kicked his motorcycle to life and clattered into the darkness without a backward glance in my direction, the red tail-light blinking farewell till the gloaming enveloped it, too, and I was left all by myself, once again.

It may have been Raj Singh's solecisms, or S.K. Gupta's repetitions, or Rajesh Mehra's ill-timed, stage-whispered asides, or the strange encounter with Police Sergeant Mann or, possibly, some heady combination of all these, that strengthened my resolve to change the rules of the game when it came to my next conversation with our guest-in-residence. Or, it may just have been the sight of him, sitting in my favourite armchair, in air-conditioned comfort, fresh out of a shower, a chilled nimbu pani by his side, while I still carried the stress of a long, unproductive day at the office, and the pervious grime of the streets, on my back. Whatever it was, I was suddenly injected with a streak of irresponsible, devil-may-care flamboyance.

'Why so late?' Surjo Sengupta asked, taking a long draw of his nimbu pani, and a long look, of some distaste, at my bedraggled appearance.

'An unscheduled meeting,' I informed him, although I was quite certain that he had little interest in knowing what had kept me, or how my day had gone, or what I had been doing to get through it. Possibly, what concerned him a great deal more was that he hadn't had a captive audience for his rambling musings for some length of time, Rita having perfected the art of looking tremendously busy, with housewifely duties, when she was not.

I was right.

'Quickly, then,' he said, motioning urgency, somewhat ineffectively, from the depths of my armchair. 'Freshen up. I've been waiting for you.'

That sounded ominous. It also predicated a long night ahead for me, unless I could outthink and outmanoeuvre him from hitting his normal, uncontrollable conversational momentum.

'Dinner at nine-thirty,' shouted Rita from her refuge in the kitchen. 'You must be ravenous.'

I admitted that I was, the lunch served by Mrs Dalal in office having neither captured my heart nor my imagination.

'Come along, come along,' urged Surjo Sengupta, impatient that I should be dawdling when good, wholesome talk-time was ticking away.

Accessorised in my newly-acquired flamboyance, I decided to be contrary and dawdle some more. When I re-emerged from our bedroom, it was well past nine-thirty and Rita had dinner on the table. I had by-passed the pre-prandial exchanges adeptly, and Round 1 could be awarded to me, albeit on points. Surjo Sengupta must have felt the same way because he was unusually silent through dinner, except for the occasional reminiscence about how things were done in Paris, much to Rita's mounting but still-concealed annoyance.

'Dinner's the one meal of the day when the whole family makes it a point to eat together,' he reminisced. 'So, there's a bit of ceremony that accompanies it. The table's fully laid. It's usually four-course, at least. Non-vegetarian, of course. Prime cuts of beef. Fish. Lobster. Leftovers go into our Sunday buffet, so nothing's wasted.'

It was ironical that Surjo Sengupta should decide to hold forth on the joys of non-vegetarianism on one of the few nights in the week that Rita, newly-educated on the menace of bad cholesterol, insisted on serving vegetarian.

'Wine, of course, is an essential accompaniment. French, naturally, ha ha. Red with meat, white with poultry and fish. The glasses are different, you know. Wine in the wrong glass can ruin its taste completely.' This last bit of information was delivered in a conspiratorial tone, as if he was privileging us with a secret that generations had gone to their deaths protecting.

By the time dinner concluded, I was fully primed, a ticking time bomb waiting to explode on an unsuspecting and, hopefully, unprepared Surjo Sengupta.

'How's Dipen?' Surjo Sengupta opened predictably, and battle was joined even before he'd finished taking his first post-dinner puff of a coloured, French cigarette.

'Fine. He's doing extremely well. Still a prodigious writing talent,' I dived straight in without inhibition.

'So, you do get to meet him?'

'Of course. At least once a fortnight. Usually, at that tea shop in Gariahat. You know the one—Tea Centre, where young intellectuals gather?'

'Yes, nice to know that it's still popular. So, when was it that you met him last?'

'Not more than a week before your arrival. We spent a couple of hours together, over loads of tea. He's in the middle of writing a new book. Read me a couple of chapters from it. Wants to write a play next and direct it himself, maybe.'

'Oh! That would certainly be something new for him. Does his writing still lean heavily on Leftist politics?'

'Yes, but there's a social voice that underlines his work these days. There's a greater exploration of human relationships, and behaviour, than just pedantic doctrines and -isms.'

'Very interesting. That's one way for him to be appreciated by a wider audience. You know, this is the one thing that you sorely miss in Paris, the company of people who speak your language.'

I presumed he meant 'language' in a philosophical, rather than a literal, sense. I detected wistfulness in his tone, indicating that I might be getting the better of him, for once. The thought propelled me to advance, even more adventurously, for the coup de grace.

'Would you like me to set up a meeting for you?' I asked, slyly, knowing that I was flirting with danger, but caring little, so flush was I with adrenaline and the scent of my first victory.

'Would you? That would be wonderful. I met Dipen last eighteen years ago. After my departure, we just haven't managed to stay in touch. He mightn't even remember me too clearly, after all these years.'

'Don't worry,' I consoled him, magnanimous in anticipation of victory. 'I'm sure Dipen has time for old acquaintances, despite all his recent successes. At heart, he's remained a simple man; otherwise I don't see why he should spend so much time with me.'

'That's good,' said Surjo Sengupta, on the verge of conceding defeat. 'I suppose you'll be meeting him again soon?'

'We have our usual, fortnightly rendezvous at Tea Centre coming up. The ideal place for you to meet him would be at the Book Fair, which starts tomorrow. Poets, writers, film-makers, all kinds of intellectuals, gather together, every day, for the entire duration of the exhibition.'

'I was planning to do just that. If you could tell him to expect me? Wouldn't do for me to arrive completely unannounced, not after a gap of eighteen years.'

'Consider it done,' I said with barely-concealed glee, deciding that all that magnanimity-of-victor-over-the-vanquished stuff could wait till I'd savoured my conquest just a little.

'Thank you,' said Surjo Sengupta, flattening his King on our conversational chessboard, in defeat. 'I think I'll call it a day. Good night.'

'Good night,' I returned, as he relinquished the armchair and returned it to its rightful owner—the spoils of victory.

'Do you have any idea who Dipen is?' asked Rita, when I'd completed my summary which, in the telling, was more a ball-by-ball commentary than a précis, with several self-congratulatory annotations, in digression.

'Not the faintest,' I replied, with unflappable equanimity. 'But, the further I advanced into the uncharted territory of make-believe, the more I got to know Dipen till, in the end, I thought I knew him pretty well.'

'And, pray, how are you planning to make this momentous meeting happen, with someone you haven't even seen, let alone know, other than in your over-active imagination?'

'I'm not,' I said. 'I'm relying on, you know, this auto-suggestion thing to do the trick. Having planted the thought of a meeting in his subconscious, I'm hoping that when he goes to the Book Fair, he'll find his own way to Dipen, and his own excuse to meet him, maybe not on the first day but by his third or fourth visit, surely.'

'And what if your name should happen to come up in conversation?'

'It won't,' I replied, confidently. 'Surjo Sengupta, if I know him at all by now, isn't the kind of guy who'll be seen dead acknowledging that someone else, particularly the crass commercial type that he considers me to be, had to set up a meeting for him with someone with whom he claims an acquaintance and equality of mind: someone in his own intellectual class. If his meeting with Dipen does take place, he'll put it down to his own initiative, or coincidence, or happenstance, but certainly not to my intervention.'

'I see that the little grey cells have been working overtime,' said Rita, visibly impressed with my performance and the intuitive reasoning that appeared to have gone behind it. To tell the truth, I was pretty impressed myself.

'Elementary, my dear Watson,' I said, introducing my own favourite fictional detective to the unrolling end credits.

The rest of that week passed uneventfully.

Raj Singh's endless malapropisms no longer merited special attention because they'd been coming so thick and fast lately that they'd become routine. Equally predictable were Surjo Sengupta's ill-timed recollections of how well things were managed in Paris and, by unsaid but obvious inference, so poorly in Calcutta. It was an example of great human endurance how Rita managed to retain a grip on her composure each time such memories were recalled, from what seemed to be an unending vault of pet peeves.

Outside the home, in the unpredictable world of Calcutta traffic, I was saved further aggravation, by managing to elude any fresh encounter with Police Sergeant Harold Mann and his loyal Royal, not because I followed road rules more religiously, but because I was just plain lucky not to have been caught violating them. As P S Mann was to tell me later, at a meeting significantly less adversarial than our early encounters, there are so many rules determining how you drive or maintain a car in Calcutta, that you are sure to be breaking at least a couple of them, even when your car is standing quite still in your garage.

Back in office, a plan had begun to unfold to neutralise Big Brother Consultancy. At the core of it was something that was common to all enduring organisations (the Mafia and the Chinese Triad, for example): information. For it to be effective, you had to, first, have some idea of what your enemy was thinking. The task of ferreting that out fell on me; I needed no other qualification for the job than to have a senior BBC consultant as an alumnus of my business school.

'Get the dummy,' instructed Raj Singh, to my great concern that the stress of the impending investigation might be causing him to not only consider the extreme step of terminating a BBC staffer with extreme prejudice, but also, to expect a lowly minion, like me, untrained in the fine art of murder and mayhem, to execute the deed.

'Get the dummy?' I repeated, just to be sure that I had heard him right and that I wouldn't be haring off on a misunderstanding to do another Murder in the Cathedral thing.

'Yes, yes,' said Raj Singh, impatiently. 'They must have put together a list of questions that they want to ask us. Try and get it out of your friend so that we're prepared with our answers.'

'He's not a friend; just someone I went to business school with,' I corrected him, politely. However, I was much relieved to decode that the dummy he was referring to was not a flesh-and-blood consultant of BBC, only a draft questionnaire.

'Take the dummy out. Show him a good time,' instructed Raj Singh next, to my utter confusion, until I reasoned that he had, probably, changed definitions in-between instructions; the last-mentioned dummy *was* a flesh-and-blood BBC consultant, *not* a list of questions, and I was being instructed to woo him, with lunch and like distractions, to inveigle out of him the previously-mentioned dummy, which was, in fact, a list of questions.

'Take the dummy out to get out the dummy,' I summarised.

'Whatever,' said Raj Singh, giving me a look that discouraged further discussion on the subject of dummies, particularly at the end of a week that had had its fair share of stress-inducing moments, not the least of which was the revelation that Big Brother would, henceforth, be watching everything we did with an overly critical eye.

In the circumstances, distracted as I was by thoughts of cloak-and-dagger manoeuvres to thwart the forces of wickedness that, for once, were not headquartered in our factory, I was quite unprepared for a renewal of my unfinished discussion with Surjo Sengupta on the subject of the litterateur Dipen. It was the last thing on my mind when I returned home, the first being a vodka-tonic that I planned to linger over, after I had repossessed my favourite armchair from our guest should he have beaten me to it again. He hadn't, which was comforting. What wasn't, was the pall of gloom that greeted me.

Surjo Sengupta sat, silent and motionless, in our living-room, his gaze transfixed on a fixture on the opposite wall that hardly merited such close scrutiny. Rita hovered, uncertainly, in the territory between the living-room and the kitchen, the expression on her face suggesting that she'd rather be somewhere else altogether, probably walking a dog who was already stunned speechless by the amount of exercise, and attention, he'd been getting recently.

'What's up?' I whispered, as we huddled, like conspirators, out of Surjo Sengupta's hearing.

'I have no idea,' she whispered back. 'He returned from the Book Fair an hour ago and has been sitting, immobile and wordless, ever since.'

'Guess old Dipen didn't give him time of day,' I concluded, sagely. With a vodka-tonic, and the weekend, beckoning, I wasn't about to allow a morose Surjo Sengupta to dampen my spirits.

'How was your day?' I chirped cheerily, determined to alleviate the shroud of despondency that Surjo Sengupta seemed to have pulled over himself and everything else around him.

He heard me, as if through dense cloud cover; a pair of dull eyes turned ever so slowly in my direction.

'Dipen,' he murmured.

'I was thinking about what we discussed the other day,' I confidently resumed from where I'd left off a few days ago, like a batsman who has hit a purple patch and can do no wrong, inning after inning. 'The Book Fair mightn't be the best place for a one-on-one meeting, after all. Too many people around, too many distractions. It would be better if I were to speak to him for a meeting at a more appropriate place—maybe the tea-shop?'

'Dipen…,' started Surjo Sengupta, his voice trailing to silence, again.

'The tea-shop is a good idea,' I argued, convincingly. 'It's informal. But it is private too, if you take one of the family cubicles. I've always found Dipen pretty relaxed and communicative there.'

'Dipen...,' started Surjo Sengupta again, but I plunged right back encouraged by the signs of returning life that I saw in him.

'Let's wait for the Book Fair to get over, which is only a matter of a few days more. I'll put in a call to Dipen before that, of course.'

I congratulated myself on the perspicacity that had helped me uncover the cause of Surjo Sengupta's despondency—his inability to forge a bond with a leading light of modern Bengal's literary renaissance, despite his pretensions and posturing of belonging to the same intellectual brotherhood. And here was crass, commercial, Philistine me, as far removed from modern Bengali literature as chalk is from cheese, about to make it happen for him, although for the life of me, I still didn't know how. But that was a fight to be fought another day. For the moment, nothing could weaken the sense of superiority that I had achieved after days of being at the receiving end of his.

'Dipen's dead,' announced Surjo Sengupta, in a sombre tone of voice that brooked no argument.

'Dead? Who's dead?' I blurted in confusion, clutching at the back of the nearest chair for support.

'Dipen's dead,' repeated Surjo Sengupta, shedding his gloom with remarkable agility.

'I don't believe it. When?' Having found the back of a chair to clutch, I was now desperately reaching for straws. 'It must have been very sudden.'

'If you can call nine months sudden,' said Surjo Sengupta, dejection fully replaced by aggression.

'Nine months?' I heard a despairing moan which, I surmised, was mine because it was certainly not Surjo Sengupta's, for his demeanour had metamorphosed from inconsolable lament to maniacal triumph, in the space of a few short exchanges.

'He died nine months ago,' said Surjo Sengupta, in a voice that left no room for dispute, or negotiation.

'Nine months? Was it really that long ago that I met him last?' I groped my faltering way to the solace of my favourite armchair and crumpled into it. 'It seems like it was yesterday.'

Surjo Sengupta stood up, so that he could look down on me with the increased condescension that height imparts. He gave Rita a sympathetic glance, which said, in no uncertain terms, that he fully understood what it took to suffer a moron as a life-partner. Then, with one last look of the deepest reproach in my direction that irredeemably condemned me to a succession of purgatories, he retired to his appointed bedchamber, no doubt to contemplate my dubious origins and those of Buddha's Mongoloid features.

NINE

The Piss Project

In celebration of a narrow escape from the tightest of corners and the comeuppance dealt to Veekay, in the end, Anoop Chowdhury granted Rahul an additional day in Bombay, in a rare gesture of generosity.

'To enjoy the delights. On the house,' he said, with an exaggerated twitch of the right eye that resembled a leer more than it did a wink, 'while I return to the salt mines of Calcutta.'

Whether there were any delights at all to be enjoyed or, even if there were, whether he had the time, or the inclination, to enjoy them, Rahul Banerjee was relieved that he didn't have to return with Chowdhury on another uncomfortable flight of shared fright.

'Don't do anything I wouldn't,' said Anoop Chowdhury, as he climbed into a waiting yellow-and-black and was whisked away in a puff of carbon monoxide fumes, leaving Rahul to consider the huge range of options encompassed in *that* bit of advice.

The previous night, after many pegs of whiskey, a drink that he said he preferred over gin post-sundown, Anoop Chowdhury had got into a protracted confabulation with the maître d' who, on being probed in what was thought to be a man-to-man manner, had waxed eloquent about this new place in the suburbs called Nandi the Bull, which had this fabulous floorshow that carried on till the wee hours of the morning and to which you were admitted by way of the kitchen since the front shutters were brought down at midnight, in strict compliance with prevailing law, although the police had been taken care of, and into confidence, just in case. In response to another searching enquiry, the maitre d' had quickly assured Chowdhury that he had it, from the most reliable of sources, that the Nandi girls were top drawer and thoroughly professional, always willing to go that extra mile, in pursuit of excellence in their art which, Rahul had surmised from the faraway look that came into Anoop Chowdhury's eyes, probably meant that they took *all* their clothes off, whereas the girls at Mandarin retained some minor semblance of modesty, although what both establishments had in common was that entry to them, for those who wished to partake of fare not on the regular menu, was by way of the kitchen. So engrossed had Anoop Chowdhury become in the maître d's exposition on the relative merits of Nandi the Bull vis-à-vis Mandarin that Rahul had been certain that he'd cancel his scheduled departure the next morning, on some pretext or other, and stay back for a boys' night on the town, before returning, sated, to the safe haven of his family home in North Calcutta. But, as Rahul was to realise the more he got to know Anoop Chowdhury, bhadraloks of his kind tended to live their lives by proxy. The closest they got to a life dramatically different from their own was by way of anecdotes shared with men more of the world than they, like maître d's of downtown hotels who, probably, had such a variety of questions directed at them in any event that nothing surprised them any more, certainly not how far down strippers at Nandi the Bull were willing to dress.

Early in the day, there was a call from Veekay, who was short to the point of rudeness; as well he might have had reason to be, after the shocks to his system delivered the previous evening.

'You guys are really the limit,' he said, his tone suggesting that this was meant in no way to be a compliment.

Rahul attempted to alleviate his suffering.

'Listen,' he reasoned, patiently. 'We had the group in place, just as we'd planned it, but some last-minute cancellations happened. You know how it is. People agree to come and then change their mind, realising that they have better ways to spend their spare time than discussing wall paint with strangers. We had the option to either cancel the group, or continue, replacing the missing participants. We chose to do the latter. I don't think there was anything principally wrong in picking people off the streets, as long as they met your predetermined profile. In sampling methodology, you can't get more random than that. Picking you was a genuine mistake, although you must agree that you do fit the profile. So, hey, we must have been doing something right!'

'No, I meant later. After it was all over. What you said.'

'Oh! That. Can you blame us for wanting to protect our livelihood and our reputation?'

'Any which way? Even blackmail?'

'Wouldn't you?'

Vishal Kaushik was silent for a while, although Rahul could hear his breathing across the wires.

'Will I get something on which I can base my advertising campaign?' he finally asked, a plaintive note replacing the earlier aggression in his voice. 'My job depends on it.'

Veekay's naïveté was almost endearing. It made Rahul Banerjee feel like an old, experienced hand. What he'd learnt, within a short career span, but what Vishal Kaushik seemed unaware of, still, was that a job in Calcutta's corporate circles was seldom lost because you couldn't do it; by that count, there wouldn't be many who would survive. There was a greater chance of losing it if you had bad table manners, an unfortunate dress sense, inadequate social graces or a poor handicap in golf; or, all of the above, in which event you were doomed forever and needed to urgently consider an alternative career, like trading. Or market research.

'Of course,' Rahul Banerjee assured his still-innocent client. 'One false start does not a disaster make.'

'What happens to the Bombay groups?'

'We'll do them when we're finished with the ones in Calcutta and Delhi. By then we'd also have smoothed out the kinks.'

As it transpired, they didn't have to return to Bombay for the ICC wall-paint project. The findings in the other cities so closely mirrored the expectations of their client and, by some happy coincidence, Anoop Chowdhury's, that the groups in Bombay were considered redundant and dispensed with. Though it meant a reduction in the budget apportioned to Rexxon, Rahul had the distinct feeling that Anoop Chowdhury was, actually, quite relieved not having to return to the scene of his earlier trials. As was Veekay, for not having to return to his, although he never exhibited quite the same enthusiasm for later groups that he'd done for the earlier ones. Obviously police arrest and blackmail, albeit of a mild variety, had left an impression more lasting than one had imagined. On the upside, his golf handicap certainly improved, as he found more time to spend at Tolly and Delhi Gym, having relieved himself of the duty of shadowing

Rexxon to various focus groups, where total strangers met, in strange surroundings over indifferent tea and snacks, to espouse their views on the merits and demerits of his paint. His baritone improved, too, as he got many more opportunities to put it to practice, most often at watering-holes that every jaunt around a golf course inevitably led to.

Without Veekay hounding him, Anoop Chowdhury became a different man altogether, particularly on his home turf in Calcutta; although, truth be told, he wasn't particularly off-colour in Delhi either, except for one day at Imperial Hotel, when only three participants turned up in place of the dozen expected. Some local residents, with time on their hands, loitering aimlessly in the hotel corridor, were pressed into service and the problem was resolved to everyone's satisfaction, particularly Rexxon's.

There was a new confidence and purpose in Anoop Chowdhury's moderation of groups, which essentially meant that he guided them in directions that suited his own preconceived notions and quashed them, mercilessly, if they didn't, unless it was a particularly bizarre line of thinking that afforded some entertainment, but no real value, in what had become increasingly repetitive and predictable sessions. The only time that Anoop Chowdhury's new-found confidence suffered a knock, and Rahul found his Bombay incarnation re-emerging, was when they received intimation that Veekay would be attending one of the Delhi groups, after all. Fortunately, Anoop Chowdhury had downed only one gin-and-tonic when Veekay called back to say that he had changed his mind, his guilt for spending more time on the golf course than his job, no doubt magically dissipated by the worthwhile distractions of the Delhi Gym bar. In celebration, Anoop Chowdhury downed a second g-and-t and, for added reassurance, a third and, literally, weaved his way through the next group where, to the confusion of participants, he solicited opinions on every known variety of paint, including the kind that women put on their faces, to the near exclusion of the type that ICC wished that people would put on their walls, preferably in countless numbers. When Rahul reminded him, sotto voce, that he might wish to return to the road that ICC was paying them to travel, Anoop Chowdhury assured him, in a return stage whisper, that it was no longer necessary. He'd already got all that he was ever going to get out of the groups and his report for ICC was written, in his mind, if not yet on paper. The sole purpose of persevering with the remaining groups, he confided, was to keep Rexxon's cash register tinkling which, from a shareholder's perspective, was as good a reason as any.

As an interested party, Rahul had to agree that the logic was irrefutable.

When Rahul Banerjee entered the Rexxon office the day after his return from Bombay, he detected an air of optimism that had been missing previously. The field team was present in full strength and he was engulfed by a wave of 'Good morning, sir' that he had some difficulty swimming his way out of. Even before the waters had subsided, came another of tidal proportions from the inner sanctum.

'Come in, come in. We have great news for you,' chorused Tapas Pan and Anoop Chowdhury. They had similar broad grins on their faces, leaving Rahul to wonder who had got a bigger share of the cream. Pan flashed a piece of paper, inundated with his usual, indecipherable doodles and some figures in black, obsessively underlined to highlight them.

'Between ICC and our on-going projects, we should turn enough of a profit to be able to shift to a new office,' announced Anoop Chowdhury.

'Not any old office,' clarified Tapas Pan, 'but one off Park Street that I've had my eyes on for a long time.'

'That's good to know,' said Rahul, realising not for the first time that, as an equal shareholder in the enterprise, there was still a lot that he didn't know about what his two partners were up to. 'I suppose there will be enough surplus generated, on a continuing basis, to justify the significantly higher rent?'

'If we just keep one ICC coming our way every other month, the urine project will take care of the rest,' said Tapas Pan, with supreme conviction.

Which, Rahul Banerjee thought, was as good a time as any to ask what the urine project was and what a field team of a dozen girls did to keep themselves busy through an entire month since, to the best of his knowledge, although he'd certainly not mind being corrected if his premise was inaccurate, there didn't seem to be enough market research work to keep a team that size productively occupied for a week, let alone, a month.

Tapas Pan exchanged a quick glance with Anoop Chowdhury who, quickly, assumed an air of nonchalance, which suggested that queries of this kind did not deserve the attention of someone of his seniority; they were best handled by minions, a category to which he was quite prepared to relegate Tapas Pan, if only to save himself the embarrassment of having to engage in a discussion on private bodily functions, and by-products thereof.

'The urine project is the backbone of Rexxon,' announced Tapas Pan grandly, mixing metaphors and human anatomy.

'And what kind of marketing research is it?' asked Rahul, with the slightest tinge of sarcasm.

'The kind that pays for our overheads and groceries,' Pan replied, reading the irony and retorting with some of his own.

Rahul realised that if he was going to get to the bottom of it, it wouldn't do to bait Tapas Pan. With seeming contriteness in his voice, he said, 'If it's of such crucial importance to Rexxon, I'd certainly like to know more about it.'

That he had been accorded centre stage was enough to appease Tapas Pan's ruffled sensitivities.

'The urine project is about collecting urine,' he said, precisely.

'The synergy with market research is quite obvious,' interjected Anoop Chowdhury, in the event that Rahul was too imperceptive to see it. 'They are both about collecting, really. One, data, and the other, well, urine.'

'And why, exactly, do we want to create a reservoir of urine?'

'Not just any old urine,' said Tapas Pan, warming to his task. 'The right stuff.'

'Oh. That's commendable. And what do you define as the right stuff?'

'The urine of pregnant women.'

'You can see where market research comes in, can't you?' interceded Anoop Chowdhury, in plaintive justification. 'Identifying pregnant women, to start with. Next, tracking them down from the patients' lists of gynaecologists and obstetricians. Then, setting-up a regular collection mechanism.'

'That certainly requires a special set of research skills!'

'From the morning's first output,' continued Tapas Pan, ignoring the exchange of marketing research bona fides. 'Calls for a great deal of precision.'

'Theirs in giving, or ours in collecting?'

'Both, actually,' said Tapas Pan, unruffled by Rahul's sarcasm and reaffirming his abiding interest in, and ownership of, the piss project.

'But remind me again. Why, exactly, are we collecting urine from pregnant women every morning?'

'Because a big pharma company needs it. Omron pays us big bucks to supply urine to them, regularly. Buckets and truckloads of the stuff. Collected from Calcutta and neighbouring districts, every morning. From wherever we can track them down. Pregnant women, that is.'

'And why is Omron pissing away its money?'

'It isn't. On the contrary, it's making lots more out of it.'

'Oh! It sees piss as the commodity of the future, does it?'

'A hormone extracted from the urine of pregnant women is a vital ingredient in a pill that Omron manufactures to treat infertility,' offered Anoop Chowdhury, by way of a clarification, and a salve for Rahul's increasing derision, which had started taking bite-sized chunks out of Tapas Pan's composure.

'It can be a lifetime project for us,' said Tapas Pan, enthusiastically, visualising a market research empire built on piss and pregnancies.

'So, the raison d'être of Rexxon's existence is piss collection,' summarised Rahul. 'Why not? That, too, can be a legacy for future generations.'

'It's easy money,' said Anoop Chowdhury, defensively. 'Tapas has the process so well streamlined that it requires only very cursory supervision. Leaves the two of us to pursue more elevating initiatives.'

'Good business is about making good money,' announced Tapas Pan, wounded by Anoop Chowdhury's attempt to ingratiate himself with Rahul by suggesting that his primary responsibility was less uplifting and inspirational than theirs. 'With the Omron assignment, we have an absolute money-spinner on our hands.'

Rahul Banerjee baulked at the imagery that came to his mind, unbidden.

'Look at the diversification possibilities,' continued Tapas Pan, showing the heaviness of purpose of a single-minded steamroller. 'On off-collection days, we have the services of twelve young women fully at our disposal.'

'To do what with?' asked Rahul Banerjee, dreading the answer but some streak of masochism getting him to ask the question anyway.

'Who knows? To start an escort service for visiting businessmen, perhaps?' said Tapas Pan, with a seriousness that was alarming.

'You're kidding, right?'

'Of course,' interposed Anoop Chowdhury, quickly, on Tapas Pan's behalf, uncomfortable with the direction in which the discussion, and Rexxon's future, seemed to be heading.

'Well, not entirely,' said Pan, an idea proposed in perverse jest beginning to take a more definitive shape in his mind. 'It certainly merits some consideration.'

'Why not?' Rahul Banerjee found that his only defence against the maddening, and strangely destabilising, influence of Tapas Pan's unique corporate vision was derision and self-deprecation. 'The three new P's of marketing research, according to Rexxon: piss, pimps and prostitutes.'

'And porn,' said Tapas Pan slyly, adding a fourth and, having played what he considered a definitive part in the evolution of the firm's future business strategy, broke into cackles of unrestrained glee which, to Rahul in his nervous state of mind, sounded decidedly demonical.

That edge of uneasiness stayed with Rahul Banerjee right through the day, despite Anoop Chowdhury's valiant attempts to engage him in discussions on subjects that were far removed from the piss project and, he hoped, capable of distracting Rahul from Tapas Pan's recent revelations: the standard of first division, inter-club football in the city, for example, or the state of West Bengal politics, or the condition of the Bengali film industry post the demise of its only real star, Uttam Kumar. But, in Rahul's somewhat jaundiced perspective, all of them, somehow, signalled piss, or variations thereof. It did not help that Tapas Pan, having completed the task of adding up the millions their firm was poised to make, and unable to contain his ebullience at the results he'd conjured, waded in unannounced, from time to time, with his own brand of logic, which tended to be so obfuscating as to discourage further discussion.

'Bad football is *purposely* played to turn people off football and move them to cricket. The establishment makes a great deal more money out of cricket than they do out of football. It's an international conspiracy that overrides local preferences.' Other than lowering his voice an octave or two, to emphasise the words, he did not bother to elucidate who the 'establishment' were and how, exactly, they had mounted this seemingly all-pervasive cricket conspiracy to kill football in the city.

'The Left will rule West Bengal, as long as the middle-class Bengali continues to feel guilty about making money and thinks passion and poetry can be found only in poverty. The Bengali intellectual perpetuates this false conviction through his writings and films.' Tapas Pan's fix for a political change in the State was through muzzling of the intellectual class, and its subversion, by a flood of contra-culture, either from another part of the country—preferably affluent—or overseas, as long as it was not China.

'Uttam Kumar died to keep his image untarnished and become the legend that he is.' To Anoop Chowdhury's question whether

Tapas Pan was implying that the great Bengali movie star might have caused his own death to preserve his image, he countered with one of his own: 'Isn't it better to be a dead superstar than a living also-ran?'

In the face of similar, incontrovertible logic, discussion ceased abruptly on any subject with which Tapas Pan had even a nodding acquaintance—and there weren't many with which he didn't. Finally, Anoop Chowdhury gave up trying to save the situation from the damage caused by Tapas Pan's disclosures. Rahul returned to his own, private hell where graphic manifestations of phrases like 'pissing it all away' and 'pissing in the wind' dominated.

And Tapas Pan, oblivious to the devastation that he'd caused, or the mental detritus surrounding him, sneaked frequent glances at his watch to determine how far away from lunch they still were.

TEN

The Big Move

During the week, the Big Move, to environs more salubrious, was completed, spearheaded by Tapas Pan, who showed almost as much enthusiasm supervising the shifting of furniture as he had ordering biryani.

The building on Middleton Street was relatively new, its surroundings clean and all the bars in the vicinity—and there were quite a few on adjoining Park Street—certainly more wholesome than Ruby.

The top floor—seventh—that Rexxon occupied was a brand new addition to the building. It was bare. It was also very hot. In his hurry to complete the premises and rent it out, the builder had opted for a temporary roof that he'd made out of corrugated asbestos sheets, instead of the usual mortar, steel and cement. His choice of roofing material may also have had something to do with his wanting the authorities to deem it a temporary structure, permission for constructing which was always easier to obtain than for something more permanent. This would have been an important consideration for the builder, as Calcutta Corporation, at their most cooperative, were not; even when a large, public transaction had been facilitated by a small, private one, as was usually the case. It also meant that, to perpetuate the myth of impermanency, the building's lift did not go any higher than the sixth floor: the top floor had to be accessed via a narrow flight of stairs.

'We'll have to sweat it out for seven days or so,' announced Tapas Pan, grabbing a seat near a window. 'That's the earliest they can install the air-conditioners.' As usual, he did not clarify why the Great Move could not have been delayed by a week.

The field team had been allotted a room of its own, separated from the directors by an intermediate room which, Tapas Pan explained, was meant for client meetings. Whether or not it was used for that purpose, it certainly helped to have it there: it gave the directors more privacy than the green, vertically-challenged curtain had in their previous office.

Despite the waves of warm air that the ceiling fans circulated, they could not dissolve the look of contentment on Anoop Chowdhury's face. With the perspiration on his brow shining as much as the gleam in his eyes, he surveyed busy Middleton Row and Park Street from his seventh floor perch.

'Saheb-para,' he breathed. White-man's neighbourhood.

'I told you, Anoop-da, we'd do it one day,' said Tapas Pan, in a tone that was a mix of awe and self-congratulation.

At last, Rahul Banerjee understood why the Big Move could not have waited another seven days. For his middle-class, North Calcutta partners, it had waited nearly forty years already. For them, there was nothing more inspirational than to own an address, albeit a temporary and tenuous one, in the erstwhile habitat, and playground of the British where, despite the intervening two score decades, the Raj still echoed, in the names of the roads, buildings and restaurants: Park Street, Camac Street, Harrington Street, Theatre Road, Middleton Row, King Edward's Court, Flury's, Blue Fox. For Anoop Chowdhury and Tapas Pan, 7th Floor, Burlington Chambers, Middleton Street, Calcutta, was as close to heaven as they were ever likely to get, even if it was a heaven sans air-conditioning.

But for Rahul Banerjee, the Big Move was just another confirmation of the Great Divide—the irreconcilable difference in mind-sets—that existed between him and his partners, one that was widening with each passing day.

North Calcuttans were the original inhabitants of the city—poets, philosophers, royalty, landed gentry, freedom fighters—founder members who were, so to speak, the city's history. They helped build it, lane by lane, cobbled street by cobbled street. They wove its social fabric, endowed it with its unique amalgam of art, literature and theatre and gave it its political voice and leadership. In comparison, South Calcuttans had assimilated themselves into the city much later being, mostly, Hindu immigrants from what was East Pakistan before it became Bangladesh. Because of their delayed entry into Calcutta's bubbling life stream, South Calcutta residents tended to be viewed, by their North Calcutta counterparts, as pretenders to, and usurpers of, the heritage that they believed they'd bestowed upon the city. This rivalry was unspoken, for the most part, except when Mohun Bagan and East Bengal were engaged in a rough-and-tumble scrap on a football field, at which time it was given voice to, in the most raucous and combative of fashions.

While a North Calcuttan revelled in his past and carried vestiges of turn-of-the-century morals, and mores, into his daily life, including the quaint practice of determinedly following a social calendar separate from that of his spouse's, a South Calcuttan wore his liberalism, and his modernity, on a sleeve and believed himself to be the vanguard of the city's future that included its seamless integration into the soon-to-arrive Global Village.

So, for example, while commercial theatre thrived in the sprawling, art-deco halls of the North, experimental drama took to the streets, and the small, open-air auditoria of South Calcutta, with audiences sitting on hard, un-upholstered wooden benches, not the plush, velvet-encased, cushioned seats that North Calcutta theatres offered. So, while short back-and-sides continued to be a fashion statement among the youth of North Calcutta, their South Calcutta brethren tended to be significantly more hirsute. So, while Rabindrasangeet and Nazrulgeet continued to dominate musical soirees in the North, adhunik gaan (Bengali pop) invaded indoor stadiums and arenas in South Calcutta, and groups doing covers of The Beatles, Dylan and Hendrix filled the spaces in-between. It was no coincidence that one of the more enduring symbols of modernity—the cinema—held sway in South Calcutta; in those days, one couldn't go much further south, without sinking into the oblivion of marshland, than the ubiquitous Tollygunge Studios, where South Calcutta denizens, like Satyajit Ray and Mrinal Sen, crafted productions for international recognition and renown.

Nowhere was this Great Divide more apparent than in their respective attitudes to social interaction. A servant to tradition, the average North Calcuttan was of the staunch, and often inflexible, view that minding the domestic roost was the duty of his spouse—by an accident of birth and the institution of marriage—whereas, tackling the world beyond the threshold of their front door was his prerogative and responsibility. With domains thus delineated, the North Calcuttan would be spotted at public places, like bars, restaurants and office parties, generally on his own, or in the company of male friends. The spouse was flashed occasionally, either at a cinema that was attended by the whole family, or at a wedding where, too, the women gathered separately, only to be united with their respective husbands when it was time to go home. On the other hand, the South Calcuttan, in an overt, often in-your-face demonstration of his liberal-mindedness, produced his spouse at every public assembly to which they were jointly invited and even at those where they were not. And, to the obvious discomfort and ill-concealed envy of his northern neighbour, he co-mingled freely with members of the opposite sex at social get-togethers, drawing from them oohs and aahs of appreciation at his ready wit and worldly humour, while his northern brother propped up the bar, at a distance, in the company of his own gender.

Anoop Chowdhury epitomised the average North Calcuttan while Rahul Banerjee was his polar opposite, being not only a resident of South Calcutta but a prabashi (meaning 'foreigner', which was what all Bengalis who didn't reside in West Bengal were, to those who did) to boot. So far, if a clash of cultures had been avoided, it was because it was still too early in the game for their inherent differences to surface. Nor did Rahul, as a prabashi, have any hereditary interest in local league football for *that* to become a catalyst in an irreversible widening of the divide.

With the adeptness of a practiced magician, which he certainly was when it came to conjuring profit forecasts, Tapas Pan cut into Rahul's reverie and produced half-a-dozen, freshly-minted visiting cards and handed them around ceremoniously. Anoop

Chowdhury gazed at his, with great reverence, mouthing the address silently, over and over again, till he was sure that he had it right and that it would trip smoothly off his tongue, if someone were to ask him for it.

'We should invite Veekay over,' he announced. 'In fact, we should throw a party for all our prospects. Once we have air-conditioning, of course. No better way to inform them of our new address.'

'Burlington Chambers, Middleton Street,' intoned Tapas Pan on cue, by way of a rehearsal.

'Burlington Chambers, Middleton Street,' repeated Anoop Chowdhury, reverentially.

They turned to Rahul, in unison, inviting his participation in the impromptu initiation ceremony where, it seemed, the address of the new office had to be repeated, like a mantra, to solemnise and sanctify it. For some inexplicable reason, it was a benediction that Rahul Banerjee couldn't find within himself to provide.

The air-conditioners arrived some days later, although manoeuvring them up the narrow flight of stairs was a feat that took most of a day to perform and stretched Partho's field supervisory talent to the limit. They were installed under Tapas Pan's eagle-eye. It was another story that they failed to start because, as it was subsequently discovered, the temporary seventh floor structure had been granted, befittingly, a temporary electricity connection only, which was nowhere near robust enough to take the load of the five tonnes of air-conditioning that Tapas Pan had ordered, in a moment of excessive enthusiasm. With air-conditioners occupying all the windows, there was no access to outside air, or light, when the power supply tripped, which was often, particularly when the sun was at its highest and had metamorphosed the asbestos roof into one large solar-heat panel. It was, therefore, not an uncommon sight for Rexxon directors and employees to be sitting in a dark, airless, mercilessly hot office, dehydrating rapidly, while the rest of the world went quite happily about its business on the six floors below and the bright streets outside. Of course, in the midst of fanning themselves frenziedly with whatever was closest at hand, Anoop Chowdhury and Tapas Pan had, at least, the solace of Burlington Chambers, Middleton Street to fall back upon. Unfortunately, that was of little comfort to Rahul and none at all when the unbearable heat was accompanied by an even more unbearable stream of expletives from Tapas Pan, questioning the forbears, indeed the very legitimacy, of people responsible for Calcutta's electricity supply. On such occasions, he actually wished he were back at the B.B. Ganguly Street office where, if nothing else, electricity was assured and, if Tapas Pan were to turn violent, Lal Bazaar was close at hand.

Few things test one's threshold of tolerance more than heat, humidity and entrapment in an airless room. Tapas Pan's was at bootlace level. Each time the ceiling fans stopped—even as they began winding down to stillness—he'd emit a nasal scream, the intensity of which was determined by the timing of the power cut, early afternoon meriting the most intense. While he was fairly impartial in his choice of expletive, some—like *bokachoda* (dumbfucker) and *saala haraamjada* (bloody bastard)—were his personal favourites, if one were to go by the number of times, and the passion with which, he used them. Anoop Chowdhury, on the other hand, would go completely silent, as if in counterpoint to Tapas Pan's primal scream. This stillness would last a minute or two, as if in sympathy for someone who had died, which wasn't far from the truth because something, if not someone, surely had: the power supply, except that, like a coward, it died a thousand deaths in an average month. With each death, Anoop Chowdhury's involuntary tics and unintended snorts would start, accompanied by self-flagellating slaps to the neck with a handkerchief, either in atonement for past sins or to dam perspiration at its source. The blame game would inevitably follow.

'You should have checked the power situation before you installed five ACs.'

'Why do I have to do everything?'

'Because you consider yourself the most practical.'

'And you think I'm not?'

'I didn't say that.'

'Why don't you tell me, Anoop-da, because I can see that you want to?'

'Fact one: we are in a temporary structure without a conventional roof.'

'That has nothing to do with air-conditioning.'

'Precisely. At least we agree on one thing. Fact two: we have five ACs but no electricity to run them. Fact three: even when there is electricity, it's never enough to run five ACs.'

'The problem's not with five ACs. It's with the electricity supply.'

'Brilliant. That's another thing we both agree on.'

'So, we'll just have to get another connection.'

'If it's that simple, why haven't we got it already?'

'Apply, apply, no reply. These things can't be done the normal way, with a formal application!'

'How then?'

'By lubrication.'

'And?'

'Who do you think I've been screaming at these last few days?'

'Why don't you tell us.'

'The guy who's been lubricated. He's promised to have the second connection for us within seventy-two hours.'

'Starting when?'

'He's late already.'

'How do you know he'll deliver at all?'

'Because he'll have a broken leg if he doesn't. To start with.'

'Meaning?' Rahul Banerjee jumped in.

'A small detail that you needn't concern yourself with. But, rest assured, it'll happen because I get things done.'

'I never doubted it. Thinking is what I do, but I can't do that in this heat,' Anoop Chowdhury's petulant justification for spending another day unproductively.

'Things will work out as long as I do what I do best and the two of you stick to your jobs.'

At the end of this exchange—or something similar—Rahul Banerjee would have a new doubt about the strange glue that bonded his partners together, and a fresh worry about his role in the firm, for he couldn't imagine what it was that was expected of him, other than being a diversionary bait for troubled clients. As far as his co-directors were concerned, one was as blasé about taking up a business of ill-repute, or a pastime that entailed the breaking of bones, as someone else would be about taking up golf, or philately; another had so buried himself in thought as to have rendered himself comatose, a condition that wasn't helped any, by his undue affection for Blue Riband gin. With men of such strange talents at the helm of affairs, it did not bode too well for their entrepreneurial future, or togetherness.

At these times, particularly when his mind was nearly as heated as the room around him, which was almost always, Rahul would wonder whether he was becoming a victim of his own self-fulfilling prophecy: that, within days of resigning his marketing manager's job in preference for a business partnership, he had regretted his impulsive choice and mentally condemned it to failure and, thereafter, was only picking up cues that were relevant to an outcome that he believed was predetermined, if not, preordained.

In retrospect, Rahul Banerjee would be hard pressed to pinpoint exactly what triggered the thought in his mind that market research with Chowdhury and Pan was not something he was prepared to commit a working lifetime to; in fact, not even another six months. It may have been the unfocused focus group in Bombay, or it may have been the revelations about the piss project, or it may have been the differences that were emerging everyday in the way he and his partners looked upon life, or it may have been a combination of all these factors reaching flashpoint one hot, power-less afternoon in their new office on the 7th floor of Burlington Chambers, Middleton Street, Calcutta.

But, as Tapas Pan let fly the inevitable stream of invective, directed, as usual, at the invisible man, who had still to deliver on the promise of a new electricity connection, and let it be known to everyone in his decibel range—which was considerable—that his patience had been tested to its limit and bones would now have to be broken in a way that made repair impossible, and as Anoop Chowdhury, in defence against the heat of the day and Pan's vitriol, found solace in a pool of escapist thoughts, primary among which must have been the dancing girls of Nandi the Bull, Rahul Banerjee quietly gathered his own thoughts and wrote, in longhand, his resignation from the Board on a sheet of yellow legal pad that was standard stationary for directors of Rexxon Consultancy Services. In so doing, he found his feet.

It would take him another six months to find his freedom.

ELEVEN

Enter Big Brother

L ike obedient school children, we assembled in the auditorium on the eighteenth floor, though, to the best of my knowledge, children of the obedient kind weren't given to chain-smoking, as some of us seemed to be doing, probably more out of nervousness than rebellion, although being called to a meeting at 8:30 on a Monday morning was certainly something to rebel about.

A white-sheeted table, with five empty chairs behind it, stood on an elevated dais. Rajesh Mehra was offering odds on who would occupy the chairs. Since the study was, purportedly, about improving the Sales–Works interface, Raj Singh and S.K. Gupta were certain candidates for two of the five positions. I guessed Big Brother would be represented by at least another two. That would leave the fifth chair for one of the Board members of TGEPC—probably the Executive Director—without whose blessing it would be difficult to harness everyone's cooperation and get a study of such sensitivity off the ground.

Who knows, I might have made a few bucks if I'd taken on Rajesh Mehra, who was backing the Managing Director for the fifth chair. My reasoning was that the MD, having come up the TGEPC way, unlike the ED, who'd been transplanted from another group company, was unlikely to want to associate himself with a study that had the potential to become unpopular among people he'd grown up with, both in years and hierarchical status. As it turned out, neither of us would have won.

Al—short for Aloke, which I thought was abbreviated enough not to require further verbal surgery—Bombat, the owner of Big Brother was, like his name, abbreviated. But, to compensate, he bustled extensively, either because he wished to divert you from his lack of inches, which, he might have thought, detracted from his becoming the imposing presence he wanted to be, or because he simply felt he had to, to lend credence to his self-propagated image of being a mover and a shaker of some calibre. He was also as bald as a well-scrubbed billiard ball, a condition from which he wished to distract you—unsuccessfully, as it turned out—by wearing a well-manicured and -tended beard, a small island in a sea of face, where your attention tended to be drawn more to the expanse of water than the sliver of land.

His assistant on the TGEPC study was Anil Pratap, the person who I'd been to business school with. I remembered him to be a quiet, soft-spoken fellow who was given to keeping his own company and spending longer hours in the institute library than on its playing-fields. While he offended nobody, I didn't recall him filling anyone with a great deal of pleasure, either. I didn't think BBC would have made him any different from his institute days.

Raj Singh bustled in—Al Bombat's affliction must have been contagious—with S.K. Gupta in tow, struggling to keep pace.

They climbed the dais and took their respective chairs. Cigarettes were extinguished and the buzz that had filled the auditorium in their absence subsided.

'Gentlemen,' said Raj Singh, very precisely as it turned out, since neither Sales nor Works had any lady executives, an unfortunate state of affairs, which always fuelled prolonged lamentation amongst us in the lunch-room.

'Gentlemen,' echoed S.K. Gupta.

'I'd like to introduce Mr Al Bombat and his colleague, Mr Anil Pratap, of Big Brother Consultancy,' announced Raj Singh with the fanfare of a barker at a freak show, inviting you to view the bearded lady and her two-headed accomplice. The flourish, I thought, was wickedly intentional. 'Al and his team will be with us for the next three months to suggest ways in which we can improve our efficiency. Over to you, Al, my pal.'

'Al, my pal,' said S.K. Gupta and enjoyed the sound of it so much that he said it again, almost reverentially. 'Al, my pal.'

Aloke Bombat was, no doubt, expecting a somewhat lengthier introduction and Raj Singh's short Master of Ceremonies act caught him a little by surprise. To give himself time to gather his thoughts for his opening—possibly, defining—statement, he pulled out a pipe from an inside pocket of his nattily-tailored, pin-striped jacket and tapped the tobacco in its bowl, with controlled savagery. Having tamped it to submission he, then, lit a fire to it with a special lighter that had a thick, focused flame, much like a miniature blowtorch. From behind a cloud of aromatic smoke, he made his opening remarks, while Raj Singh coughed in erratic punctuation.

'Gentlemen,' said Aloke—Al-my-pal—Bombat in a voice that had strains of an imported nasal twang. 'You must be wondering what I'm all about and what I'm doing here.'

He paused to suck hungrily at the stem of his pipe and for Raj Singh's ill-timed fit of coughing to abate. Smoke swirled around them like a minor twister.

'Not really,' volunteered Rajesh Mehra, with pretended ingenuousness. 'We mightn't know everything that one should know about you, but we certainly know why you are here.'

'Yes?' twanged Al Bombat, like a guitar that had lost a string. From the deliberate manner in which he was strangling the pipe in his hands, it was apparent that he wasn't entirely pleased with having to cope with audience interaction so early in his opening statement.

'To suggest ways in which we can improve our efficiency for the greater good of the company,' said Rajesh Mehra, in a monotone that was generally associated with the permanently brainwashed.

Raj Singh broke into a renewed bout of coughing to camouflage his amusement.

'Quite so,' said Aloke Bombat, fuming almost as much as the tobacco in his pipe. He shared a whispered aside with his colleague, Anil Pratap, and then returned to his interrupted, opening salvo.

'I'm going to say it like it is,' he re-started, aggressively. 'It's believed at your company's highest level that you guys have become too comfortable, with an economy of shortages, to function effectively and efficiently, in the age of competition that's just around the corner. Your actions and mind-set are geared for rationing, not selling. That's the general belief. It may, or may not, be the reality. I've been entrusted with the job of finding out. If it is, indeed, true that your systems, procedures and organisation are incapable of responding to the needs of a competitive environment, then, we've got to equip you for it. Otherwise, you chaps will lose your way and get left behind. You wouldn't want that to happen, would you?'

In case his rhetorical question elicited another unwanted response, Aloke Bombat hurried on.

'You guys know your business best. So, you understand your problems best. I don't have a magic wand. All I can be is a catalyst in the process of course correction. I can only point you in directions that require attention. The solutions will, necessarily, have to emerge from your own understanding of the business.'

And so it went for another hour, self-deprecation mixed with self-admiration, censure with praise and castigation with commendation. In tenor, straightforward plain-talking was interspersed with peaks of evangelistic zeal and, in accent, Ludhiana intermingled freely with Louisiana. Al-my-pal Bombat's recovery from a stuttering, interrupted start was quite commendable. If nothing else, the man was a master of oration. The pity of it was that very little, if anything, of what he said was true.

Raj Singh rolled his eyes, exaggeratedly, at the falsehoods and inaccuracies that, he believed, were being propagated on stage, but could do very little about, other than to wish that he were somewhere else; S.K. Gupta was just happy that he was away from the heat of a production furnace; the rest of us had a diversion from our daily routine, which wasn't entirely unwelcome, and Al Bombat thought that he had a captive audience—a belief that encouraged him to introduce risqué anecdotes into his peroration, in an ineffectual attempt at bonding, as he warmed to his subject.

And right through that first, introductory session, the chair that I had guessed the Executive Director would occupy, remained empty, as if distancing itself from the players and the performance on stage.

My meeting with Aloke Bombat was a fortnight later. By then we knew, more or less, which way the study—investigation, really—was heading. Clearly, it was *not* going around the corner behind which competition was believed to be lurking. Nor did it seem to have very much to do with equipping us for a new tomorrow. On the contrary, it appeared to be entirely focused on the Old Yesterday.

Big Brother was allotted the Sales meeting room on the fifteenth floor for the duration of their stay, which meant that we had one place less to sneak to for a soothing cigarette, or a have-you-heard-the-latest huddle. It was, mostly, occupied by Anil Pratap and a couple of his minions. Aloke Bombat made occasional visits, usually when a personal interview with one of us had to be conducted, preferring to spend more of his time on the higher floors. His visits would normally last a couple of hours but, in no case, extend into the lunch break. Aloke Bombat was extremely particular about his lunch—where he had it (Bengal Club) and who he had it with (directors of assorted blue chip companies which still retained their head offices in Calcutta and were, therefore, prime candidates for his particular brand of management counselling).

When I walked into the Sales meeting room, I was greeted by a cloud of Amphora pipe tobacco smoke from behind which a smiling Al-my-pal Bombat emerged like a good-humoured apparition. Next to him sat an equally good-humoured Anil Pratap. Obviously they had a lot more to smile about than I did because, at home, Surjo Sengupta was continuing *not* to be amused about most things; evidently, the Dead Dipen episode still rankled.

'Hey, I believe you were with Anil at the institute. That makes us like *that*.' Like *that* was accompanied by an emphatic crossing of the index and forefingers of Bombat's right hand, indicating that we had a special kinship not shared with anyone who *hadn't* been to business school with someone from the Big Brother family.

'So, we can have a free and frank discussion,' chipped in Anil Pratap, which I read as an invitation to spill the beans, in case I had any to spill. That's what I read into the 'frank' part; 'free' probably meant that I wouldn't go entirely unrewarded, if the beans were found to be worth the spilling. Who knew, I might even be recommended for a promotion.

'As one of the upcoming stars of TGEPC, I'm sure you'll agree that the old order needs to change,' said Al-my-pal Bombat, with friendly, almost chummy, persuasion, implying that any change, if it were to happen, would be hugely beneficial to those who'd contributed to it.

'If old order means the way we do some of the things we do, certainly,' I said, cautiously.

'C'mon,' said Al Bombat, pretending impatience at my slowness to grasp the kernel of his argument. 'You know that he has got to go—Raj Singh. And that old fart who's been giving him protection all these years.'

'Mazoomdar, your MD,' clarified Anil Pratap in case I hadn't quite grasped who the old fart might be, as if there were many others holding positions of eminence in TGEPC who fitted that colourful description quite so aptly.

Just like that, it was out in the open. And for the agenda to be revealed, I hadn't had to take the dummy out, not even once.

'Let's get on with it then,' said Aloke Bombat, casually, as if I'd only imagined the exchange of a moment ago. 'Tell me, how many more executives have your bosses lost lately?'

Behind a huge balloon of Amphora tobacco smoke, I saw a sly smile wreath Al Bombat's face, and mischief, Anil Pratap's, telling me that they already knew the answer, and warning me, in the friendly manner of alumni, which at least one of them was, that I'd better be careful who I placed my money, and faith, on.

TWELVE

Missing in Inaction

My first immediate boss at The Great Eastern Pipe Company (TGEPC) was Amar Puri. Within a few days of my joining, I discovered him to be extremely proficient at solving the daily newspaper crossword, preferring the *Telegraph*'s over the *Statesman*'s because he completed the former well before the first tea break, an hour into the day, whereas the latter often remained unfinished till late into the afternoon, by when his enthusiasm, effort and ability had all slackened. As we got to know each other better, he took to involving me in his crossword-solving pursuits. Many an afternoon was happily, and productively, spent with our heads together cracking a fourteen across or a twenty-one down that had eluded our individual ability but could not stand up to the might of our collective intellect.

It was in the course of throwing crossword clues at each other that I first began to suspect that Amar Puri might be slightly hard of hearing. This was confirmed when my cheery 'good mornings' often elicited only monosyllabic grunts, a 'what?' or a 'when?' and, on occasion, a 'how?', that discouraged any further conversation. After a number of such indeterminate exchanges, I decided to dispense with the convention, preferring to nod silently and emphatically when I saw him rather than shout a greeting, which, in the manner of its delivery, might have converted it from the friendly salutation that it was meant to be to an offensive reprimand. And forever closed the door to our continued exploration of literary conundrums on afternoons—and there were many such—when the wheels of The Great Eastern Pipe Company did not need any help from us to keep them on the rails and rolling.

Unfortunately, the nature of our relationship—boss-subordinate—required that there be something a little more substantial between us than just courteous nods, wordless greetings and the quiet pursuit of the daily crossword. Our close proximity to the babus was not conducive to loud conversation, otherwise that might have been the simplest solution. As it was, Romen-babu and his under-occupied ilk had no qualms about eavesdropping on us in their unremitting efforts to uncover the secrets of the 'management class'. We certainly did not want to make it easier for them to invade our fragile privacy, particularly when we were deep in the mysteries of the morning crossword. Also, as I discovered, Amar Puri had moments when his hearing was sharper—or so it seemed—than at other times. It was extremely disconcerting to be interrupted in the middle of an especially loud sentence by a tetchy 'Why are you shouting?' and then, on obediently lowering one's voice, to be admonished for doing so. It did not make for fluid, seamless and meaningful discussion.

I complained as much to Rajesh Mehra one day, after an especially frustrating endeavour to solve the *Statesman* crossword, prolonged beyond the limits of my patience by the 'stop-go' conversation that accompanied it. While this unfortunate affliction, at so early an age, was certainly deserving of sympathy, I said, something, surely, could be done about it? Particularly if, one day, God forbid, we were required to address matters somewhat more critical to the well-being of TGEPC than getting the *Telegraph* done before Alam, the peon, served us our first cup of tea of the morning?

Rajesh Mehra nodded, sagely.

'Thereby hangs a tale,' he said, and proceeded to tell it.

'In the Ice Age,' he began, lighting a cigarette, settling comfortably into his executive chair and sweeping several memorandums marked URGENT off his desk with a flourish that he'd later regret when he had to retrieve them, 'TGEPC didn't have a formal orientation programme for sales trainees. Our batch—recruited directly from college campuses three years ago—was the first to benefit from a formal, time-bound training programme. All trainees joined on the same day and, unless there were mitigating circumstances that required someone's training period to be extended, graduated together to the level of sales officers, admittedly the lowest end of the management totem pole but a position from where, thankfully, the only direction was up. But, why am I preaching to the converted? You know all this, having yourself spent nine months shuttling from department to department, and function to function, before getting your final posting, so to speak.'

I nodded in agreement while Rajesh Mehra used the intercom to inform Reception that he was engaged in vitally-important discussions from which he wouldn't want to be distracted for the next couple of hours, even if someone were to claim that it was a matter of life and death since we all knew that nothing in the affairs of TGEPC ever was.

'Before us, things weren't particularly systematic, either,' he continued. 'Recruitments happened ad hoc, anytime during the year, since they depended less on where the actual vacancies were and more on who had to be accommodated from which 'old boy network'. Retired generals, senior bureaucrats, octogenarian directors, they all had sons or nephews who had either completed their basic education, or failed to, and needed to be found something that would keep them occupied at least, if not entirely honest. With their antecedents spoken for, fluency in the English language, usually, was sufficient qualification for them to secure a position in the Sales department. A reasonable handicap in golf was always a bonus and could get you a higher starting salary than someone without it.

'Given the circumstances of his employment, a job had to be fitted around the fresh recruit rather than it being the other way around. The primary objective of the inductee's training schedule was to keep at bay, for as long as one could, the decision of what his job was actually going to be. This had to be done delicately, without ever suggesting to his patron—the retired general, senior bureaucrat or venerable Board member, as the case might be—that there was anything wrong with the employee himself that stood in the way of his achieving glory faster, in the exacting world of commerce.

'Ambiguity about the actual duration of the training period, therefore, was intentional. I believe it varied anywhere between six months and a couple of years! How short—or long—it was depended upon the frequency with which a patron enquired about the well-being of his ward and the extent of influence he exercised over the affairs of the company. For example, a retired General, who'd become chairman of some industry body or other, was more influential than, say, one growing prize-winning pumpkins in his kitchen garden; or, a senior bureaucrat who doled out manufacturing licenses than, say, a Board director who'd resigned by rotation and, for some unfathomable reason, was not seeking re-election.

'In Amar Puri's case, it was unfortunate that his benefactor passed on within a few months of Puri joining TGEPC. With his demise—more unfortunate for Puri than his dearly departed sponsor, who'd, no doubt, travelled to a happier hunting ground than the one he'd abandoned his protégé in—Puri's progress in the company fell off the radar screen. Not the kind to demand attention or seek the limelight, Amar Puri stepped quietly into the Twilight Zone one day, unknown to his bosses—the duo of Mazoomdar and Raj Singh—and, possibly, himself.

Rajesh Mehra paused dramatically to stub out his cigarette and light another.

'What do you mean?' I asked, on cue.

Taking a long, satisfying draw on his freshly-lit Wills Navy Cut, Rajesh Mehra said, 'They lost him. To add insult to injury— I'm not quite sure whose—they didn't even realise that they had!'

I waited for Rajesh Mehra to take full satisfaction from his dramatic moment, which he did, puffing contentedly at his cigarette and tossing the smoke out in concentric loops through pursed lips.

'Months passed,' he said, having had his fill of the ill-concealed impatience in my eyes that urged him to continue. 'If my sources are to be believed, one whole year, until the next batch of trainees joined. Over the traditional welcome lunch that old man Mazoomdar hosts for fresh recruits at Bengal Club, someone innocently asked him how the previous batch—Amar Puri—was doing. For reasons that we all now know, that casual query brought proceedings to a bit of a standstill. About to launch into his customary "we-are-one-big-happy-family" speech, Mazoomdar stumbled, turning to Raj Singh for an explanation, as he's prone to do whenever he's stumped for an answer. Raj Singh, of course, didn't have one, which is his usual state whenever the old man nudges a particularly nasty ball into his court. He hurriedly excused himself from the table in the middle of his mulligatawny soup and did not return either for the main course or dessert. Mazoomdar himself was so distracted, I'm told, that he abandoned the closing act he's so fond of—the one where he shakes each new recruit's hand in both his, looks him in the eye with patriarchal benevolence and assures him of an exciting future. Even before the dessert plates had been removed, he'd rushed back to office for a huddle with Raj Singh, which continued well into late evening.

'While Mazoomdar was still distractedly going through the motions at Bengal Club, Raj Singh had already initiated a search for the missing sales trainee. He was constrained by the fact that he had to do things quietly and discreetly. A direct, purposeful approach might have sent the wrong signals to those who mattered—the Board of Directors, for one, and, certainly, the labour union, who'd just have one more stick to flay an "unfeeling, inconsiderate Management" with when it came to negotiating the next pay rise. If it was ready to treat its own people so shabbily, they'd say, imagine what it had in store for the non-management staff!

'On the positive side, it was quickly ascertained that definite traces of Amar Puri's existence remained, a great relief to those who'd begun to believe that he may have disappeared totally, like some alien abductee. Finance confirmed that his salary had been religiously credited to his bank account, every month, for the preceding twelve months. The bank, in turn, confirmed that his account was still active. Next, the fact that his family hadn't raised any alarms meant that nothing untoward had happened to him: it could be safely assumed that he was leaving for work every morning and returning home every evening. The question was, where was he going everyday? It wasn't a question that you could ask the family. It wouldn't have, exactly, suffused them with confidence and a warm feeling towards the company to find out that it had misplaced one of its managers for a year! "Excuse us, we have a Mr Amar Puri on our rolls and have been unfailingly paying his salary for the last twelve months but we don't seem to know where he's working or what he's doing. Can any of you help?" '

Rajesh Mehra paused, theatrically.

'What's this going to get me?' he asked. 'This re-telling of TGEPC's colourful past?'

'Other than an enraptured, captive audience, you mean?' I asked.

Mehra was an amateur thespian, partial to bedroom farces. He usually played the cuckolded husband, a role that gave him license to improvise, ad lib and ham outrageously, which invariably he did, to upstage the main protagonist and get more laughs out of the audience than the hero could, despite having the better lines and the bigger part. Rajesh Mehra was a player in constant search of an audience and nothing pleased him more than to know that he had one.

'Quite,' he acknowledged, happily, lit another cigarette and returned to his narrative, which I could sense was approaching the great denouement.

'Finance was asked to peruse travel statements of all sales personnel for the preceding twelve months: a travel expense audit, they were told. Had Amar Puri been sent to Works, or one of the regional offices, or on a market survey—the latter a favourite when senior management had run out of ways in which to keep a fresh recruit gainfully employed and out of its hair? No clues there: everyone in Sales seemed to have a travel voucher against his name, except the missing Amar Puri.

'Weeks passed, during which Mazoomdar got increasingly agitated by the lack of progress, Raj Singh bearing the brunt of his escalating displeasure. At one point, in a moment of desperation, the old man even contemplated contracting a detective agency to assist in the investigation. He must have back-tracked imagining the adverse publicity that it would get the company—a gang of insensitive ex-policemen, more accustomed to dealing with petty criminals and straying husbands than respectable executives, plodding heavily, and indiscriminately, through the offices of TGEPC, upending every applecart in sight, in search of an elusive officer-trainee.

'Another fortnight passed with no sign of hide or hair of A. Puri.

'Then, one day, quite by happenstance, Raj Singh visited the TGEPC warehouse in Kidderpore, a visit that he seldom, if ever, made. This time he was forced to. Some very expensive pipes had been rejected and returned to the warehouse and, given the importance of the customer, it behove Raj Singh to go and see what the complaint was all about, first-hand. He wasn't planning to spend much time there—it was the middle of summer and the premises weren't air-conditioned. And it was in a dingy part of the city. It must have been a great comfort for him to know that The Tolly wasn't far from where he'd be going and, on his way back, a detour that included cold beer and hot kebabs might not be out of place, as just compensation for the discomfort he'd be enduring in the service of the company.'

Rajesh Mehra's telephone rang, interrupting his narrative. It was a colleague who wished to know how much longer he'd be before he was available to discuss some urgent issues. Mehra wished to know whether it was a matter of life and death and whether heavens would fall if the discussions were postponed to the next day. Assured that it wasn't and they wouldn't, he returned to his story.

'You've been to the warehouse during your travels,' he continued, peering at me from behind a screen of cigarette smoke. 'You know what sort of a hell-hole it is: a hot, cavernous, aircraft hangar-type space, where row upon row of steel pipes are stacked, and the constant, mind-numbing din of them being lifted, loaded and stored, fork-lift trucks banging around on the shop floor, trolleys clanging overhead.

'When Raj Singh entered, pipes were being stacked and the noise was loud enough to be almost painful. As he recoiled from the combined onslaught of heat and sound, he happened to turn his eyes heavenwards, in supplication, perhaps. An overhead trolley was busily tracking the ceiling, from one end of the hangar to the other, its pincers expertly lifting pipes from one stack and piling them on another. And busy behind the controls, manoeuvring the trolley with skill and great precision, was his missing sales trainee: Amar Puri.'

Having delivered the denouement, Rajesh Mehra paused for applause. I gave it, dutifully.

'You don't say!' I exclaimed. 'Exiled to the warehouse for a year!'

'Not exiled, misplaced,' corrected Rajesh Mehra.

'As part of his orientation programme, Amar Puri had been allotted a week at the warehouse, after which he'd been forgotten. The week completed and with no new directives from his bosses, Amar Puri, had returned to the warehouse— his last, official posting—day after day, week after week and month after month like a good foot soldier who follows orders, even when there aren't any, without question or protest. With mostly unskilled labourers for company, he'd found distraction in the daily crossword, developing quite a talent for it, as you now know. However, that was still not challenging enough to engage him an entire day. Taking the amiable and accommodating warehouse manager's permission, which wasn't too difficult to get, he'd learnt to work, first, the fork-lift truck on the shop floor and then, a few months later when he'd accumulated sufficient confidence in his abilities, the overhead trolley.

'Between the crossword in the mornings and the fork-lift trucks in the afternoons, he'd seen a year through. Except that, without the benefit of ear-muffs and immersed as he always was in the constant din of pipes being stacked, he'd lost a bit of his hearing, a handicap that came to light only months later because, in the environment of a warehouse, you have to shout to make yourself heard, in any case.

'Immediately, not even waiting to investigate the complaint that he'd gone for, and selflessly sacrificing beer and kebabs at Tolly, Raj Singh escorted Amar Puri back to TGEPC, their first stop, on return, being Mazoomdar's office. No one quite knows what transpired in that meeting but it is speculated that Puri was assured something akin to lifetime employment, and the best medical care, on the condition that he bury this unfortunate incident in the darkest recesses of his mind, which he did; though, as these things have a funny way of doing, bits and pieces surfaced at various points in time and got woven together into an urban legend, almost, one of many that haunt TGEPC.

'So, what do you think of that!' Rajesh Mehra exclaimed in conclusion, probing to know whether his story had got my complete, undivided attention. It had, but I wasn't about to tell him that.

'Did he get the medical attention that he was promised?' I asked.

'I believe he did,' replied Mehra. 'But when the only permanent cure on offer was a hearing aid, some misplaced sense of vanity made him decline it. Of course, the less-kind among us believe that it's Amar Puri's way of keeping the company in a constant state of guilt, which can be a nice little lever to pull when the going really gets rough. As for me, I think it has other advantages too. For example, when a boss is screaming, as bosses are prone to do, and the rest of us are quivering like leaves in high wind, it's just normal conversation for Amar Puri.'

'Or, it can be a nice little device to tune out of a conversation when you're tired of it,' I supplemented. 'Or, you can fall back on it to deter people from starting a pointless conversation with you, in the first place.'

If we had given wing to our imagination, no doubt we would have discovered many more ways that a hardness of hearing can, actually, be quite beneficial in the workplace, not the least being able to complete the daily crossword without unwanted interference from talkative colleagues wishing to share the latest slice of office gossip with you. But our flight of fancy was prematurely aborted by the insistent ring of Rajesh Mehra's telephone; it was Reception wanting to know whether his wife should be given the prescribed brush-off or permitted entry, though, to be fair to her, she hadn't ever claimed that it was a matter of life and death that had brought her to his office door, merely the need for a ride back home should her busy husband be about finished with his day in office.

With his tale told, Rajesh Mehra was.

Soon it was pretty clear that either someone was leaking TGEPC's less-savoury secrets, like an irresponsible sieve, or Big Brother Consultancy was uncannily prescient about these matters, which, if it was true, explained the wariness with which most people viewed Bombat and his team. I was inclined to think it was the former, although that did not get me to drop my guard each time Al-my-pal found some flimsy excuse or another to call me into the Sales conference room that they'd almost permanently commandeered and engage me in casual-seeming discussions, all of which, somehow, inevitably led to Mazoomdar and Raj Singh and their rumoured misdemeanours.

It wasn't as if I was the only canary that Big Brother wanted to cajole into song. The same modus operandi was applied to Chaks, Rajesh Mehra and the others too. Clearly the big guns were out and Emem (as Manab Mazoomdar, the managing director, was popularly known) and Raj Singh were in the cross-hairs. The blatant-ness of the approach suggested that Big Brother had the implicit support of someone in the highest echelon; whether that 'someone' was acting in his individual capacity or in consort with others was still unclear.

While none of us was particularly enamoured of either Emem's management style, which bordered on dictatorship, or his corporate vision, which, at the best of times, was myopic, we all had a bit of a soft corner for Raj Singh who, unless under a specific directive from Up Above that he just couldn't ignore, usually adopted an easy-going, laissez faire attitude with us, to compensate for Emem's often-unreasonable rigidity, no doubt. Unfortunately, in the matter of corporate vision, he was equally near-sighted although he made up for it with his unique brand of solecisms that always gave us something to cheer about when the business of selling pipes was getting us down, which was often.

That, we thought, was reason enough to do something to disrupt Big Brother's transparent plot to extract so-called evidence, from straws of gossip, to overthrow the current Masters of our Sales universe. TGEPC would be half the place it was without the entertainment that Raj Singh's inadvertent malapropisms often provided.

Who else, when asked to thank a group of visiting thespians from the UK, who'd just completed a strenuous, if not exactly exhilarating, performance of Orwell's *Animal Farm*, would call it an 'allergy' when I had scripted 'allegory' for him to read?

'The performance was an allergy,' he proudly announced, much to the horror of Mr John Taylor and his band of young, enthusiastic actors and, thereafter, misreading the chagrin on the director's face to be gratitude, continued, with irrepressible vigour: 'A two-hour allergy that, I'm sure, none of us will forget in a hurry.'

Who else, when agitated by Emem's insistence that we change the way we'd been doing something successfully for years, would jump up in the middle of a well-attended conference to shout, 'Let's not give the baby a bath,' and plunge into the hiatus created by his pronouncement to say, 'Unless we know where to throw it'?

It was time for the good guys to bring out their whitest hats and no one wore one whiter than Mr Samar Bose, 'Esbee' to those favoured by his friendship but always *Mister* Bose to the less privileged.

Mister Bose was the Mr Big of the Sales department. He'd joined TGEPC when the British still ran the company and had climbed up the corporate hierarchy, rung by rung, till he was, now, a divisional head, a level below Raj Singh's and a couple under Emem's. On merit alone he would have outpaced them both, except that he possessed an undisciplined streak of irreverence that, often, made him go against the grain of accepted corporate behaviour to the detriment of all those whose grain he rubbed the wrong way and, unfortunately, to his own disadvantage too, since the people who bore the brunt of his derision, usually, were more accustomed to being genuflected upon than crucified.

All it required for Mister Bose to don his white hat was the slightest whiff of injustice. And if ever there was a stink, it came from the Sales conference room where Al Bombat and Anil Pratap pushed, prodded and probed to find sufficient empirical evidence and cause to administer a brand of justice all their own.

'It must be Ramaswami up to his old mischief,' said Mister Bose, in his famous baritone, referring to the executive director, when we'd finished telling him about Big Brother's modus operandi and the pre-determined direction in which their investigation seemed to be heading. 'He's always wanted Sales to report to him directly. Maybe he's got some people from his previous company in mind, who he thinks will be more loyal to him than Emem and Raj. Not that I'm holding a brief for either!'

He swivelled his chair around to give us a view of his broad back while he contemplated a more soothing and sylvan one outside the bay window of his office. Tendrils of cigarette smoke circled his head like flawed haloes.

'But it's such an amateurish, elaborate, heavy-handed and pricey way of doing things,' he growled, the words bouncing back to us from the glass opposite. 'Typical Ramaswami.'

Not having any personal experience of the executive director's management style, Chaks, Rajesh Mehra and I had nothing to offer by way of comment. Nor were we certain what was giving Mister Bose greater cause for umbrage: the clumsiness of the effort or its expensiveness. We waited in silence while he continued his meditative survey of the Calcutta Maidan, blowing imperfect rings of cigarette smoke. Then, he suddenly turned to face us again, the chair squeaking in protest under the strain of the abrupt movement and his weight.

'We'll just have to take the Mickey out of them, won't we?' he said, grinning broadly, a mischievous glint in his eye.

From his suppressed excitement it was clear that not only had the hat been pulled out of safekeeping and polished to a blinding whiteness, but it had also been donned at a buccaneering angle, which signalled that battle had truly been joined and no prisoners would be taken at the end of it, if Esbee was allowed to have his way, which, in most circumstances, he was.

THIRTEEN

The Country Spirit

As it transpired, no legs had to be broken nor lives extinguished, to get an additional electricity connection for 7th floor, Burlington Chambers; it just took a few weeks longer than it should have, as all things involving the local municipality did. By the end of the waiting period, Rahul Banerjee's vocabulary of Bengali swear-words had expanded substantially, under Tapas Pan's unintended tutelage, although he had yet to perfect the exact manner of their delivery, extending the sibilants, in words such as saala, for example, to make them literally sizzle with menace, or booming the consonants in words, like bokachoda, to transform them into bludgeons of destruction. While it often crossed his mind to break the news of his impending departure to his fellow-directors, better sense advised that he should wait until sanity had, hopefully, been restored along with the air-conditioning.

In the meantime, Tapas Pan's urine undertaking continued to cover Rexxon's cash flow requirements adequately, though not extravagantly. The occasional market research job from a client, who required data cheaply to support a decision he had already made, or disprove one someone else had, kept alive the myth, at least in Rahul's mind, that he was engaged in an activity of some consequence, if not respect.

For instance, the findings of the ICC groups having happily coincided with Veekay's boss's own prognostications, earned him a lecture on the wisdom that came from direct field-selling experience, and a congratulatory pat on the back for not sullying that hard-earned knowledge by attempting new-fangled ways of doing things, as some inexperienced business school graduates were prone to do. With his future thus secured and, possibly, on the road to advancement, Veekay began to show a willingness to forget the past, particularly his brush with the Bombay police, and entrust more work to Rexxon, so long as they were willing to suffer his artificial baritone. Having endured Tapas Pan's continuous, high-pitched swearing for weeks, Rahul found that he actually welcomed the change; or, perhaps, it was just that the air-conditioning at ICC never failed. Whatever the reason, Rexxon's job bag seemed reasonably full for the time being, which meant that Tapas Pan's diversification proposal, to start an escort service for visiting businessmen, could be relegated to a remote back-burner, much to Rahul's relief.

With the restoration of air-conditioning, in the fourth week of their stay at Burlington Chambers, came a new optimism.

'I think we have Veekay wrapped up,' announced Anoop Chowdhury, as if he were a package for despatch to some far corner of the universe. 'He'll definitely give us the job to measure the effectiveness of the launch campaign.'

'*His* campaign,' Rahul Banerjee pointed out. 'It must be seen to be working, if we are to secure that promotion for him.'

'He should get it if we can show that enough people saw his advertising, liked it and remember the fundamental benefits of the new brand,' said Anoop Chowdhury, with the wisdom that comes from years of experience. 'After all, Veekay can't be faulted if Sales haven't been able to convert the potential, or Distribution reach the product far enough, or R & D design it to meet consumer expectations!'

'It's nice to be able to write a research report even before the research is done,' said Rahul, with a heavy helping of sarcasm, which went largely unnoticed, Anoop Chowdhury having suddenly found something, or someone, more deserving of his attention seven floors below, and Tapas Pan taking that precise moment to step into the conversation with a query that, as usual, bore little relevance to the subject under discussion.

'Ever had bangla?' he asked.

'Bangla?'

'Country liquor, hooch' said Tapas Pan, grinning, with barely-concealed glee, now that he had everyone's attention. 'The spirit of the masses,' he hissed, overwhelmed by an abundance of sibilants.

'Can't say I have,' admitted Rahul.

'Not even in college? When your pocket-money ran out, but your thirst didn't?'

'Not even then. We may have down-traded the brand, but not the category,' Rahul Banerjee reminisced, wondering what had brought this on.

'What about you, Anoop-da?'

Chowdhury tore himself away from his long-distance appraisal of college girls, in miniature, at the gates of Loreto House on Middleton Street.

'Maybe, once,' he said. 'Didn't much care for it.'

'Why not?'

'Rough. Smelly. Strong. Left me with the mother of all headaches.'

'Precisely,' said Tapas Pan. 'Now, all that's about to change.' Briefly, he outlined how.

At the top of the quality pyramid, he said, was imported foreign liquor, exorbitantly priced in the official market since the category attracted huge import duties, and of dubious quality, when sourced from your friendly, neighbourhood smuggler. It was surmised that there was more Scotch consumed in India than distilled in the whole of Scotland. Then, there was the category called 'Indian-made foreign liquor', or IMFL, which comprised brands manufactured by reputed Indian companies that satisfied the thirst of a majority of urban Indians. But the largest market, many times the first two categories combined, was for country liquor, which was produced by State- and district- specific distillers, and was, usually, unbranded, though sometimes, they carried numerals to denote either their quality or their potency, one was never quite sure which. It was retailed out of Government-designated country liquor shops and was the thirst-quencher of choice of blue-collar workers, truckers, non-discerning alcoholics and a significant proportion of the Bengali intellectual-class, who consumed it either as a badge of their Bohemianism or because their writings didn't sell well enough to fund their habit. Finally, there was country liquor of the illicit variety—true-blue hooch—surreptitiously and illegally distilled from items of uncertain origin into a final product of even greater dubiousness.

If national players having distribution muscle, marketing clout and deep pockets were to enter the country liquor market, not only was there a great deal of money to be made, but also the quality of the category itself could be substantially improved, weaning consumers away from all the unhealthy stuff that found its way into State-level markets from small-time distillers, who had very little respect for quality and, often, put customers' lives at risk with their untested products. People who knew about these things, said Tapas Pan, implying that he knew people who knew, believed that a whole new category, between IMFL and conventional country liquor, could be created that offered the potential to be many times as profitable as IMFL.

Tapas Pan had the attention of his fellow-directors, although Rahul Banerjee was still not certain what a treatise on alcohol distillation and consumption had to do with Rexxon's marketing research pursuits. But, after the recent revelations of the piss project, he knew that he shouldn't be surprised if a connection, however tenuous, were to be finally established.

'Imagine a category that has all the qualities of IMFL, but isn't IMFL,' said Tapas Pan.

'Why not lower-priced IMFL brands?'

'The typical country liquor customer wouldn't find it affordable,' explained Tapas Pan, 'because IMFL, by definition, attracts high taxes and duties. To by-pass them, the new product must remain firmly within the category of country liquor yet retain all the qualities of IMFL.'

'Why would the authorities give someone a licence to produce something that they know is IMFL thinly-disguised as country liquor if the over-riding motive is to by-pass taxes?' asked Rahul.

'They would, if they were to be assured of revenues far in excess of what they make from the sale of conventional country liquor alone. And, of course, if some benefits were to accrue to those responsible for handing out the manufacturing licences,' said Pan having, obviously, thought the matter through at some length.

'Yes, this is all very interesting but where, exactly, do we come in?' asked Anoop Chowdhury. Rahul was surprised that he hadn't been taken into confidence already, unless this was another little improvised act for his benefit.

'Through someone in Omron, who knows the owner of the company that's been granted a licence, I've set the ball rolling,' said Tapas Pan, affecting an air of superior nonchalance.

'Rolling where?' asked Rahul, not entirely surprised that piss and booze should have found a common meeting-ground in Tapas Pan's scheme of things.

'Distributing the stuff, of course,' said Pan, a little annoyed that something so obvious should have eluded Rahul. 'In Calcutta and neighbouring areas. We already have vans to collect urine. We can use the same vans to distribute hooch when they are sitting idle!'

'If not the same bottles,' said Rahul, not quite under his breath, unable to stifle his dismay at the direction in which Rexxon was being inexorably steered, but Tapas Pan was too impressed, by his own strategic acumen, to let the intended irony distract him. Instead, he turned to Anoop Chowdhury for approbation.

'So, Anoop-da, what do you think? At a distribution margin of ten percent, and the huge potential that a market like Calcutta offers, imagine what Rexxon stands to make!'

Anoop Chowdhury imagined. From the nervous twitch that teased the corners of his mouth and the sniffing fit that convulsed him soon after, Rahul surmised that the figures he'd totted up in his mind had impressed him enough to cause the kind of stress that comes from too much anticipation. When he finally surfaced from his sea of sniffles, he turned to Rahul, a little guiltily, aware that the memorandum with which he'd persuaded him to join

Rexxon was being tossed to the four winds, and replaced by something much too bizarre to be immediately recognisable.

'There's a lot of money to be made,' said Anoop Chowdhury, rationalising a decision that he was readying himself to make, already carried away by Tapas Pan's infectious enthusiasm for drowning Calcutta in a flood of alcohol: a Brown Revolution that would make the Green Revolution of Punjab, or the White of Gujarat, pale into insignificance.

'So is there, in selling smut,' retorted Rahul.

'Exactly,' pounced Tapas Pan, enthusiastically. 'In fact, I've been giving *that* a lot of thought, too...'

'Quite so,' said Anoop Chowdhury, hastening to stop his diversification guru from unshackling his creativity on the subject of pornography, and how Rexxon stood to benefit from peddling it.

'It's worth a shot, isn't it?' asked Chowdhury of no one in particular but, from the tinge of plaintiveness in his voice, it was apparent that he hoped that Rahul would come around to their way of thinking, eventually. 'With Tapas generating surpluses out of these projects, we can really pick and choose the research projects we associate ourselves with. Be ruthlessly selective; apply new techniques; maybe, set new standards.'

'You actually think that will ever happen?' asked Rahul, disbelievingly.

From the furtive look that sneaked across Anoop Chowdhury's countenance, like a guilty delinquent, and the manner in which Tapas Pan suddenly searched for deliverance in the indecipherable hieroglyphics of his doodle-pad, Rahul Banerjee knew that they didn't.

Almost as if it was preordained, a meeting was fixed with the soon-to-be Booze Baron, for a week later, in Durgapur, a few hours' train ride from Calcutta, where his empire was located.

FOURTEEN

Den of Inequity

'He's called De-da,' said Tapas Pan, with an air of self-importance, as the train pulled out of Howrah Station and began its three-hour journey to Durgapur. The self-importance came from his having initiated, what he considered, a momentous meeting with someone who, he believed, had the resources and stature, if not the respect, to be Rexxon's greatest benefactor. Obviously, his investigation of De-da over the past seven days had revealed nothing to dilute the initial enthusiasm. Or diminish his vision of where the firm would be headed if the venerable De-da were to be riding alongside it. On the contrary, the mere mention of the name seemed to fill him with awe, although Rahul Banerjee suspected that some of the reverence was born out of the anticipation of flooding Rexxon in a sea of money, even as Calcutta was submerged in an ocean of hooch.

'He is like an elder brother to his employees—as much a simple worker as they are—not a boss, except that, as the eldest member of the family, he has certain additional responsibilities. Fulfilling them, naturally, entitles him to some additional privileges,' said Tapas Pan, his eulogy to De-da losing some of its gravity for having to be shouted above the heightening clatter of the train as it picked up speed.

'And what, exactly, does De-da do?' asked Rahul Banerjee. 'When he's not performing his brotherly duties, that is?'

Annoyance streaked across Tapas Pan's face at this show of disrespect for his recently-excavated idol.

'He is into banking, manufacturing, mining and aviation,' said Tapas Pan, dusting off the imaginary dirt that Rahul had thrown on his idol's face. 'You name it, he's in it. Just that he doesn't talk about it. Keeps a low profile.'

'So low as to be invisible,' said Rahul. 'Almost as if he wants to hide, which can't be entirely out of an innate sense of modesty, can it?'

'It isn't easy to be a successful businessman in a Communist State,' offered Anoop Chowdhury as an explanation for why De-da and his diverse business interests seemed to be such a closely-guarded secret. Rahul Banerjee wondered how you could be successful in public pursuits, like banking and aviation, if no one knew that you existed. He voiced his doubt but, in Tapas Pan, he encountered a staunch advocate of the De-da school of business, unfazed and unmoved by any contrary opinion, however worthy of consideration it might appear to be.

'His banking business rides on the back of a mammoth direct contact network,' said Tapas Pan, with the conviction and passion of the recently-converted. 'When you have one-to-one interactions with your entire client base, on a regular basis, why would you need to advertise? Or, when you run a cheap, no-frills airline service, connecting upcountry destinations in the Eastern and North-Eastern parts of the country, for which you already have enough takers, why would you want to talk about it?'

'An airline that literally flies under the radar,' said Rahul Banerjee, deciding that further discussion would serve little purpose, nor make issues any clearer, since Tapas Pan was firmly in the grip of an irrational and overwhelming enthusiasm for De-da's cause, completely blinded by the glister of all the gold that he saw in his mind's eye, at the end of the country liquor road.

They rolled into Durgapur station at ten o'clock, which gave them eight straight hours with De-da before it was time to catch the train back to Calcutta; adequate, presumably, to conclude their deliberations. The agenda, as Rahul understood it, was for De-da to map out his plans for the new liquor products and understand from Rexxon how they'd go about distributing them, if they were to be awarded the contract. According to Tapas Pan, there were no contenders for the franchise, except the distilling company itself. However, in Tapas Pan's understanding of how the company was run—an understanding that he claimed to have gained through meticulous background research—if Rexxon were to credit half its commission earnings back to one of De-da's many personal accounts—as one of the additional privileges that De-da, no doubt, felt he was entitled to, for fulfilling his extra responsibilities—the company would disqualify itself from the two-man distribution race, leaving Rexxon to romp home, uncontested. Not one to let an opportunity for corruption slip through the cracks, Tapas Pan, after obtaining a predictable two-third majority from the Rexxon Board, had let it be known to the secret grapevine, that Rexxon would be honoured to share De-da's largesse with whomever he might care to designate. That done, the Durgapur meeting was expected to be a mere formality, an occasion for De-da to get to know his prospective business partners, and vice versa. Or, so Tapas Pan believed.

They emerged from Durgapur station into the glare of a summer morning and the cacophony of cycle rickshaws, street hawkers and red-uniformed, arm-banded railway porters. From amidst the bustle of arriving and departing passengers emerged a tall man, in white uniform and peaked cap, who strode purposefully in their general direction holding aloft a placard. The sign read 'DeEn Welcomes Pan'.

Pan preened.

'DeEn. De Enterprises. Clever, isn't it?' He raised his hand to be recognised as *the* Pan that DeEn were keen to welcome.

The uniformed man came to attention in front of them, took off his cap and suddenly clutched at his brow, to Rahul's concern that he might be suffering an attack of cerebral thrombosis, overcome by the mere sight of Tapas Pan. However, he was relieved to discover that it was only a gesture of greeting, not approaching death.

'Good DeEn,' the man in uniform said, hand to brow, in an unusual, but distinctive, salute.

'Good DeEn,' responded Tapas Pan, replicating the clutching-brow bit with a fair amount of skill, as if he'd been regularly practicing it in some secret training camp.

'That's their own special brand of welcome,' he explained, like a tourist guide highlighting the unique features of a recently-discovered civilization. 'Each time it's said, the company name gets reinforced, like a mantra. Keeps you aware, and proud, of where you work. Innovative thinking, wouldn't you say?'

'Silly as it is, you might still get away with it in the daytime,' replied Rahul, irreverently. 'But, what if you should meet someone in the evening? What do you greet them with? Good EnDe?'

The man in the white uniform, his peaked cap returned to its rightful place and his brow released from the clutch of his right hand, led them to a rank of cars—three brilliant-white Ambassadors, with exactly the same exterior trimmings and black, sun-filmed windows.

'One for each of us?' asked Anoop Chowdhury, in pleasant surprise and a great deal of awe.

'If that's the way you wish to travel,' said the uniformed man. 'Or, we could all travel in one car while the others provide escort. It's your choice.'

Not ever having had the experience, they chose to be escorted.

The fleet wound its way out of the constricted streets of Durgapur town and soon hit the highway, on either side of which stretched asbestos-roofed work-sheds and factory smokestacks. After a few miles, these gradually disappeared and they were in open territory. The air-conditioning whispered comfortingly inside their car while, outside, the heat shimmered and danced, as the summer sun climbed higher in a cloudless, bright blue sky. They travelled for almost an hour at a steady sixty kilometres. Then, the fleet exited the highway and entered a private road down which they drove for another fifteen minutes, until they ran smack into a high wall and a mammoth sculpture of Goddess Kali astride, for some inexplicable reason, a chariot, her hair flowing back from a determined and resolute face. The road contoured around the wall and the statue and, denied entry, curved back upon itself and headed towards the highway once again, almost as if in defeat.

The cars stopped, but the engines were kept running to ensure that the air-conditioning did not die. Tapas Pan gave a sigh of supreme contentment; he'd never had it so good; nor, frankly, had Rahul.

Their uniformed chaperone had a few words with the security staff, at a narrow entrance in the Great Wall, and returned to the car, necessary permissions obtained.

'We change vehicles here,' he informed them.

They left their cocoon of cool comfort and were shepherded around the huge sculpture to a turnstile, which was designed to permit entry through the Great Wall, one at a time only—for security reasons, said their uniformed escort. Goddess Kali towered above them imperiously, as they made their way past the wheels of her chariot in a silent queue.

'Good DeEn,' said the man in the white uniform, with an encore clutching-at-brow performance, his job completed, his charges now someone else's responsibility for the next leg of their journey.

'Good DeEn,' said Tapas Pan, in fond farewell, as he led the way though the turnstile, like an intrepid explorer.

And, then, they were on the other side of the Great Wall.

A single, white Ambassador, an exact clone of the one they'd travelled in, awaited them. As did an apparition in a white, blood-red bordered sari and a vermilion bindi.

'Hello, I'm Sumita,' said the vision, with a smile as luminous as the sun that beat down on them. 'Good DeEn.'

She shimmered like a mirage in a heat haze and the enthusiasm of her performance, with shapely wrist on smooth-as-satin brow, even elicited a choked 'Good DeEn' from Anoop Chowdhury who, Rahul observed, had begun to develop the nervous tics that, usually, heralded the onset of another attack of stress-sniffles. Sumita escorted them to the waiting Ambassador and bade them take the rear seat while she insinuated herself into the front passenger's, with a sexual swirl of sari.

'De-da suggests that you freshen yourselves up before the meeting,' she said, her smile as fixed as the bindi on her forehead, and no less brilliant. Correctly assuming that De-da's recommendations were unlikely to be ignored, she turned to the driver and motioned for him to start.

Acres of land surrounded them. On one side of the road, buildings were joined end-to-end, mostly single-storied, all painted the same dazzling white as the car in which they were travelling. These were offices, Sumita informed them, somewhat redundantly, identifying a sprawling three-storied structure as the Central Office, where De-da held his meetings and operated out of. The buildings on either side of it housed all the different companies that comprised De En. Time permitting, Sumita said, they would be shown the new distillery that had been recently constructed, within the premises, but at a distance of about ten miles from the Central Office, on the other side of a man-made lake.

The other side of the road was beautifully—and expensively— landscaped. Artificial waterfalls, an array of fountains, a Japanese garden, a miniature golf course, a full-size stadium—'apart from regular cricket and football matches, De-da gets artists from Calcutta to perform here; even the late Uttam Kumar came once'—and, to Rahul's increasing bewilderment, row upon row of windmills—'we generate our own electricity to compensate for any shortfalls in supply.'

'This, then, is DeEn City,' said Sumita, in conclusion, with an expansive gesture, or with as much expansiveness as the constricted confines of an Ambassador would allow. The car rolled to a halt in front of a two-storied bungalow which, to avoid any confusion among its prospective residents, had the simple, but unambiguous, legend 'Guest House' nailed to its front-gate.

'The staff will look after your needs.' Sumita turned on the hi-wattage smile again, causing Anoop Chowdhury to break out into his trademark sniffs and Tapas Pan to wonder, no doubt, what a bunch of white-liveried, red-turbaned men could do for the kind of need that he'd developed since he set eyes on her at the altar of the Goddess Kali. Sumita looked at her wrist, the same that had been intimate with her forehead some minutes earlier, and said, 'The car will be back for you in one hour exactly. Noon?'

Then, with a companionable 'Good DeEn', she was gone, and that was the last they saw of her that day. Or ever.

As promised, the car returned before the clock in the lounge had completed chiming noon. By then, Tapas Pan had availed himself of almost all the facilities that the guest-house provided, including a bathtub soak, the duration of which he'd had to curtail, to his eternal regret, to give himself time to sample the other services on offer. He had tried a few anarchic shots of snooker, sending the balls in every direction but the ones they were intended for; consumed a pitcher of chilled nimbu pani, telling whoever was in the proximity of his bellow that beer would have hit the spot better, if only they didn't have a meeting with De-da later; demolished bowls of roasted cashew-nuts, merely as an experiment, he explained, to ascertain whether the refill process was endless (it was); and coaxed out of the bearers the names of recent visitors to the guest-house, turning to Anoop Chowdhury and Rahul, in pantomimed salaciousness, each time the name of a minor celebrity of the female persuasion was mentioned, particularly if her visit had entailed an overnight stay.

Anoop Chowdhury had dropped off to sleep watching the lazily-rotating windmills through the lounge-room window, a half-smoked cigarette growing ash in a crystal-glass ashtray by his side. Before that, he'd been a somewhat reluctant audience to Tapas Pan's expert commentary on each service that he'd sampled. Somewhere between a rundown on the dexterity of his snooker-play and the variety of toiletries he'd mixed to his bath, Anoop Chowdhury had found watching windmills more fascinating, although that had not deterred Tapas Pan from continuing to direct 'So-what-do-you-think?' queries at him, with the frequency of a persistent woodpecker knocking on wood, until a warbling snore told him that his audience had escaped from captivity in the only way that he knew how.

For Rahul Banerjee, the hour of relative privacy had proved useful to clear his mind of any nagging doubts that he might have still had about the decision to give his entrepreneurial urge, and marketing research, a rest. Not that too many doubts remained, with Tapas Pan having assumed responsibility for taking Rexxon down the strange road that he had chosen for it, a compliant Anoop Chowdhury in tow. However, it still left Rahul to wonder where he might seek the job satisfaction that every wet-behind-the-ears business school graduate considered his birthright, but discovered to be an elusive phantom, teasingly within his reach but, seldom, his grasp, once he'd substituted satchel for briefcase.

'Advertising,' someone had once whispered into his ear, 'gives you an opportunity for creative expression, if you're inclined that way.' It was in the midst of his silently debating whether he was, indeed, disposed that way that one of the bearers arrived by his side to say that De-da was ready to meet them in fifteen minutes and that they should be making their way to Central Office immediately, because De-da didn't like to be kept waiting, although he didn't seem to have any qualms about making others wait.

Tapas Pan, post-snooker, bathtub soak and cashew-nut consumption, was in ebullient form, which was always a worry, since, even at his most lugubrious, he was given to verbal exchanges that generally proved extremely embarrassing because of their impropriety, irrelevance, or both. Tapas Pan unchained was a loose cannon discharged. Either because this thought was haunting him, or because his sleep had been interrupted at its deepest, or because Sumita was not riding with them this time, Anoop Chowdhury was so subdued as to seem sedated. Or, without the ersatz bravado he usually borrowed from a gin bottle, he was frozen with fear at the thought of a meeting with the omnipresent De-da. On the other hand, Rahul Banerjee found himself to be surprisingly detached. Since distributing country liquor didn't feature on his personal agenda, or acquiring its distribution franchise, on his official one, he was willing to tot this one up to just another experience to reminisce about in his dotage, although he hoped that that was still several decades in the future.

At 12:15 p.m. they arrived at the doors of Central Office where Sumita was waiting for them.

Except that it wasn't Sumita, but someone who could have passed off for her twin, even at close hand, so alike were they in their appearance, attire and actions, particularly in the performance of the 'Good DeEn' ritual.

'I'm Diya,' she said, with a smile that was dazzling enough to lure Anoop Chowdhury out of the gloom that he'd descended into, and actually bring back the nervous tics to his face, which was his way of saying that all was well with his world once more.

'Are you Sumita's sister?' asked Tapas Pan, with predictable bluntness, causing Diya to lose her smile for an infinitesimal moment.

'In De-da's family, we all are,' she replied, recovering her composure, and her smile, very quickly. 'Come, I'll take you to the conference venue where the others have already assembled.'

'Others?' croaked Anoop Chowdhury, apprehensively and even Tapas Pan lost the froth of his effervescence, a fraction. 'We thought it was a private meeting with De-da,' he said.

'Nothing is private in De-da's family,' Diya replied, in a practiced tone of voice which, despite the seeming innocuousness of her words, set off Rahul's over-sensitive alarm system, albeit faintly.

They entered a cavernous conference room at the centre of which was a long, elongated table that could seat at least thirty. It was fully taken, except for three vacant positions, presumably for the Rexxon contingent, and one at its head, for De-da, presumably, going by the ornate-ness of the chair, almost resembling a throne, and the fact that all eyes were turned towards it, even though it was unoccupied.

Distanced from the oval table, on one side, were two concentric half-circles of more chairs, again fully occupied. At first glance, Rahul estimated that there were, at least, seventy-five people already seated. The conference room was done predominantly in white, including all the furniture and the drapes. White speakers—too many to be counted—adorned the walls. White microphones squatted on the table, a distance of a yard between each; De-da had one exclusively to himself. On the wall opposite his chair was a screen of cinema-hall proportions; an expanded map of West Bengal adorned the wall behind his seat, pricked with metal pins of various colours, primarily red.

The hum of conversation died with their entrance. Diya led them to the empty chairs and bade them goodbye, with a whispered 'Good DeEn'. The filter of her presence removed, seventy-five pairs of curious eyes turned in their direction, fixing them like insects to flypaper and dissecting them to the bone, with laser-like precision. Or, so it felt. The hostility came off in tsunami-like waves and the atmosphere was thick enough to cut.

'Good DeEn,' said a bearded individual, sitting to Rahul's left, in a chair adjacent to the one reserved for De-da. 'Amit Sarkar. I'm CEO of DeEn Spirits.'

Rahul couldn't stop an image, of a boardroom filled with ghosts, spectres and things unholy, from rushing through his mind. Someone extremely creative, or with an extremely perverse sense of humour, had come up with this name for De-da's new venture. Stifling endless associations of the ridiculous kind that it conjured, Rahul introduced himself, and his fellow directors, without benefit, or ritual, of the 'Good DeEn' prefix. He felt that he might implode if he heard it one more time.

The conversation with Amit Sarkar hadn't progressed beyond stilted preliminaries when Rahul heard the sound of chairs being pushed back and the clothes-rustle of people rising hurriedly to their feet. He turned, in time, to see a man of ordinary height, but extraordinary demeanour, stride jauntily into the conference room, accompanied by an entourage of what seemed like twins of Sumita and Diya and, in bizarre counterpoint, two bulky guards, wearing bristling glares, moustaches and rather ugly-looking guns.

'Good DeEn,' chorused the assemblage.

'Good DeEn,' acknowledged De-da, raising his right hand to his brow and, the salute accomplished, letting it hang in the air for a couple of minutes as if in benediction.

The blessed congregation resumed their seats and turned eyes of reverence towards De-da, who remained standing until the last of them had sat down, which happened to be the Rexxon contingent; untutored in the ways of De-da, the clan of Chowdhury, Pan and Banerjee had failed to synchronise its movements with the rest and, as a consequence, had leapfrogged to De-da's immediate attention, much like the proverbial sore thumb.

'Welcome to our visitors from Calcutta,' boomed De-da.

'Welcome,' boomed the assemblage.

That settled, De-da turned to one of the ladies, who'd taken up position behind his chair, and whispered something into her shell-like ear, so close to it that he could have bitten off a chunk if he'd wanted to. She nodded vigorously and hurried out, presumably to do his bidding, ear thankfully preserved. Then, De-da picked up one of the two cigarettes that had been placed decoratively on the blotter in front of him, giving company to a tube of mint lozenges, a pitcher of cold water, two gold pens and a book, which, Rahul later discovered, was an English translation of Hitler's *Mein Kampf* that accompanied De-da wherever he went, which could have meant either that he was a very slow reader or he drew inspiration from the physical presence of the book since he could not, anymore, from the man who'd written it.

As De-da brought the cigarette to his lips ceremoniously, the remaining lady mysteriously conjured a cigarette lighter from the folds of her silk sari and, with the practised flick of a manicured thumb, brought it to flame. She leaned forward to apply it to the tip of De-da's cigarette while the congregation watched with bated breath, as if some intricate manoeuvre were being performed on high wires.

De-da leaned back and drew hungrily on his cigarette. Like a champion underwater swimmer, he held his breath, and the tobacco smoke, for several minutes, before leaking it, in tentative dribbles, from the corner of his mouth. The assembly watched in respectful silence, as De-da consumed his cigarette over ten, long, lingering minutes. The bodyguards, their backs to the map of West Bengal, rotated their unblinking eyes, 180 degrees every few minutes, left to right, right to left, left to right, right to left. Rahul had the feeling that their stare tended to rest on the Rexxon threesome somewhat longer than it did on the others. Or, maybe, it was just his paranoia escalating.

'Respect,' said De-da, stubbing out his cigarette and inserting a mint lozenge into his mouth, to freshen it. 'It's the fabric that binds.'

Rahul was too taken aback at the unexpectedness of the statement to question what it was that needed binding and why.

'Society cannot function without respect amongst its constituents,' continued De-da. 'Respect of children for their parents, youth for their elders, wives for their husbands, husbands for their wives, employees for their company, a company for its employees. Respect is much too important to be taken for granted. I'd rather that it be obtained forcibly than not at all.'

Tapas Pan thumped the table in agreement, drawing a bemused look from De-da, and baleful stares from his bodyguards. Anoop Chowdhury clutched desperately at Pan's arm, imploring him to curtail his enthusiasm. Rahul Banerjee sneaked a glance at his watch and wondered what had brought all this on, what it had to do with drowning the State of West Bengal in country liquor, and whether they'd be in time to catch the evening train back to Calcutta.

'You have to be impartial about how you go about getting respect if, by right, it is owed to you,' said De-da, in a sonorous voice, hitting his stride and, clearly, warming to his theme. 'Get up, my sons.'

From the gathering of seventy-five, two gawky youngsters stood up. Eyes that had so far been transfixed on De-da, swivelled, in unison, towards them causing them to fidget uneasily. De-da left them hanging, in awkward limbo, for a few minutes.

'For example, if my sons do not give respect to their mother, they deserve the same punishment that an employee would get for disrespecting his organisation, or the head of an organisation for unjustifiably disregarding the rights of his employees. Lack of respect cannot be tolerated if society has to function smoothly. So, if I see disrespect, I'm not one to spare the rod, whether it's my son, or anyone else, even me, at the other end of it.'

Rahul Banerjee had a sudden, unbidden image of De-da in the throes of self-flagellation: on his knees in some bare, underground basement room, whipping himself to a foaming frenzy for not having said 'Good DeEn' to himself, watched over by two bodyguards wearing bristling glares, guns and attitude. De-da saw the beginnings of a smile on Rahul's face, paused fractionally, as if deliberating whether a smile in the middle of his sombre discourse was sufficient cause to unsheathe the rod and, then, deciding that it was not, permitted his gaze to walk away from Rahul, much to his relief. It sauntered across the gathering till it came to rest, once again, on his squirming sons who, in their nervousness had, by now, probably gouged the polish off the furniture that they were leaning on for support.

'Sit down,' commanded De-da. They sat even before the last syllable had stopped reverberating.

At that moment, the lady, who'd left to do De-da's bidding, returned, her mission accomplished. She bent at her slim waist and whispered something into De-da's accommodating ear, although it wasn't accommodating enough for one to consider taking a bite out of, unless sufficiently provoked. What De-da heard must have been overflowing with respect because he threw back his head in a rolling laugh.

'Lunch,' he announced and, with his entourage in tow, strode out of the conference room, leaving his visitors from Calcutta, and the rest of the gathering, in some confusion about whether it was another momentous truth that he'd shared with them, or an invitation. Thankfully, Diya made a timely re-appearance to clear up the ambiguity.

Even in a family of seeming equals, there must have been an unspoken caste system because, by the time they'd traversed the distance to the dining hall, the undeserving and, therefore, the uninvited had, strangely, fallen by the wayside, leaving only a third of the original seventy-five to arrive at their destination. How this was achieved within a space of just twenty minutes remained a mystery to Rahul unless, of course, there was some secret training manual, authored by De-da naturally, where food-chain positions and pecking order entitlements within the extended DeEn family were unambiguously spelt out, including who sat at lunch with whom.

The lunch-room was done, as to be expected, in white: white drapes, white linen and white-liveried waiters in white gloves. Most of the colour in the room came from the food arrayed on the table, of which there was a quantity sufficient to sate a large and exceptionally ravenous army. The main dining-room led off to an annexe where another table stood, similarly laden with food, a single place laid out at one end of it, where De-da sat, busily munching. Other than his chair, there were no others. Two Sumita-Diya clones, in crimson-bordered saris and vermilion bindis, hovered around him, like bees around nectar, except that, in a strange reversal of roles, the nectar was doing all the feeding.

The fare wouldn't have been out of place at a lavish Bengali wedding. Radhaballabi with chholar dal, fish fry, pullao, chingdi machcher malai curry, kasha mangsho, aamer chutney and mishti doi. No doubt a believer in the theory that if food has to be enjoyed, it has to be eaten with one's fingers, De-da had forsaken all forms of cutlery. In their place, the two girls dexterously crafted uniform globules of food and popped them into his mouth, daintily. De-da would masticate with supreme relish and, when done, turn his mouth playfully, from one girl to the other, for another bite-sized chunk, sometimes, in his pleasure, taking their fingers with it. The charitable sisters of Sumita would urge him on, with coy looks and trilling laughs, as they extricated their digits from his mouth and returned them to the task of feeding him.

'I don't think we'll catch the train back to Calcutta this evening,' said Rahul Banerjee, as Tapas Pan foraged among the chinaware for another prawn to add to the skeletons he'd already accumulated on his plate. 'Not at the rate at which we're going, not if the sermon on respect is resumed after the break.'

'I don't mind,' said Tapas Pan, finding peace and fulfilment in chingdi machcher malai curry. From the concentration with which Anoop Chowdhury was de-boning a piece of mutton, Rahul surmised that he didn't either, although it was a little difficult to be certain what it was that they didn't mind—the food or a resumption of De-da's diatribe.

It was after 2:30 p.m. when lunch ended. De-da had disappeared earlier through an exit in the annexe that didn't require him to cross the main dining hall. With his departure, the waiters began to show a distinct reluctance to replenish empty bowls and you could say that the game was truly up when only a few decapitated prawn-heads floated in a sea of malai curry, crumbs marked the spot where fish fry had once existed and mishti doi was introduced into the proceedings with a haste that bordered on boorishness.

'You'll return to the guest-house for rest till De-da's ready to see you again,' said Diya with a certainty that came from having, no doubt, received instructions directly from De-da.

'Do you think there's any possibility of the meeting ending by five?' asked Rahul, knowing fully well that it wouldn't, but hoping against hope that it might.

For once, Diya seemed to lose her composure. Her kohl-lined eyes rounded in surprise.

'De-da will re-convene the meeting when he's ready,' she repeated, her tone suggesting that De-da's methods were not to be questioned for, in mysterious ways, he did his wonders perform.

'Nevertheless, could you make absolutely certain, before we change our train tickets?' Rahul persisted receiving a look from Diya that she'd normally reserve for something stuck to the bottom of her shoe that refused to come off.

'As you wish,' she said, escorting them to the car that would take them back to the guest-house. On their way, they passed Amit Sarkar, who hadn't exchanged a word with them since his introduction as chief executive of DeEn Spirits, but chose this moment, unknowingly perhaps, to deliver the coup de grace on Rahul's rapidly-fading expectations.

'See you at dinner,' he said.

Rahul wasn't sure whether the malevolence that he read into what was, otherwise, a seemingly-innocuous statement, was real or a by-product of a paranoia that had, by now, achieved full-blown proportions.

As it happened, they didn't see him, or anyone else for that matter, at dinner; it was served to them in the guest-house, saving them a trek back to the dining hall, although Tapas Pan was patently disappointed at not having the freedom of choice, and the indulgence of self-help, that he'd enjoyed at lunch. Much before that, of course, they got a visit from Diya, who informed them that De-da would be honoured if they were to consider staying back which, in Rahul's mind, carried an 'if-you-know-what's-good-for-you' postscript to it that was impossible to ignore. She took their rail tickets to be changed, an act that gave Rahul the same sense of deprivation, and foreboding, that he might have got, if his passport were to be impounded, in some strange, unknown and hostile country. In exchange, they received three brown paper-wrapped parcels, each containing a pair of pyjamas, a kurta and a cotton pouch with toothbrush, paste and shaving paraphernalia. It was an ominous portent of a long night ahead.

As the minutes coalesced into hours and the call for a meeting, that they'd travelled all the way from Calcutta for, did not materialise, Anoop Chowdhury developed the nervous tremor for which the only tried-and-tested cure was the calming touch of gin-and-tonic, or whiskey, since it was well past sundown. He refrained only out of a concern that it could, as it had often done in the past, soothe him into a state of oblivion, which De-da might construe as disrespectful, encouraging him to bring out the rod that he'd expressed such a fondness for earlier in the day. Tapas Pan, after extracting all the gossip that he could out of the bearers, through a little bribery and loads of persistence, stretched out on a sofa for a shut-eye that was intended to be short but, from the rhythm and intensity of his snores, indicated quite the opposite.

Rahul Banerjee put in a call to Ratna.

'We're stuck in Durgapur,' he informed her, across the static of a poor connection.

'How so? You mean, your meeting's been extended?'

'I mean, it hasn't even started. Except for an opening discourse on respect.'

'A discourse? Who by?'

'De-da.'

'Who?'

'Never mind. Our tickets are being changed for the morning train tomorrow, departure at six-thirty. Or, so I'm told.'

'You don't sound very sure.'

'I'm not. About anything. I'm not even sure whether the meeting will take place at all!'

'When will you know?'

'When De-da calls for it. Or doesn't.'

'Who's De-da?'

'The guy we're here to meet.'

'The same guy who gave the discourse?'

'Yes, De-da does that, too.'

'Why?'

'Because he can, I suppose.'

It was around midnight when the proverbial knock on the door came. It was Diya, her demeanour just a little worse for wear, her smile a faint shadow of its former self and the enthusiasm hollowed out of her voice by the lateness of the hour.

'De-da will see you now,' she said, with a brave, but futile, attempt at replicating her zeal of the morning.

'I can't wait,' said Rahul Banerjee. And prodding his fellow-directors into wakefulness, he followed Diya to the waiting

Ambassador for what he was certain would be his last trip to Central Office that night, or ever again.

It was the same conference room, though Rahul wasn't absolutely sure whether it was the same dramatis personae. Some faces certainly looked familiar, Amit Sarkar's for one. Others were harder to place, either because faces look different in the middle of the night from what they are at the start of the day, or because some heads had been substituted, not having lasted the course, for some unknown reason.

On the stroke of twelve, as if to enhance the drama of the moment, De-da made his entrance with the same jauntiness of the morning, but a different entourage. The bodyguards had changed, as had the two women who took up their positions behind his chair. They looked a little different, too, the white saris replaced by maroon, gold-bordered ones, the vermilion bindis by midnight blue, as befitted the hour.

Looking at De-da puffing contentedly at his ceremonial cigarette after the 'Good DeEn' ritual had been enacted, once again, Rahul thought that, for someone to be as bright-eyed as this, at this time of night, required him to be either an incurable insomniac, or on some drug-induced adrenaline rush, or freshly-awakened from a recuperative nap that he'd sneaked in when the rest of the world believed him to be occupied in furthering the interests of a thriving business empire.

'Allow me to spell out my plans,' said De-da, as if there was anyone in the assembled gathering with the gumption to deny him that permission.

With sleep constantly threatening to slip under his defences, Rahul Banerjee had only a vague appreciation of subsequent proceedings. De-da, as usual, did all the talking, keeping his audience captive, and silent, by the force of his authority, if not his logic. Rahul wanted to question De-da on the choice of his brand name—Big Bull—which, he felt, suited contraceptives, aphrodisiacs and investment companies more than it did liquor, but stopped himself fearing that it might start a line of argument that prolonged the meeting beyond the departure time of their train back to Calcutta the next morning, and required them to spend another night in De-da's lair. For the same reason, he kept his silence when De-da extolled the value of key-chains, in the shape of a big bull, as promotional giveaways, along with coasters, ashtrays, napkins, tissue paper boxes and, to catch them young and at their most receptive, erasers and geometry boxes, all shaped like a big bull. Balls and all? Rahul wondered, impiously.

Suddenly, somewhere in the middle of it all, Amit Sarkar, his bearded face mottled with the passion of his belief, clambered to his feet and, in a voice choked with emotion, said: 'De-da, it's not fair.'

Rahul was wondering whether it could be that someone had, finally, found the courage to tell De-da that enough was enough and keeping everyone awake in the middle of the night just because he could, wasn't the right thing to do, when Amit Sarkar shouted: 'Big Bull's our baby. It's not fair to give it away to outsiders to distribute.'

Then, he sat down, abruptly. The silence that followed was deafening. De-da looked at Amit Sarkar, his face inscrutable. At least, to Rahul it was, although from the way others of the DeEn family were reacting—wide-eyed horror being the predominant expression—De-da must have been an open book.

De-da stared. Amit Sarkar squirmed; then, found something in his lap deserving of his undivided attention. The silence expanded, till the ticking of the wall-clock was like a metronome of doom. After long minutes of a fixed, unblinking stare, De-da turned away from his chief executive and picked up his train of thought exactly where he'd left it, as if nothing at all had happened. The room heaved a collective sigh, as if a major catastrophe had been averted and Rahul went back to contemplating the contradiction of a big bull being called a baby.

'I was wrong to have interrupted you, De-da,' said Amit Sarkar interrupting him again and revisiting the scene of his crime, as it were. 'Also, to have disrespected our guests from Calcutta.'

The room went graveyard-silent once more and even Tapas Pan who was, normally, unbelievably insensitive to his surroundings, stopped rummaging among the empty wrappers for a mint lozenge that he hadn't already chewed on.

De-da, in deliberate slow-motion, swivelled his gaze back to Amit Sarkar, a bemused smile touching the corners of his mouth. Then, he reached for the second of the two cigarettes he permitted himself for the duration of a meeting, and leaned back to catch the flame that one of the girls struck for him. He returned to unfolding his grandiose schemes for Big Bull, ignoring Amit Sarkar who, Rahul observed, was getting increasingly agitated and red in the face with each rebuff.

The same scene, then, played itself out every fifteen minutes.

In the middle of some obscure point that De-da would be making, Amit Sarkar would lunge to his feet and ask forgiveness of De-da for showing him and his guests, disrespect. The room would hold its collective breath, to the point of suffocation, until De-da had completed his preoccupied perusal of his chief executive, and release it in a breathless sigh, when he resumed his interrupted soliloquy.

And so it went, every quarter, for the next couple of hours.

'Forgive me, De-da. I have wronged you.'

Pause. Turn. Inspect. Turn. Talk.

'De-da. Punish me.'

Pause. Turn. Peruse. Turn. Talk.

'De-da, I've erred. Punish me.'

Pause. Turn. Inspect. Smile a faraway smile. Turn. Talk.

Then, as the ultimate supplication: 'Punish me, De-da. Because if you don't, I'll know that I've not been forgiven and I can't live with that.'

At this, De-da turned to his chief executive with a smile that, finally, reached his eyes. He raised his right hand and, though he said not a word, Amit Sarkar knew, as did the rest of the gathering, that he'd been allowed back on the road to redemption.

'I will punish you soon,' promised De-da and Amit Sarkar rejoiced by genuflecting in front of his saviour, so immense was his relief.

At five in the morning, with the fate of the liquor distribution business still in the balance but, in Rahul's judgement, leaning heavily in favour of the company because punishment was known to bring its own reward, much as pleasure, often, accompanied pain, De-da brought the meeting to a close, if for no other reason, but that he'd had enough of the sound of his own voice. The fact that some of his entourage—the two girls, for example— and a few of those occupying the back-rows, who believed themselves to be relatively more impervious to his all-seeing gaze, had begun to drop like flies, may have had something to do with it, too. However, not one to let things end without ceremony, De-da rose to his feet and clutched his brow in the DeEn salute. The others, practiced in his methods, followed suit and, in a single voice, except for Rahul's, which had choked on him at the bizarreness of the move, Anoop Chowdhury's, because prolonged denial of sleep had brought on a renewed attack of sniffles and Tapas Pan's, because his mouth was crammed with the last of the mint lozenges, they sang the national anthem, De-da leading with a full-throated bellow that sounded even louder in the relative quiet of dawn.

It still left them enough time to reach Durgapur Station, in a car that Diya thoughtfully arranged, to board the six-thirty Express back to Calcutta. Somewhere along the way, amidst the clatter and sway of the train and the holler of hawkers peddling tea, toast and omelettes, Rahul Banerjee announced that he'd decided to quit. It was either the ambivalent mood that lack of sleep induces, or the aftermath of the De-da experience, but Anoop Chowdhury, somehow, wasn't surprised. And Tapas Pan was too busy imagining the ways in which Amit Sarkar would be made to eat crow, to really care.

FIFTEEN

Drawing the Battle Lines

I f the plan to unravel Big Brother's conspiracy was masterminded by Esbee, the one to unstitch Surjo Sengupta's complacency owed its provenance to Rita's inspired choice of Mrs Talukdar as ammunition, even if, on hindsight, I must confess that neither of us had quite seen her as an ultimate weapon of destruction nor predicted the kind of devastation she'd end up wreaking on his psyche.

It all started with Surjo Sengupta announcing one morning at breakfast that he wanted to host a dinner for his literary friends, that is, if we had no objection to playing the role of co-hosts, which, loosely translated, meant our footing the bill, although he made it sound as if he were bestowing a singular honour on us.

'What did you have in mind?' asked Rita, heaping bacon on his egg-laden plate since, in one of his earliest confessions, he had confided to her that, despite his long residence in France, he hadn't developed a fancy for sparse, Continental breakfasts, preferring the substantial repast of his English neighbours instead.

'Maybe a dozen people in all,' he answered. 'Writers and film-makers from my student days that I lost touch with when I moved to Paris, but have managed to revive on my current visit.'

I thought that whatever else it achieved, the dinner would get me to, finally, put faces to the arsenal of names that Surjo Sengupta had dropped on me, like misguided missiles, over the last several weeks; except, of course, Dipen's, who, it may be recalled, had died without the courtesy of advance intimation, much to my embarrassment and humiliation and could not, therefore, have his name put to a face, even if he had wanted to.

'For the event to go like clockwork, there must be a proper delineation of individual roles,' continued Surjo Sengupta, deigning to include me in the conversation after several days of deliberate remoteness, which meant that he'd either forgiven me the Dipen contretemps, or was willing to temporarily overlook it, since he had to ensure my willing cooperation in his latest undertaking.

'It's settled, then. I'll send out the invitations,' said Surjo Sengupta, briskly, taking our silence for acquiescence and adding, in a fit of sudden generosity: 'If you like, you could call one or two people of your own, as long as they fit the general profile of my guests.'

'Mrs Talukdar,' said Rita, unexpectedly, although if there was anyone further removed from my concept of what the general profile of Surjo Sengupta's guests was, it was she.

Mrs Uma Talukdar was the mother of a school friend of Rita's, which put her age in the high forties, or low fifties. The wife of a tea-plantation owner, she was unfortunate to have been widowed early, when her husband, after a night of excessive revelry at the Planters' Club, took a curve in the road that was, entirely, of his own alcoholic imagining, and transplanted his Jeep from the height of a mountain road to the bottom of a precipitous ravine. According to the medical examiner, who'd earlier been a witness to the anaesthetics his friend had been ingesting with unbridled enthusiasm, old Kaypee (as Krishna Prasad Talukdar was fondly called) couldn't have felt a thing, which was, at least, of some solace to the young widow.

Of equal, if not greater, comfort was the legacy that he bequeathed her, primary among which was a bungalow in Calcutta's Alipore, and an annual income from the sale of the plantation that kept her in food, drink, the weekly punt at the Races and considerable good humour, without her having to encroach upon the principal, at all.

Since her recently-divorced daughter, Usha, lived with her, I ran into Mrs Talukdar whenever Rita felt the call of duty, which was whenever she thought that her old school chum needed some cheering to tide her over the difficult circumstances of an abbreviated marriage, although I was convinced that Usha was more relieved than sorry that she'd got the use of her own surname back. So, while Rita lightened the load of Usha's marital sorrow, I did the same for Mrs Talukdar's bar, which comprised an exquisite collection of imported liquors that I passionately coveted, but could seldom afford. Much later, I was to learn that, while Mrs Uma Talukdar was flashing me her smile, her crystal and her diamonds, her daughter, in the adjoining room, was flashing Rita her thigh, which, in retrospect, partly explained why her marriage may have hit the kind of insurmountable bump that it did.

Mrs Uma Talukdar had no such ambiguity about her own sexual preferences, or sexuality. Not having to overly concern herself with the mundane job of keeping hearth and home together, she had all the time in the world for the more enriching task of chasing beauty or, in her case, preserving it. In her youth in Darjeeling, she must have, certainly, been a head-turner, if not a heartbreaker, and the scourge of married women everywhere, especially in the Planters' Club. She was from a class that received its education privately, with a partiality for the liberal arts, from tutors who'd themselves been schooled in England. Her teachings would have included piano and dance lessons and instructions in etiquette, all of which, no doubt, stood her in excellent stead when she had to oversee the social events her plantation-owner husband was partial to, if for no other reason, but to have something to distract himself with, once the tea had been planted and set on their inevitable way to bloom, since there was little else for him to do. Fifteen years later, the habits learnt, and practiced, in her plantation days were as much a part of Mrs Uma Talukdar, as if she were still by her husband's side, inspecting the stepped tea-estates of his domain, or welcoming another line of chatty, over-dressed guests, to hers.

Even now, without an active social calendar to occupy her, she was still always impeccably turned out. I couldn't think of a single occasion when we'd caught her without her hair and make-up perfectly in place, or a cloak of some exotic fragrance, no doubt French in origin, wrapped around her. She had a preference for long, flowing dresses of a soft, form-caressing material that played mischievous tricks with your eyes in the artificial lighting that she favoured even in the daytime, which, with her drapes always tightly drawn, wasn't really very different from her nights. She never entered a room; she made an entry, her arrival preceded by a rustle of chiffon and a whiff of perfume. Seconds later, she'd glide into the room, her painted lips pursed to air-kiss, a long, onyx cigarette holder delicately balanced in one hand and a crystal tumbler of some clear, ice-chilled liquid, in the other.

'Darling,' she'd say, in a voice drenched in nicotine and alcohol, throwing an arm, usually the one that had the unlit cigarette at the end of it, around your neck in a hug of some abandon. Then, raising herself on the tips of her toes for additional purchase, she'd breathe her warm scented breath—the sweetness of juniper mixed with the earthiness of tobacco—on both your cheeks and whisper a throaty welcome that never varied in content, irrespective of the gender of its recipient: 'So good of you to come. Don't you look wonderful?' which was *not* your cue to say that you owed it all to yoga and abstinence, but to respond with something along the lines of: 'Uma'—she abhorred the use of a suffix with her name—'just look at you! Exquisite, as always.'

However, it was the otherworldliness of the time warp that she was stuck in that was, also, the source of Mrs Uma Talukdar's appeal. She was an excellent raconteur and I found her stories of the genteel world of tea plantations, of two decades ago, strange, fanciful and entirely absorbing. So did Rita, and her reason for returning frequently to the Talukdar household had, I suspect, more to do with the unveiling of a world—indeed, an age—that both of us were complete strangers to, and less with providing her daughter the proverbial shoulder to cry on, for the slights, real or imagined, that she'd suffered during her ephemeral marriage.

'Good idea,' I said, extricating myself from the breakfast table and the possibility of another lengthy lecture from our house guest—one on How to Host a Successful Dinner the Way it's done in Paris. I proposed that that had better await my return from the coalmines—an analogy that Surjo Sengupta may have taken too literally, if the distasteful expression that crossed his face was anything to go by—because I did not think that The Great Eastern Pipe Company would look too kindly upon my punching the proverbial time-clock late, with a suspicious big brother roaming its premises.

With the game truly afoot, Mister Bose, or Esbee to his friends, among whom I was privileged to number, had got into the thick of things, with infectious enthusiasm. All through the previous week, he'd sought updates from us on the progress, and line of questioning, of the Big Brother study, at meetings that were convened after office hours, or when the BBC team had left for the day. At one such update session, he finally revealed the foundations of his master-plan.

'We need to soften them up with a series of quick jabs—like mosquito bites, painless, but irritatingly itchy—before we deliver the coup de grace,' Esbee confided, in a deep, natural baritone that leant gravity to even his most innocuous statements, and these certainly weren't. 'Go for the lynchpin—Al Bombat. Knock him out and you've derailed Big Brother.'

'How?' we asked of the Oracle.

'To defeat your enemy, you must, first, understand his psychology.' Esbee was known to have said this to successive batches of fresh trainees, for whom a week with The Oracle was the only fixed part of an ever-changing orientation schedule. Like any strategist worth his salt, Esbee practiced what he preached; he'd already done his homework on Al-my-Pal Bombat and, like the ubiquitous Nero Wolfe, mayn't even have left his room to do it.

'He's a vain man,' Esbee said. 'His experience—he ran his own manufacturing business to the ground—and education—

there is a great deal of mystery surrounding some of the letters he attaches to his surname—do not qualify him to dole out the management counsel that he's so notoriously free with. But, by virtue of his head-hunting activity, he insinuates himself into the right industry circles; after that, he lets his native cunning take over. Going by his success at conning companies out of their manpower budgets, he obviously has loads of it—native cunning, I mean.'

By now, Esbee had our undivided attention: Rajesh Mehra's, Chaks' and mine. He savoured the moment by pausing to light a cigarette with great relish.

'But, he's a vain man,' he continued, in a tone of voice that Marc Anthony may have used to heap pretend praise on a fellow Roman senator, who'd recently wielded a knife with rather unfortunate consequences. 'A vanity that serves to camouflage sham, the easy, superficial success that comes from using one's wits rather than from any real merit. But, if an old adage is to be believed, easy come, easy go, too. All that it requires is a little push along the way, in the right place.'

Esbee did not expand on what, in his considered view, was the right place until he'd smoked the cigarette down to its filter, encouraging us with his silence to work it out for ourselves. We didn't even try.

'Prick the man's vanity and you've shattered the man,' said Esbee, stubbing out his cigarette, with the same deliberateness that he might have applied to Al Bombat, if he'd been around.

'How?' we chorused.

'Public humiliation,' Esbee revealed, with conviction and mischievous relish.

While he did not reveal what form this open embarrassment of Al Bombat would take, he urged us to be contrary, if not downright cussed, in our responses to Big Brother's continuing enquiries so that, sooner than later, Esbee would be called into play.

'If I know Ramaswami at all, he'll want me to set things right when Al-my-pal complains to him that you Sales boys aren't cooperating,' he surmised.

If, in the interim, we were to think of other, creative ways to rattle Al Bombat, we were free to try them out, as long as we weren't too obvious. Despite our repeated entreaties, Esbee refused to divulge any more of his master plan, claiming that success of a secret enterprise depended upon applying the need-to-know principle, strictly. To stoke our curiosity further, he mentioned, with studied casualness, that the police might have to be involved at some point in the proceedings; therefore, one of us had better cosy-up with anyone from the constabulary whom we might have acquaintance of, even if it was only of the nodding kind. I volunteered believing that I'd met Police Sergeant Harold Mann sufficient times already for the foundations of a lasting relationship to have been laid.

And so it was that the counterattack against the machinations of Big Brother Consultancy, was launched. Of course, if we'd put as much enthusiasm, and creativity, into selling pipes, as we did into the plot to demolish Al Bombat, TGEPC would have neither faced the marketing problems that it eventually did, nor would it have been necessary to solicit the motivated advice of BBC, and their ilk, in the first place. But to our young, rebellious minds, barely freed from the irresponsibility of college campuses, there were irresistible attractions in the shadow-land of after-hours intrigue that were totally absent from our day jobs. Between James Bond, Harry Palmer, George Smiley, Quiller and Jason Love our minds had been captured, and transported, to exotic locales, and situations, that bore not the slightest resemblance to the daily trade of unloading pipes of a confusing array of dimensions and specifications, to an equally confusing lot of people who were, probably, as bored of transacting commerce with us, as we of them.

Not that all of us involved in the Grand Plot could cite recent freedom from the discipline of academia as an excuse for what were, in retrospect, infantile antics: although, in the end, they did yield results that would have been the envy of most mature minds. For instance, Esbee, the mastermind behind the conspiracy, had no excuse at all for his behaviour, except that he might have suffered from a congenital delinquency of the juvenile kind, an affliction that made him a hero amongst some, and an embarrassment to most others.

It was Esbee who originated the deep breathing call over the intercom system, although it was picked up, customised and passed on with such alacrity that very few knew, or remembered, much to Esbee's relief, who had invented it originally. It was introduced when the first intercoms arrived and executives, suddenly, had the luxury of two telephone instruments on their desk, one for outside calls, for which you went through the telephone operator in the traditional way, and the other, to reach work colleagues located on the same, or different, floors of the office. The beauty of the intercom was that it bypassed the telephone operator, freeing you, finally, from her prying ear and giving you the anonymity to do things that you hadn't done before, like making anonymous, deep breathing calls.

It was a simple procedure. You picked up your handset, dialled the three-digit number of the person you wished to harass and breathed into his ear deeply, and hoarsely, like an asthmatic serial killer, when he answered at the other end. It was important for your deep breathing to be uniform so that one call was indistinguishable from another. A careless caller was one who left a clue, like a recognisable background noise, and was soon drummed out of the competition. How consummate a deep breather you were, depended upon how long you could retain your anonymity, and how high up the organisational ladder you could call without being recognised, because if you were, your future in TGEPC would be in great jeopardy, assuming that you were left with a future, at all. The intensity of your adrenaline-rush depended upon a *combination* of both who you called, and when; for example, a deep breathing call to the executive director, Ramaswami, when he was in the middle of a meeting with another Board member, ranked pretty high, particularly because Ramaswami had the habit of hanging on to his end of the line, suffering the deep breathing in silence, while he tried to work out who the anonymous caller might be. Not that he ever succeeded.

Rajesh Mehra had added his own bells and whistles to the concept, having the courage to actually go vocal, sometimes banking on his mimicking ability to retain anonymity. His most effective ploy was to dial his intended victim and bark a peremptory 'Come' when the line was picked up. His tone was ambiguous enough to confuse even the wariest of targets: usually, the conclusion reached was that it was the boss calling. The trouble was that most of us had so many that it was difficult to be absolutely certain which one it might be. As a consequence, the victim would rush into the most obvious room first. Greeted by a blank, often irritated, stare—because most bosses disliked unannounced intrusions when they were occupied with navel-gazing, practice-putting or social-calendar-finalising—he'd return to his table in confusion, his actions covertly watched by Rajesh

Mehra, the originator of the anonymous call, from behind some convenient, potted plant, or filing cabinet. Then, just as his target had begun to relax, he'd call again, his camouflaged voice, even more impatient: 'So, what's keeping you?' And off would go his victim, once again, in futile search of a boss who demanded his immediate presence but preferred to remain inconveniently incognito.

This was the tactic that was unleashed on Al Bombat, both to rattle him and also ascertain who he'd rush to for sympathy, thereby putting to rest all speculation about who was the puppet-master pulling his strings. So, one late morning, almost as soon as Al Bombat entered the Sales meeting room, the intercom trilled.

'Al,' said Bombat.

'Come, quickly,' said Rajesh Mehra.

Chaks and I loitered in the corridor, innocently.

Al Bombat rushed out of the meeting room. He stopped to look up and down the corridor. Then, as we ducked back into the Sales staff section, he bustled to the 'Executive Lift' and pressed the call button impatiently, several times, as if that would get the elevator up to him faster. He waited for it, his left foot tapping, peering through the glass from time to time, to see if he could will the lift to climb more quickly, in his agitation not realising that some things, like sundown, just can't be hurried.

'I think he's headed upstairs for Ramaswami's room,' I relayed to Rajesh Mehra. He quickly activated his sleeper agents on that floor.

When we returned to the corridor, Al Bombat had gone. A few minutes later, Mehra received a call on his intercom: a short, bald man, wearing a beard and a worried expression, had entered the executive director's room, found it empty and, now wearing a confused look, was on his way back to the Sales floor by way of the stairs.

'It *is* Ramaswami,' I informed Esbee, who nodded sagely, as if he'd known it all along as, indeed, he had.

Rajesh Mehra, in the meantime, was making his second call. 'What's keeping you? Boardroom, not my room,' he barked, much to Esbee's perverse satisfaction. He was never one for not appreciating an improvement, even if it was on something that he'd himself developed originally.

Chaks rushed into Esbee's room, looking delighted. As I recall it now, there was certainly a lot of rushing about that first day that we launched our counter-offensive.

'He's off again,' he informed us. 'Emem's in a meeting with some overseas visitors in the eighteenth floor Boardroom. I don't think he'll take too kindly to being interrupted by Al-my-pal.'

Chaks' forecast was accurate. As we heard it later from Emem's secretary, who owed a certain allegiance to Esbee, having started as his assistant before her career grew faster than his did, Manab Mazoomdar was most displeased to have had his discussions with his foreign Principals disturbed by a strange-looking man somewhat agitatedly demanding to know where Ramaswami was, as if a man of his exalted position had nothing better to do than to keep tabs on the whereabouts of his executive director. Even more galling had been the strange-looking man's insistence that he'd been called to a meeting in the Boardroom, when it was amply clear to anyone, with even the remotest of intelligences, that the only meeting taking place in the Boardroom was the one that Emem was chairing and Ramaswami was certainly not a part of it, nor anyone else whom he might have invited.

Irritated by his subordinate, Anil Pratap's, innocent query as to where he kept disappearing to, for short, unexplained bursts of time, and a little out of breath from having had to tackle the stairs twice in quick succession, Al Bombat decided to do an early lunch, from which he did not return till the next morning.

Round One was ours.

As, indeed, were Rounds Two and Three.

Action Stonewalling started in right earnest. Questions from Al Bombat and Anil Pratap were parried by counter questions. In the guise of conciseness and clarity, our answers tended to be monosyllabic. Even the most self-opinionated among us—Rajesh Mehra, for one—suddenly stopped having opinions about anything, not even whether we fancied our chances in the World Cup in England. If we were asked to hazard a guess, or speculate— usually on matters relating to who we thought was dragging the process down, or might have a hand in the till, or took favours from obliging dealers—we'd desist, saying that we didn't have the imagination for it because, if we had, wouldn't we be doing something more fulfilling than peddling pipes?

We could see the frustration building in Al Bombat because, if it was his, and his master's, intention to suggest that Emem and Raj Singh suffered from moral turpitude and were, therefore, not suited to lead an organisation as honourable as TGEPC through the last two decades of the century, they needed irrefutable evidence, irrevocable proof, or the unshakeable testimony of credible witnesses, the last being a little easier to concoct than the first two. Unfortunately for them, they were getting neither.

As the Oracle had predicted, a truce was called and it was Ramaswami who called it, hoisting, if not a flag exactly, a white handkerchief which, in the circumstances, was sufficient. Esbee was invited to his room and, over Darjeeling tea, Flury's pastries and pretended bonhomie, the first two of which he had several helpings of, requested to extend to Big Brother the proverbial hand of cooperation and, to Bombat, his own, because Al was mightily peeved, as well he had reason to be, by the treatment meted out to him, so far.

'We are entering the most critical phase,' said Esbee, sombrely, when he returned from his tea tête-à-tête. 'We have to be very careful. The last part of the operation is extremely delicate.'

As usual, we were left to wonder at his perspicacious wisdom and what the hell he was talking about.

SIXTEEN

The Last Supper

At breakfast, on the day of Surjo Sengupta's Grand Party, he decided to hold forth, at his usual length, which was considerable, on what hospitality and social graces entailed, despite my vehement protests that I had this absolutely crucial business meeting that I couldn't afford to be late for.

He dismissed my urgency with a sniff and a supercilious smile. 'I am sure your business won't run away,' he said, glibly, as though his lecture would. Sipping his second cup of Darjeeling, and smoking his first cigarette of the day, he launched into a dissertation on what it took to host the perfect party or, at least, one that would be remembered and talked about, in hushed tones of reverence, for months after it was over.

'Speaking from experience,' the party guru said, 'the first requirement is that the hosts know what their respective roles are, and play them accordingly.'

'Like a good play,' said Rita, with ersatz chirpiness.

'Precisely,' said Surjo Sengupta, like a fond teacher to a favourite pupil, the kind who always sits on the first bench, takes copious notes and raises her hand enthusiastically every time a question is asked; everything that Rita was far removed from, in her own student days.

'Where I come from, the role of the lady of the house is to circulate among the guests, make polite chitchat and ensure that the supply of food is adequate and continuous. Naturally, that part is yours.' Surjo Sengupta, playing casting director, bestowed his munificence on Rita, the expression on his face suggesting that he might have made the casting coup of the decade.

'Since I'm the official host of the party, my role is pivotal,' he continued, awarding the plum job to himself. 'It's my task to meet and greet the guests, make sure they are comfortable with each other, keep the conversation, and the liquor, flowing and, all in all, ensure that everyone's having a jolly good time.'

I was about to thank my forefathers that I had been written out of the plot when Sengupta turned a baleful eye in my direction.

'Your job is to make sure that the drinks are served properly and re-filled timely. That's of the essence. If a party has to be successful, glasses must never remain empty.'

Then, in what was nothing but a blatant vote of no-confidence in my ability to spot an empty glass, even if it were to be dangled in front of my face, and some kind of vengeance for the Dead Dipen incident, which he had obviously not forgotten, or forgiven me for, Surjo Sengupta proceeded to give a practical demonstration on what it took to spot, and replenish, a glass that needed replenishing, without making an obvious song and dance about it.

'Service is a critical component of a successful party,' Sengupta explained to me, father to idiot child. 'The best service is a service that's unobtrusive.'

Since he, apparently, had no faith in my ability to be discreet, if not altogether invisible, Surjo Sengupta proceeded to demonstrate how I would be tipped off when someone needed another drink, much to my increasing horror and Rita's enjoyment.

'Keep your eyes on me at all times,' he instructed. 'When I turn my face in the direction of a particular guest and pull the lobe of my left ear lightly, you'll know that his drink needs attention.' Not trusting me to understand verbal instructions, Sengupta acted it out, jerking a chin in Rita's direction and pulling at his left ear lobe, in dramatic exaggeration rather than studied casualness.

'What's the right ear for?' I asked, to avoid any confusion when we had to do it for real in the evening.

'That's a last resort, when I think someone's had enough and any more is going to ruin the rest of his evening,' said the party sage.

He looked pleadingly at me, willing me to use my apology of a brain to its fullest.

'Please don't confuse signals. We don't want the bar to close on people even before they've got going, ha-ha.' His attempt at levity was, somehow, lacking in conviction.

He moved on, like a coach who's done the best he can for a team at the bottom of the league table.

'I strongly suggest that the food is ordered in,' he said, as my heart sank, like an overweight stone, at the thought of the bill. 'You can get it on your way back from office. That'll leave Rita free to do up the place a little, set the table, rearrange the furniture, if required. Without any cooking smells haunting us.'

'Wonderful,' Rita said, pleased in spite of herself at not having to slave in a kitchen to feed Surjo Sengupta's motley friends.

'And costume; very, very important.' Sengupta rounded his eyes to emphasise how important he thought clothing was in the successful execution of a dinner-party; as much as it was, I thought, in staging a play, which was what this seemed to be turning into, except that this piece of supper theatre would only have actors, no audience.

'Something cool, something light. Chiffon, perhaps? And a touch of spicy perfume?' he queried, looking at Rita for endorsement of his choice for her. He turned to me, started to say something and then, changed his mind. I guessed that he'd decided to give up on being able to rescue me from the depths of my sartorial inelegance.

'I am a stickler for punctuality,' said Sengupta, as if there was anything left that he wasn't a nit-picker for, particularly if it was someone else's nit he was picking. 'I've asked everyone to come by seven-thirty. Allowing some lax for Calcutta's unpredictable traffic, I expect everyone to be in by eight. One hour for drinks, dinner served at nine, everyone out by ten-thirty and us in our beds by eleven. Makes for a perfect evening. Just like we do it in France.'

'Wonderful,' repeated Rita for want of anything better to say, speechless as we both almost were, at the precision, if not the perfection, of Surjo Sengupta's plan.

'Wonderful,' I echoed, hoping that approbation might help me escape further lecturing on exactly how things were done in Paris. Unbidden, the adage about what happens, oftentimes, to the best laid plans of mice and men, flashed through my mind; and, that too, without any interference from the likes of someone like Mrs Uma Talukdar, who could always be relied upon to put a whole new spin on things.

It was a miracle of sorts that I returned home with the food without either destroying it, or myself. The day in office had flashed by, as most days did these days, in a succession of meetings, none of which had anything to do with the commerce of selling pipes. There were updates to provide Raj Singh and Esbee, information to deny Anil Pratap and Al Bombat, diversions to waylay Romen-babu and his ilk (who had begun to suspect that something momentous was going on in the 'management class'), and speculations to conjure with Rajesh Mehra and Chaks, about what was Esbee's devious plan for Al Bombat's downfall. In the midst of all this, I could be forgiven if I were to forget which earlobe pulled in which direction signified what. But, so dramatic had been Surjo Sengupta's enactment of the morning, that I had not.

Nor, that the responsibility for picking up peas pillau, mutton do piazza, fish fry and aloo gobi curry from Teen Murti, near the TGEPC office, was, also, mine. Mounds of the good stuff, in huge dekchis that took up the entire rear, and a front bucket-seat, of my Standard Herald, were ready for me to collect at six. But, as I discovered, collection was the easy part.

The tough part was to drive all the way home, transporting dekchis that had a dubious sense of balance, inherently, without overturning them each time I braked, which was frequently, or ran over a speed-breaker lying in ambush, which was often, too. For the most part, I had one hand on the steering-wheel and the other behind me, in stunt driver fashion, holding down the lid of a utensil that contained mutton do piazza, which, I'd discovered early in the proceedings, had the greatest propensity to slosh. This securing hand was removed only to execute a nifty gear change, or to placate a dekchi of aloo gobi in the front seat, when it expressed the same tendency to spill as its non-vegetarian counterpart in the rear, which, thankfully, was not simultaneously. It was a wonder that I reached home without doing myself, or my Standard Herald, injury, navigating the streets of Calcutta, with only one hand on the steering wheel when, at the best of times, it required both, if not ten, as Goddess Durga was prone to use, on her annual visits to the city. It was an equal marvel that the only thing I spilled in the process was perspiration, not gravy.

For a feat of such dexterity, endurance and heroism, the least I expected, when I heaved the dekchis up three flights of stairs into our flat, was a nod of acknowledgement, if not open admiration. Instead, seeing my bedraggled and sweaty presence despoiling the sanctity of the party-room, which had obviously been worked upon in my absence going by the evidence of all varieties of flowers and foliage that sprouted from every conceivable nook and cranny, Surjo Sengupta gave a grimace of displeasure, the kind that one usually reserves for the lowliest of insect classes.

'Hurry up, hurry up,' he said, as one would to a particularly recalcitrant beast of burden. 'It's seven already. My guests will be here soon.'

Disappointed as I was by this greeting, his use of the personal pronoun didn't go entirely unnoticed, and I was in a temper as filthy as my appearance, when I stormed into the relative privacy of our bedroom.

'This is it,' I announced to Rita, who was trying out some clingy chiffon thing in front of a full-length mirror. 'I've had it up to here! Please don't stop me if I strangle him before the night is out.'

'You mightn't have to. Maybe someone else will do it for us and save you the bother,' said Rita, with an equability that was commendable in the face of my venomous mood. As usual, she was right.

When we re-emerged from our bedroom, which had, increasingly, become our sanctuary, Rita sheathed in chiffon and I attired in a manner appropriate, hopefully, to pass Surjo Sengupta's demanding sartorial standards, it was seven-thirty on the button.

To add insult to injury, our house guest was lounging in my favourite armchair in a white linen suit—costume, as he called it—freshly bathed and cologned, wearing a smile of smug satisfaction. He had reason to be happy. Everything was moving like a well-oiled machine, the room creatively rearranged, the food in place, the host and hostess looking suitably gracious and the barman bedecked and put in his place, in more senses of the term than just the literal. All it required for Surjo Sengupta's cup of joy to brim over was for his guests—we had begun to accept them as that—to keep to the time that he'd fixed for them.

They did not.

At eight, when no one had arrived, Surjo Sengupta lost a little of his composure. He straightened in his chair, eyes repeatedly flicking to the front door, ears attuned for the bell to ring.

'Must be the traffic,' he said, in self-consolation, when it didn't emit the tiniest of tinkles. We agreed that that, indeed, must be so.

At eight-thirty, Surjo Sengupta catapulted out of his chair, too distracted to react when I moved, with practiced deftness, to recapture it. He paced the carpet, much like he had the floor of YWCA when I'd first made his acquaintance. The same look of extreme stress displaced the smugness; a similar uncertainty, the earlier confidence.

'What's keeping them? Do you think they can't find the place?' Though rhetorical in nature, his questions were directed at Rita; I was still persona non grata.

Rita murmured something about our place being pretty simple to find, which did little to smooth his furrowed brow, let alone fill a cup that now contained next to nothing of joy.

At eight-forty five, he exploded.

'This is why nothing's ever going to change in Calcutta. No discipline, no commitment, no sense of social etiquette.'

He went on to enumerate all the things that Calcutta was sadly missing, and theorised at length on why the city's future was extremely bleak, and why those of sound mind would, ultimately, leave her shores for greener, and healthier pastures, if they, like him, hadn't already. Then, finally, he stopped in his pacing to give me a look of abject misery.

'Pour me a drink,' he said despairingly, and I leaped to throw him a lifeline because, by now, the thirst had got to me, too.

'Who needs them?' Surjo Sengupta asked, after he'd taken a long, ameliorating draw of his vodka martini, which, in the circumstances, was, certainly, less shaken, or stirred, than he was. 'We can have a jolly good party all on our own. Lots more for us to drink and eat.'

Rita, in between sips of her drink, reminded him that the amount we'd ordered, it would take us a week of eating the same food, every meal, to finish it, which mightn't keep us jolly for all that long.

At nine-thirty p.m., Surjo Sengupta was, still, far from being jolly, although he was perilously close to the bluster that comes, like a false dawn, from downing too many martinis in too short a time.

'I don't care,' he said, as if anyone did. 'It's my party and it's a party I will have.'

Though his logic was somewhat suspect, we decided against questioning it, in case it gave him cause to draw us into a meaningless argument when we were so much better off being silent, non-participating spectators.

'In another half-an-hour, Rita will serve dinner,' said Surjo Sengupta, sticking steadfastly to his original scheme, despite the disruption caused by an absence of the guests for whom his grand plan had been designed in the first place. 'We shall enjoy it. And liqueur and cigarettes, thereafter. Get out of these dressy costumes, make ourselves comfortable and chat to our heart's content. Even if someone does ring the doorbell this minute, we won't let them in. No one is welcome to Surjo Sengupta's party two hours late. Not even the Queen of England.'

The doorbell rang.

'Open the door, open the door,' said Sengupta, barely able to contain his excitement, or his voice. 'Hurry up, hurry up. What's keeping you?'

I was back to being the recalcitrant beast of burden. I got up to open the front door, while Sengupta smoothed his countenance, his linen suit and what remained of his hair and watched me with the fixed stare that a hunting lion gives its unsuspecting prey before it leaps for the kill, although, in my case, I was sufficiently forewarned, if not yet adequately forearmed.

It wasn't the Queen of England, but Mrs Uma Talukdar was a close approximation.

'Hello, darlings,' she trilled, as she traipsed into the room on a cloud of satin and scent. 'Sorry I'm late. Where's the party?'

Before I could tell her that she was looking at it, Mrs Talukdar had me in a hug that almost knocked the breath out of me, planting light, perfumed kisses on my cheeks as I struggled for air.

'Where's Usha?' I managed.

'How can one be naughty, dear boy, with one's daughter hovering around?' asked Mrs Uma Talukdar impishly, releasing me and turning her exuberance on Rita. From the corner of my eye, I saw a look of great consternation suffuse Surjo Sengupta's face. It turned to absolute horror when, done with Rita, Mrs Talukdar turned her attention on him, as he tried to make himself invisible with no real success.

'And who's this?' asked Mrs Talukdar, genuinely interested, although Surjo Sengupta, three martinis down and sans his guests, was a shadow of his usual dominating, self-confident self.

Rita made the introductions.

'A poet! How divine,' warbled Mrs Talukdar and would have clapped her hands, if it wasn't for the cigarette she was holding. Seeing that Surjo Sengupta wasn't in any hurry to get up, she plonked herself in his lap, to his utter astonishment.

'Light my fire, darling,' she demanded throatily, putting the cigarette to her lips and drawing his face close to hers with the help of a purposeful wrist.

Fumbling nervously, he did. Jouncing in his lap to his added discomfiture, Mrs Uma Talukdar drew on her cigarette and let the smoke out of her mouth in teasing trickles, her eyes never leaving Surjo Sengupta's, although he tried slipping his away, many times. Then, as unexpectedly as she had found his lap, she got out of it, leaving a lot of emotional debris behind.

'Who's fixing me my vodka-and-tonic?' she asked, with a coquettish turn of her head.

Even though I hadn't received the predetermined tug-of-left-earlobe signal from Surjo Sengupta, I volunteered, and got another hug from Mrs Talukdar in the bargain, as she settled down to make the most of a party that wasn't going anywhere in a hurry. In a stage whisper that would have reached the next neighbourhood, she turned to Rita, conspiratorially, and said: 'You should have told me that there was no party and it was all just an excuse for me to meet this dear man. A poet? I love poets because they are so sensitively vulnerable from being unpublished and unread!'

Surjo Sengupta cringed and tugged reflexively at his left earlobe signalling that his drink needed rapid refilling. I obliged.

The rest of the evening went in a blur because, each time I refilled Surjo Sengupta, Mrs Talukdar, or Rita's glass, I freshened my own. However, despite how confused some things became with the gradual, but inevitable, emptying of the vodka bottle, some others remain indelibly etched in my mind.

For one, not a single of the dozen guests that Surjo Sengupta had invited to his homecoming party turned up. Despite all his pretended nonchalance, and false bravado, that must have hurt deeply. If the fundamental reason for his return was to try and revive old ties and uncover old roots, he'd drowned testing the waters.

For another, Mrs Uma Talukdar genuinely believed, at least, that evening she did, that in his vulnerability—and Surjo Sengupta could not have been more woebegone than he was that day—lay his appeal and moved in on him, with a sense of purpose that had Sengupta's equanimity in complete disarray. After disconcerting him, with another uninhibited leap-into-the-lap performance, she withdrew a silver snuff box from her bag and, to the loud shredding of his middle-class Bengali morality, extracted from it stuff of dubious identity, which she, then, proceeded to insert into her cigarette, with great industriousness.

As Surjo Sengupta watched with mounting horror, Mrs Uma Talukdar lit up and the sweet smell of marijuana climbed for dominance over the scent of her perfume. She smoked two tokes in a row, separated by a fit of almost uncontrollable giggles, which had Surjo Sengupta squirming in his chair and seeking solace in his glass.

Seeing his discomfiture, Mrs Uma Talukdar patted him consolingly on the wrist and said, 'Don't fret, darling man, nothing ever happens to me with plain old grass,' and proceeded to prepare and smoke another, after which she went abruptly silent.

A few moments later, she let out a stifled shout: 'It's turning, it's turning.'

'What is?' I asked through my personal cloud of vodka fumes, not entirely sure whether it was a good thing or not, whatever it was that was turning.

'My head, it's spinning three sixty degrees, over and over,' said Mrs Uma Talukdar, getting unsteadily to her feet and, like an errant homing pigeon, stumbling in the general direction of Surjo Sengupta, who tracked her uncertain progress with trepidation.

'Is that a problem?' asked Rita, concerned that her only guest of the evening might soon be rendered hors de combat.

'No, that isn't a problem. I can live with my head spinning three sixty degrees, like a top,' said Mrs Talukdar, to our short-lived relief. 'But, what I can't live with is the creaking noise it makes when it spins! That's got to be stopped. O, the noise, the noise.'

I had an image of Quasimodo—Anthony Quinn, to our generation—holding his ears and rushing helter-skelter, his hunchback bowing him down to half his height, as the bells of Notre Dame tolled, unceasingly.

'Can we oil it?' I queried, impractically.

'Don't be daft, dear boy,' Mrs Uma Talukdar dismissed my suggestion without a second thought. 'The only way for the creaking to stop is for the turning to stop. The only way for the turning to stop, is for someone to hold my head rock steady.'

For someone who was several vodkas and three tokes down, her reasoning was infallible; such was the greatness of the woman.

The last and, indeed, most lasting image I have of that evening, as Rita and I prepared to give our guests the slip and sneak, hopefully unnoticed, into the sanctuary of our bedroom, is that of Mrs Uma Talukdar, sitting in Surjo Sengupta's lap, back to front, her head in the firm grip of his steady hands, smoking an unadulterated cigarette for a change, the smoke from it wafting back to water his eyes since, with both his hands occupied, Sengupta could do little to avoid it. Later, we learnt, that they'd sat in that frozen tableau until the early light of dawn when the effects of marijuana on Mrs Uma Talukdar's brain, finally, began to subside.

Over a late breakfast the next morning, Surjo Sengupta announced, with profound regret, that he couldn't continue to give us the pleasure of his company because something unexpected had come up, which required him to return to Paris post-haste and that he would be catching the train to Delhi that very evening, if we didn't have any objection, that is.

In a tone of voice that respected the significance of the occasion and the enormity of his decision, we said that we did not, although he would be sorely missed. I might have been wrong, but I thought I heard him murmur something about our loss being substantially greater than his which, if he truly believed it, meant that Mrs Uma Talukdar had had an even greater impression on him than we'd first imagined.

, On the downside, Rita served peas pullao and mutton do piazza every day, every meal, for the rest of the week.

SEVENTEEN

Crime and Punishment

'So, what are you thinking of doing?' queried Anoop Chowdhury, staring out of the window, as he habitually did, whenever he accosted a subject that he considered too delicate to handle. Outside, the first rains of the season lashed the city, like an angry, unfettered beast, growling, as its wet claws raked the streets and sent people scurrying for the safety of shop awnings and building porticos. Rainwater converted roads to rivers through which cars stumbled their cautious way, headlights glowing like fireflies in the murky midmorning, the unwary among them trapped into immobility, bobbing like buoys in the middle of the waterlogged streets, their engines flooded.

'I don't really know,' said Rahul Banerjee, with candour. 'I was thinking of giving advertising a try.'

'Advertising?' snorted Tapas Pan, the vehemence of his grunt unambiguously establishing where *he* stood on the subject. 'Why advertising?'

Rahul Banerjee had found that since he'd announced his decision to quit Rexxon, his fellow directors seemed more interested in *where* he was going rather than *why* he was parting ways with them.

'Why not?' answered Anoop Chowdhury, in Rahul's defence. 'Look at the positive side: we would have an insider in place to give us marketing research work.'

'Not very likely,' Tapas Pan snorted, having perfected the act through much repetition. 'Advertising types don't like doing research, if they can help it, in case it blows up their carefully-constructed theories about the consumer.'

'Or, is it because they suspect that research people are too concerned about keeping the marketer happy to be genuinely objective about advertising?' countered Rahul Banerjee, the ICC project still fresh in his mind and a trifle irritated by a holier-than-thou attitude from someone who, usually, kept marketing research on a back-burner, preferring to dabble in piss and alcohol instead, just because they brought in more money.

Anoop Chowdhury turned from his contemplation of the rain.

'Everyone in advertising can't be tarred by the same brush,' he said, wisely travelling the middle road. 'There are some who find substance and challenge in criticism and there are those who don't.'

'Name some who do,' challenged Tapas Pan, belligerently.

'The fact that the largest market research company in the country belongs to an advertising agency should speak for itself,' said Rahul Banerjee.

Tapas Pan emitted a grunt of derision, but refrained from joining further battle on the subject of advertising agencies and the dubious value that they attributed to research, if any at all.

However, he could not restrain himself from hurling one last weapon of intended destruction.

'Anyone who can speak English properly, dress smartly and drink heavily can be a success in advertising,' he said. 'So, there's no reason why it shouldn't work for you.'

While Rahul Banerjee was still deciding whether to take that as a compliment, albeit left-handed, or to respond with a barb of his own, Anoop Chowdhury executed a dexterous verbal feint by announcing that there was no earthly hurry to inform prospective clients—the likes of Vishal Kaushik, for instance—of Rahul's impending departure and that he'd make the news known to them, eventually, at what he considered to be an appropriate juncture.

'Till then, it should be business as usual,' Anoop Chowdhury proposed.

'Good,' said Tapas Pan, although it wasn't very clear what he was giving his seal of approval to: the proposal to keep Rahul's imminent exit a closely-guarded secret or the edict that the show must go on, as if nothing had changed.

'I haven't given up on that liquor distribution deal yet,' he said, with the tenacity of a bulldog that has a bone in its maw. 'We might still swing it, if we have another meeting with De-da where Rexxon is represented at full strength.'

Rahul groaned inwardly at the prospect of a second encounter with De-da but realised that, as long as he remained a director of the firm, he had to play by its rules. Outside, the rain continued to pelt, as if it had a point to prove, which it probably did.

'He's coming,' announced Tapas Pan, a couple of days later, reverence in his tone and worship in his eyes, as if God Himself were arriving to take stock of the situation, after seventy-two hours of incessant rain had converted many of Calcutta's roads into swollen rivers. If there was no let-up soon, the Army might need to be called in, to evacuate buildings in low-lying areas, and boats requisitioned, as they had been some years ago, to ferry stranded commuters. It was as good a time as any for Him to descend, though why He should have thought it necessary to tip off Tapas Pan about his impending arrival, Rahul Banerjee couldn't begin to imagine.

'Who is?' he asked.

'De-da,' revealed Tapas Pan. 'He's arriving tonight and has agreed to see us tomorrow morning at his office on Lower Circular Road. Saves us an outstation trip.'

'How do you keep such close track of his movements?' asked Anoop Chowdhury, not looking as pleased as he should have that a visit to Durgapur had been saved. Perhaps he had been hoping to meet Sumita of the brilliant smile again, if for no other reason but to bask in its sunshine.

'Amit Sarkar,' said Pan, smugly, referring to the chief executive of DeEn's liquor venture who, at their last meeting, had been the single-most vociferous opponent to the idea of outsourcing distribution. 'He and I have kept in touch; still can't say that we are actually friends, but we seem to be getting there.'

Tapas Pan never ceased to amaze Rahul. Only someone with his bizarre talent could establish or, even, claim, a friendship with someone who, only days earlier, had been a sworn enemy, willing to sacrifice everything, including his standing and future with De-da, to keep them out of his domain.

'Has he got his punishment?' asked Rahul, curiously.

'Not that I know of. Not till the day before when I spoke to him last. He's in Calcutta too, in advance of De-da's visit,' said

Tapas Pan, revelling in his role of keeper of DeEn's secrets or, more appositely, DeEn's travel log.

'Since you seem to know it all, what's the purpose of De-da's visit?' asked Chowdhury, still smarting at having been denied the opportunity to renew his acquaintance with Sumita and others of her sisterhood.

'A private matter,' said Tapas Pan, lowering his voice, conspiratorially, for no apparent reason that Rahul could see. Either Pan was revealing less than he knew, or he knew nothing at all and this was just his way of pretending that he did.

The next day, though overcast and dreary, was relatively dry, the periods of dryness interspersed by short, smart showers, which kept people guessing and umbrellas in business. The streets were still flooded, but the water level was subsiding on the main, arterial roads, which gave Anoop Chowdhury the courage to offer his vehicle for transport. Rahul rejoiced because it meant that he didn't have to drive, a role that was usually his, since neither Chowdhury, nor Pan, could.

Anoop Chowdhury had acquired a personal car too late in his life to want to go through the pain of learning to drive and getting a licence from the Regional Transport Office, who weren't the most accommodating at the best of times. Rahul suspected that it also had something to do with his inherent nervousness; if the slightest stress caused him to break out into prolonged sniffles, driving in Calcutta's chaotic traffic would have, certainly, caused him to breakdown more often and incur more lasting damage, if not to his body, then to his psyche, than his car.

On the other hand, Tapas Pan never tired of reiterating, particularly when a sparse marketing research order book came up for discussion, that he hadn't been able to afford one yet, so the question of his learning to drive did not arise, although that situation was poised to change, with the piss project continuing to drip its considerable largesse into the coffers of Rexxon and not needing to be split three ways for much longer. Added to that, if he could swing the country-liquor distribution deal, he'd not only *not* have to restrict his choice of vehicle to the three, measly models on offer from local manufacturers, but also *never* need to dirty his hands on a steering-wheel, either, as he'd always have a chauffeur on call. If ever there was a motivation that drove Tapas Pan to return to De-da, even after it was more or less certain that the decision to outsource distribution had been dropped, it was this: the thought of lounging casually in the rear seat of an imported car and weaving smoothly through Calcutta traffic in the capable, white-gloved hands of a white-uniformed, peak-capped chauffeur, the cynosure and envy of passing eyes, particularly those of Rahul Banerjee and his kind, whose ability to speak English, with the fluency that came from an English-language education and without the exaggerated sibilants, misplaced consonants and rounded vowels of a Bengali accent, gave them access to, and acceptance in, circles that were, currently, out of Tapas Pan's reach.

They made their way towards DeEn's office on Lower Circular Road, in sudden bursts of rain and an uneasy truce. Tapas Pan sat hunched forward in the front seat, next to the driver, and Rahul, in the back with Anoop Chowdhury, who, for the most part, kept tensely quiet, except to issue sharp instructions of caution each time he thought they'd run into an open manhole, or an inattentive pedestrian in rolled-up trousers and shoes laced around the neck for safe-keeping. Progress was slow. With water swirling around them and threatening to seep inside, or flood the carburettor, the car was in second gear for almost the entire journey, clutch half-pressed and accelerator flattened to avoid sucking in water through the exhaust pipe. They groaned their way towards their destination, the engine overheating, like Tapas Pan's temper, and clouding the windows and their spectacles, making the morning seem even drearier and more indistinct than it already was. To complete their misery, it started to rain again to coincide with their arrival at the DeEn office.

'I hope it's worth the journey,' murmured Rahul Banerjee under his breath, as they sat in the car waiting for the downpour, and their mood, to lighten.

'How do we play it?' asked Anoop Chowdhury, in nervous aftershock, still tense from the arduous, forty-five-minute navigation of Calcutta's flooded thoroughfares.

'Doesn't that depend a lot on what game De-da decides to play today?' asked Rahul, with the wisdom of past experience.

Tapas Pan glowered. Clearly, he was no longer willing to carry the cross of other people's doubts, particularly someone's who had abdicated his responsibility to the firm. If battle had to be done, he, like the boy who stood on the burning deck whence all but he had fled, was prepared to do it alone, except that he had to, first, find a way around the lake of water that separated him from the battleground. In frustration, he glowered some more.

'A little water isn't going to kill us,' he said and, in his impatience throwing caution to the winds, abruptly opened the door and stepped out to find himself knee-deep in a pothole. Stunned, he stood there, like a foreshortened shadow, the rain plastering the thinning hair on his head into wet, longitudinal, wayward strips, like black Band-aid, untidily applied. Then, soaked to the skin, he clambered out and ponderously limped in search of shelter, a wounded amphibian, water ballooning at his heels and in his wake.

Its perverse purpose served, the rain stopped as suddenly as it had begun. Under Anoop Chowdhury's continuous barrage of contradictory instructions, the driver somehow manoeuvred the car through the water and past the camouflaged potholes to the building's portico, and temporary refuge. Chowdhury and Rahul disembarked.

'You can't attend a meeting with De-da in the state you're in,' said Anoop Chowdhury, looking unhappily at Tapas Pan as he unsuccessfully tried to shake the wetness out of his clothes and finger-comb his hair into some semblance of order.

'Nothing that a pedestal fan can't cure,' said Tapas Pan optimistically, and went in search of one.

They entered the reception area of DeEn's Calcutta office. An expanse of marble ran headfirst into a glass table atop a platform of granite, behind which sat a Sumita Sister. Anoop Chowdhury brightened perceptibly. So did Tapas Pan, noticing a large fan next to the platform, aimed in no particular direction, but humming vigorously all the same. He homed in on it with purposeful strides and, reaching it, commenced a libidinous salsa, synchronous with its movements, in an effort to dry his clothes, watched wide-eyed by Sumita, who happened to be Shilpi, if the pin on her blouse was to be believed.

Politely deflecting her ritual of the DeEn salute and the accompanying 'Good DeEn' with a more conventional 'Good Morning' of his own, Rahul enquired of her when De-da would see the contingent from Rexxon, if at all, while Anoop Chowdhury simpered, in a quick return to the form he had shown in Durgapur, and Tapas Pan flapped about untidily, like something caught in high wind.

'He hasn't come in yet,' said Shilpi of the ready smile and, as it transpired, ready information. 'He's here to attend a private wedding; so, he mightn't be spending too much time in office.'

'A wedding?' Curiosity got the better of Tapas Pan. He paused in his gyrations to glance at Shilpi, his hair standing on end, not out of any excitement but only the contrary blasts of an overactive, oscillating fan. 'Whose?'

'A senior colleague of ours,' Shilpi volunteered. Obviously, there were no secrets within the DeEn family.

'Whose?' persisted Pan.

'You mightn't know him because he spends most of his time in Durgapur,' said Shilpi, dancing teasingly around the corners of the great denouement for no reason that Rahul Banerjee could determine, except that she was one of those people who had a linear and logical, but infuriatingly slow, way of getting to a conversational destination.

'Whose?' Tapas Pan's impatience was beginning to mottle his complexion with spots of red which, along with the manic gleam that it was bringing to his eyes, was sufficient cause for Shilpi to hasten to the end of *this* verbal highway. Tapas Pan, half-dried and half-fried, was not to be denied.

'One of our chief executive officers,' said Shilpi quickly. 'Amit Sarkar.'

'Amit Sarkar?' In Rahul Banerjee's experience, limited though it was, there were very few things that disturbed Tapas Pan's equilibrium. This seemed to be one of them.

'Amit Sarkar?' he echoed. 'But, I spoke to him only the day before! He didn't mention anything about getting married!'

'It was all a bit sudden,' said Shilpi, uncomfortably, perhaps beginning to realise that she had revealed more than she should have to a bunch of absolute strangers.

'Sudden?' said Rahul. 'This is like shotgun!'

Shilpi's gaze drifted beyond the three strangers crowding her desk and widened in recognition. Rahul Banerjee turned to see Amit Sarkar enter the reception area, with a timing that was almost uncanny in its precision. He strode in their direction. Several yards behind him walked a lady who, as she drew near, Rahul recognised, as one of the two women who'd been feeding De-da his lunch in Durgapur to the accompaniment of many coy looks, trilling laughs and nibbled fingers.

Tapas Pan pounced on Amit Sarkar with his customary bluntness, like a clumsy bear on an unsuspecting prey.

'Saala,' he greeted, with embarrassing familiarity, grabbing Sarkar's right hand and pumping it up and down with a vehemence that could have dislocated a shoulder. 'You've been keeping it a secret, this big news!'

For a man who'd just been united in holy matrimony, Amit Sarkar didn't seem either particularly pious, or particularly pleased. On the contrary, he looked downright uncomfortable, more so, with Tapas Pan continuing to pump his hand and showering words of congratulation, as if he had broken some long-held world record.

'Won't you introduce us to boudi?' Pan released Sarkar's hand reluctantly, as his wife of a few hours drew abreast.

Close up, boudi (elder sister-in-law) was not as young, nor as innocent, as her trilling laughs and decorous glances had made her seem in Durgapur. Distance, and the context of the occasion, had given her an advantage that proximity, and the absence of one, could not. Not that he was an expert on such matters but, despite the camouflage of cream and colour, Rahul surmised that she may have already bid goodbye to the best years of her youth.

'This is Dolly,' said Amit Sarkar, as one might, if pushed to the wall against one's will with a gun of excessive calibre rammed against one's head.

'Hello, Dolly,' said Tapas Pan, enthusiastically, flicking water from his hair in all directions, like a large dog fresh out of a shower. 'Congratulations.'

Anoop Chowdhury and Rahul extended more subdued versions of their own. But Dolly had little time for them. With a small shake of her coiffured head, where drops of rain glistened like tiny shards of glass, she swished past them and out of the reception area.

There was an uncomfortable silence. Sarkar fidgeted, Chowdhury sniffed, Pan picked at his shirt to assess how much it had dried and Rahul Banerjee wondered whether the story that was beginning to unfold in his mind was real, or just the bizarre imaginings of a blooming paranoiac. Shilpi trespassed into his impromptu contemplation of life, especially the part that had to do with the concept of crime and punishment according to De-da, by whispering that he was on his way, in a voice that left no doubt as to who *he* was.

'It's time,' said Rahul Banerjee gloomily, as if Armageddon had arrived.

Armageddon that day came in the shape of De-da in white—white shirt, white trousers, white vest, even white shoes. In sharp contrast, was the blackness of his hair which, most likely, came out of a bottle, and his mood which, probably, did as well. Despite the joyfulness that an occasion, such as the wedding of a near and dear, connoted, De-da seemed unhappy. His affliction was selectively contagious: his ubiquitous bodyguards, in obedient empathy, wore expressions as grim as the guns they carried; however, the girls who accompanied him—a different pair from the ones that had done service in Durgapur—wore their usual, dazzling smiles hoping, perhaps, that some of their sunny disposition would, eventually, rub-off on their employer, because if it did not, they would have failed in their duty, which would be a crime befitting of a punishment that only De-da could conceive.

De-da and his entourage entered the room where the Rexxon contingent and Amit Sarkar were seated. Despite the smallness of the audience, the ritualistic placement of two cigarettes, a tube of mint lozenges, a pitcher of cold water, two gold pens and an English translation of *Mein Kampf,* on a spotless blotter, had not been dispensed with. They awaited De-da, just as they had in the conference room in Durgapur.

But, today, De-da was preoccupied. While the guards and the girls took up their customary position behind him, he took his chair with a minimum of ceremony and only the most perfunctory of 'Good DeEns'. He put a cigarette to his lips and waited for one of the girls to light it for him. Then, he drew on it deeply and luxuriated in the smoke that he held back in his lungs for longer than Rahul had seen anyone do.

'Well?' he asked, looking in Amit Sarkar's direction and ignoring the Rexxon team as if it wasn't even there. 'Are you happy now?'

Amit Sarkar stumbled to his feet. A look of pure devotion suffused his face.

'Thank you, De-da. Now, I know that I'm truly forgiven,' he said, in a voice thick with gratitude and emotion. Then, he clambered out from behind the table and flung himself prostate in front of De-da's chair. De-da raised his right hand to bless him.

His genuflection completed, Amit Sarkar returned to his place, tears in his eyes and, with great deliberateness, shook Rahul's hand with both of his, then Chowdhury's and, finally, Tapas Pan's, as if he were thanking them for giving him the opportunity to sample De-da's forgiveness and the quality of his mercy.

'Bring in your wife,' summoned De-da.

As if on cue, Dolly entered and, with markedly less devotion than Amit Sarkar had shown, bowed her head in front of De-da for his benediction, which he proceeded to give, in his usual manner. However, perhaps because Rahul was watching out for it specifically, he thought he caught a touch of sadness in De-da's eyes, the kind that you might see in a father's when he's giving away a daughter in marriage or, a lover's, when he's bidding his beloved a reluctant farewell. Then, just as suddenly as it had appeared, it had gone, leaving Rahul to wonder whether he'd imagined it all.

De-da got up to go. Tapas Pan hurriedly struggled to his feet, his clothes squishing wetly, his damp face rumpling in panic.

'De-da, we haven't discussed the distribution issue yet,' he cried.

'There's nothing to discuss,' said De-da, in a voice that brooked argument only on pain of grievous assault, if not permanent damage. 'It stays in the DeEn family.'

Like everything else, thought Rahul Banerjee, including forsaken Dollys.

Tapas Pan watched, wide-eyed, wide-mouthed and slack-jawed, as De-da, his private agenda completed, and his customary jauntiness staging a gradual comeback, made for the exit, his bodyguards, both guns and girls, in tow.

'But...,' he tried one last time.

De-da stopped in his tracks. Slowly, he turned and cast a long, lingering look at Tapas Pan, damp clothes, damp hair, dampened spirits, and all. His jaw tightened. His eyes hardened. He started to say something. Then, with visible effort, he wound down and, actually, smiled, although very little of it reached his eyes.

'You are very wet,' he said and walked out the door, leaving Rahul to wonder whether he had meant 'behind the ears', or merely the obvious.

'What was all *that* about?' asked Tapas Pan, seriously confused, on the journey back to the office. It was still raining, heavier than it had been, and the water levels on the streets were rising again. 'Why were we called for a meeting in the first place?'

'Only to witness some power play,' said Rahul Banerjee. 'Not because he was re-thinking his decision about outsourcing distribution. He always meant to leave it with the company.'

'What was all that forgiving shit with Amit Sarkar about?' Subtle behaviour not being his strongest suit, Tapas Pan got particularly upset if someone else's actions weren't as obvious as his own.

'Don't you understand?' said Anoop Chowdhury, finally breaking the silence that he had immersed himself into with the arrival of De-da. 'He was administering the punishment that he'd promised Sarkar in Durgapur. Without which Sarkar would never have known whether he'd received De-da's forgiveness or not.'

'Punishment? I didn't see any of that,' blurted Tapas Pan, annoyed that he wasn't getting what the others seemed to be. 'Lots of feet-touching and blessing, but no punishment that I could see.'

'The punishment was getting Amit Sarkar to marry Dolly,' explained Rahul, patiently. Beside him, Anoop Chowdhury sniffed noisily, either because the truth, in all its embarrassing nakedness, was finally out there, or because the car had swung dangerously close to an open manhole which, if they'd hit, would have done as much damage to their bodies as the recent encounter with De-da had done to their minds.

'You call that punishment?' Tapas Pan chortled, disbelievingly. 'Pray that I should ever get so lucky!'

Then, receiving no response from his colleagues, the penny dropped, if not fully, the greater part of the way.

'I don't understand,' said Tapas Pan, just beginning to. 'Who's Dolly?'

'Dolly, I guess, is someone who became tiresome for De-da, or someone De-da tired of,' said Rahul Banerjee. 'Yet, some convoluted sense of propriety—fair play, if you will—demanded that she be looked after, economically, at least, if not emotionally, considering that she'd given some of the best years of her life to the enterprise, so to speak. And what better way to do that than to marry her off to one of your more successful, senior executives and keep it all within the extended DeEn family.'

'Saala,' breathed Tapas Pan, for once appropriately.

'Bugger,' said Anoop Chowdhury, in emphasis, but totally out of character.

Each immersed in his personal thoughts and imaginings, there was hardly any conversation for the rest of the journey. The rain continued to relentlessly hammer on the roof of the car, a staccato drum beat. The windshield wipers slapped in harmony, although they did little to improve vision, so heavy and continuous was the rainfall. Driving was reduced to guess-work, the flickering red tail-lamps of cars in front the only guide, albeit uncertain, to the road ahead.

But, at least, the car had the red tail-lights for navigation.

Rahul Banerjee had nothing. The road in front of him was unlit, uncharted, unknown. He wasn't even sure if it was there at all, and even if it was, whether it was any better than the one he had recently travelled. But, as the torrential rain flooded the streets of Calcutta, it also cleansed his mind and the one truth that surfaced, with sparkling clarity, even as they limped hesitatingly into Middleton Street, was that he was done with DeEn.

And, he was definitely done with Rexxon.

'We've arrived,' said Anoop Chowdhury, releasing his tension by unclenching his fists and his silence.

Rahul Banerjee found himself laughing, in carefree relief, even though he knew he hadn't.

EIGHTEEN

The Final Patsy

Afterwards, when it was all over and we met at Tolly on a Sunday morning, over endless pitchers of beer and platters of kebabs, we spoke of it in hushed tones and wondered, with awe and reverence, how smoothly things had actually gone when, in retrospect, it had been an operation of knife-edged uncertainty, depending as much on providence for its success as on our collective intention and individual abilities. If, on that fateful, rainy night, Lady Luck had decided *not* to smile on us, it could have blown up in our faces, with very unfortunate and lasting consequences, not the least of which would have been a one-way ticket to a professional limbo that would have made Amar Puri's unintended confinement in a pipe warehouse for a year seem like a smart career move, in comparison.

Being the only TGEPC witness to the event—other than Esbee, of course—I found myself cast in the role of Reluctant Hero although, truth be told, I had known as little about what that evening had in store for us as, perhaps, our prey. However,

I wasn't about to let a small thing like that dampen my enthusiasm for narrating the story whenever I got the chance, particularly when the role of effusive raconteur was accompanied by free beer, and adoring looks from colleagues' wives, who, at the end of it all, saw me as this Great Mastermind, busily spinning a wondrous web of mystery and mystification into which villains of every creed, colour and devilry fell, with increasing befuddlement and regularity. Much as I would have loved to believe that that, indeed, was the case, nothing was further from the truth, although my natural reticence discouraged me from contradicting people when they reached that conclusion, with only the mildest persuasion from my side.

If there was a brain behind the events of that evening, it was Esbee, although he completely disassociated himself from them, as soon as they were over. If one made the error of judgement to press him for details, he'd assume an inscrutable look and resort to the kind of expressive deep breathing that warned of dire consequences if you were stupid enough to persist with your enquiries. Even I, despite being a willing accessory before, during and after the fact, received little from him by way of an explanation as to how he'd orchestrated the whole thing and whether he'd had a contingency plan to fall back upon if our quarry had not taken the bait, or behaved differently from the way that Esbee had wanted him to.

'It was a plan based on the psychology of the individual,' was all that he'd volunteer to Chaks, Rajesh Mehra and me in the privacy of his room. We had to be satisfied with that and believe that everything had, indeed, been planned to the last detail, when I knew full well that they hadn't. But if a bit of self-delusion helped one to assume the stature of a corporate cog of consequence, I was willing to live with that.

I had just finished my morning's first cup of tea when Esbee summoned me to his room. The rain was coming down in unending sheets, which meant that the babus had forsaken their ledgers for long-winded discussions on how they would return home before all the roads water-logged, and what would be the right time for the office to shut—not too early that they should miss out on the contracted rounds of free tea and biscuits, yet not too late that the journey home should actually become difficult, with roads under water and buses and trains not plying. Three-thirty p.m. was emerging as the popular choice when I entered Esbee's office.

'It's tonight. The end-game,' he said, mysteriously. 'Are you ready for it?'

I assured him that I was as ready as I'd ever be, but I could be readier, if I only knew what I had to be ready for.

'Some male bonding,' he said, in his trademark baritone. 'I've just received a final, desperate plea from Ramaswami, to intervene immediately and correct a relationship that's gone completely off-the-rails, or so he thinks. Al-my-pal can't seem to make any progress because of what he calls "stubborn and sustained non-cooperation" from Sales. Ramaswami finds himself in an embarrassing position—which is something I can't be too unhappy about—because he initiated the study in the first place, and has been touting its importance and relevance to the Board of Directors, apparently, over their indifference to it.'

'Exactly as you'd anticipated,' I said, respectfully. A corporate prophecy of such accuracy deserved all the respect it could get.

'Thanks to all the successful stonewalling you chaps have been doing,' said Esbee, as always, willing to give credit where it was due. Then, he lit a cigarette and drew on it deeply, his eyes, and his mind, distant.

'To set-up the détente, I've proposed to Al Bombat that we meet for drinks first. At Trinca's. Catch up on some good music, a floorshow, let our hair down, talk out our differences,' he said.

'Trinca's?' I asked, surprised. 'I didn't know you cared for that sort of thing!'

Esbee smiled a mysterious smile from behind a screen of cigarette smoke. 'There's a lot that you don't know,' he said, which, I had to agree, was very true. 'There's a Patsy who comes on at ten. I believe she's quite sensational.'

Esbee was not one for loose, unsubstantiated comments. If he believed someone to be a sensation, it was only because he *knew* that they were so. Patsy had been checked out personally, there was little doubt about that.

'Al-my-pal was very hesitant about having you around,' continued Esbee. 'Said that this was something that needed to be discussed amongst like-minded seniors, that you were an interested party and, therefore, a part of the problem we were meeting to resolve. I assured him that you had my complete trust and could keep your mouth zipped, if I asked you to. Also, that I didn't drink and drive, and if we were going to make a *real* boys' night out of it, I'd want to have someone around who could drive us home, if we got plastered, as I was hoping we would. That seemed to clinch the argument.'

'Which means that, as the designated driver, I'm stuck with plain soda,' I said, morosely.

'I'm sure you can risk a beer or two,' smiled Esbee, consolingly. 'How's your police contact coming along?'

'Reasonably,' I informed him. Over the previous weeks, I had made a number of visits to Lal Bazaar and, on the excuse of TGEPC wanting to make a contribution of structural pipes for the upkeep of the Police Club, in return for some free publicity, of course ('Calcutta Police trusts TGEPC pipes. Shouldn't you?'), had struck up an acquaintance, of sorts, with P S Harold Mann. While we were still far from being buddies, we had got on to first-name terms, on a trial basis, although I was still far more comfortable with the formality of 'Sergeant' than the intimacy of 'Harold', or 'Harry'.

'What's his usual beat?' asked Esbee.

'Park Street, Calcutta Maidan, the riverside,' I answered.

'Right up our street, then,' said Esbee, satisfied. 'Tip him off to keep a lookout for us. We might have need of him before the night is through.'

And that was all that Esbee would divulge, although, later, when I re-told the story, it was as if I'd known all along what it was that Esbee had in mind and that it had really come as no great surprise when things culminated the way they did.

On the dot of eight p.m., Esbee and I were at the door of Trinca's. It was still raining, though intermittently and not half as heavily as it had been for the better part of the day. Park Street was relatively empty, the rain keeping most people indoors, except for the most hardened of drinkers and those, like us, who had their own secret missions to accomplish. The colourful neon signs bounced off the puddles on the road; directly opposite us was the YWCA, where I'd met Surjo Sengupta for the first time. It was ironical that, almost at the spot where one misadventure had begun, another was, possibly, ending.

Al Bombat was late, which was cause for some discomfort because loitering aimlessly on Park Street in the night has certain disadvantages, particularly if you are of the male gender and are unescorted by either female or family. Within minutes of our arrival, a couple of dubious-looking characters had sidled past, with the casualness of fellow window-shoppers, offering to introduce us to the kind of girls who'd make our wildest dreams come true, if only we were prepared to live them. We said that we were not. Unfazed, they suggested that we might like to study the a la carte menu, no strings attached, if for no other reason, but to marvel at the choice of wares available: white-complexioned, wheat-complexioned, dark-complexioned; English-speaking, Bengali-speaking, non-speaking; secretaries, stewardesses, singers, starlets, schoolgirls; young, mature, naive, experienced, chic, gauche; all we had to do was ask. We said that we'd rather not. With a contemptuous remark about our virility or, in this instance, the lack of it, they slithered away in search of greener pastures, leaving Esbee muttering something about the lengths to which one had to go when duty, or Raj Singh's burning bacon, beckoned.

Just about when panic had begun to lay siege, and I to wonder whether our guest had had second thoughts about a night on the town with the enemy, a yellow-and-black grunted to a stop in front of us, spewing smoke, water and, eventually, Al Bombat. He raised a hand in greeting and, with a broad buddy-to-buddy smile wreathing his features, strode in our direction, ducking his bald head under the awning of Trinca's to get away from the rain.

'Hi, guys,' he said, with exaggerated bonhomie. 'Sorry I'm late. Had a little trouble getting a taxi in this rain. As you can see, I followed your advice, Esbee. Didn't bring my car. Can't have our style cramped, can we?'

Esbee agreed that it did not do to restrict one's natural panache, particularly on an evening that cried out for excess. With that, and a lot of heavy back-slapping from Al Bombat, we entered Trinca's.

We were assaulted by a high wave of sound and a low cloud of cigarette smoke. From the small entrance lobby, there were two paths that you could take: one, the left, took you to a bar around which was festooned a semi-circle of high-hipped barstools, most of them occupied by people who preferred liquid sustenance over everything else. Not for them the distractions of food and music; the sight of alcohol being poured in front of your very eyes with hardly a moment's delay between your asking for it and it being served, was heaven, or as close to it as you could get without travelling six foot under, in a box.

The other, on the right, took you to a larger room where you could drink, dine and, of course, see the floorshow. For that main event, there was a dais raised high enough for everyone in the room to get an unrestricted view.

As we entered and stood uncertainly in the lobby, we were taken custody of by someone called Michael, who wore a tuxedo, somewhat frayed at the sleeves and an ingratiating smile, somewhat frayed at the edges. He guided us to a table close to the dais—'for the best view in the room', he confided—and rushed off to get us our first drinks. At my order of soda, Al-my-pal shouted, to make himself heard above the noise of a group called 'The Flintstones' performing an exceptionally enthusiastic version of *I'm not a stepping-stone*, that I'd better stop being a party-pooper and switch to Scotch, like everyone else, if I knew what was good for my health, ha ha.

We settled into our chairs as, almost by magic, whiskies appeared before Al Bombat and Esbee, and a glass of iced soda before me, with a slice of lemon swimming smoothly on its surface. With an energetic clinking of raised glasses, we toasted to our, and TGEPC's, health and to a new, improved beginning to our relationship. 'The Flintstones', in empathy, switched to *I'm a believer*.

Esbee had, no doubt, taken good care of both Michael and our waiter in advance, for they spent almost their entire watch hovering attentively at our table, making sure that there were no unnecessary pauses in our drinking and that one drink always flowed seamlessly into the next. Esbee was at his magnanimous best: platters of mixed kebabs accompanied each round and, before long, I'd graduated to beer trusting that frequent visits to the toilet would keep my head sufficiently clear for the drive back home, irresponsibility at one end compensated by responsibility at another.

I don't think many differences got ironed out that evening, or were even discussed. The wall of sound that 'The Flintstones' created, moving with equal energy, if not ability, between 'The Monkees' and 'The Rolling Stones', discouraged any conversation that required more than hand gestures or monosyllabic shouts. From time to time, Al Bombat would lean towards Esbee, conspiratorially, and whisper at length into a proffered ear but, going by the whooping laughter that he'd succumb to immediately thereafter, and the pained expression that would cross Esbee's face, I guessed it wasn't corporate confidences that he was sharing, only the latest off-colour jokes. The number of times he leaned into Esbee increased with the number of whiskeys he consumed, until Al Bombat froze into a permanent tilt out of which he emerged only when an MC announced, with manufactured exuberance over a rising roll of drums, that the moment that we'd all been waiting for had finally arrived and that the one and only Miss Patsy would now put in her appearance.

'Boss,' said Al Bombat, reverting to type and the comfort of the language he'd been born to, with the approach of drunkenness. 'Jum gaya hai.'

Esbee agreed that it, indeed, had frozen to perfection which, loosely translated, meant that it couldn't get any better than this.

The house-lights dimmed, plunging the room into night and converting people into indistinguishable silhouettes. An anticipatory sigh coursed through the room, like a charge of electricity. The anonymity that the darkness provided encouraged the more uninhibited among the audience to emit whistles and hoots of 'C'mon Patsy, do your thing'. These soon trailed into fitful silence, to the accompaniment of embarrassed laughter and nervous coughs.

We waited, Al Bombat fidgeting in impatience, slurping whiskey in anticipation.

Then, suddenly, a single beam of light came on and bounced across the dais, as if desperately seeking something. Out of the darkness, drums rolled, booming to a deafening crescendo. With their final crash, a guitar twanged to life. To its sinuous play, Miss Patsy shimmered onstage. The audience went into a frenzy of applause. Al Bombat jumped to his feet. Even in the gloom I could see the beads of perspiration on his bald head, glistening in the overspill of the stage lights.

Miss Patsy was truly sensational. She was lean, tall and toned. The sheer black skirt and top she had poured herself into clung to her like a sheath, emphasising every curve in her body. When she turned, the audience gasped; her blouse ended, where no self-respecting blouse should have, exposing the naked, tightly-toned expanse of her back, tiny muscles rippling under the surface of her fair skin.

'Jum gaya hai,' repeated Al Bombat, awe constricting his vocabulary, and his voice, as Miss Patsy undulated and shimmered before our table, close enough to touch. Michael had promised us the best view in the room and, indeed, it was.

Her face serene and contented, in sharp contrast to the sensuous gyrations of her body, Miss Patsy proceeded to divest herself of some of her excess clothing, to the accompaniment of drum-rolls that emanated anonymously, but appropriately, out of the dark. First to go were her elbow-length, black gloves, one glove at a time, slowly peeled off one arm, then the other, hanging to the tips of her fingers, as if for life, and then, wafting to the wooden floor, like dead, autumn leaves. Done with the gloves, Patsy turned her back to the audience and stepped, teasingly, out of her little black skirt, one long, reluctant leg at a time, posing to beam buttocks, in frilly, white panties, at an appreciative audience, before swivelling to face us again, her hands climbing to her black blouse to play shyly with its buttons.

Al Bombat was breathing with difficulty and, despite the several drinks he'd downed, his voice, when it emerged, had the rasp of a match being lit.

'Jum gaya hai, boss,' he whispered hoarsely, at a loss for anything new to say.

Onstage, Miss Patsy, her tongue lasciviously licking her lips, proceeded to pop the buttons on her black blouse, in sync with the thud of a bass drum and howls of 'Do it, do it' from an audience that had found its voice, but lost its balance.

Miss Patsy glimmered and shone in the focused spotlight. She swayed languorously and rippled out of her blouse. Then, she stood there in front of us, rising above our table, all five feet eight inches of her, in white brassiere, frilly panties and high heels, the sweat glistening on her skin, and a myriad hidden muscles tensing and releasing below it, as if she were winding down from a hard-run race. She twisted around, a wide expanse of back directed at an audience that, by now, had lost both its balance and its voice. She clasped herself in a tight embrace, long fingers stroking the clasp of her brassiere, painted nails flashing a warning that no one was in any mood to heed. The drum-roll started, surging towards a climax. Beside me, Al Bombat was statue-still, mumbling hoarsely what I thought was an incantation for her to turn, turn, turn.

With a click that matched the sharp intake of the audience's collective breath, Miss Patsy undid the clasp of her brassiere; her legs splayed, her back to us, still. Then, to a loud crash of cymbals, she twisted to face us and, before our eyes could even begin to adjust to the new image, all the lights went out and we were plunged into pitch blackness, our retinas retaining the last impression they'd registered—that of a white bra unfastening.

A buzz of inconsequential small talk, and an epidemic of dry coughs, broke out when the lights came back on. The dais was empty, as were our glasses. And so were we.

Al Bombat was a further two whiskeys down and I had graduated from beer to vodka-tonic when, at a pre-arranged signal, Michael rushed to our table and held a long, whispered conversation with Esbee, the hushed tones and expressive hand gestures suggesting that a special dispensation was under hard negotiation.

'Only for you, sir,' said Michael, finally, palming a few crisp notes of unknown denomination and hurrying off with the air of someone who had just granted a concession that had the potential to alter lives, if not change them irrevocably.

'Well?' asked Al Bombat, turning to Esbee, eyes brimming with anticipation and voice with hope.

'Patsy's agreed to spend some time with us,' announced Esbee, importantly, as if he'd secured an exclusive commercial franchise which, in a fashion, he had.

'Maan gaye, ustad,' slurred Al Bombat, his hand searching for a non-existent drink. If the table hadn't obstructed him, he might have fallen prostrate at Esbee's feet, in genuflection to someone whom he'd begun to acknowledge as being vastly superior to anything that he could, ever, hope to be.

'As long as we behave ourselves,' warned Esbee.

'Whatever you say, boss,' said Al Bombat, acquiescing to keep a disorderly libido in check, an easy choice when, in his current state of priapic disarray, he was willing to commit his very soul to the devil.

At the stroke of midnight, as 'The Flintstones' completed a last, lacklustre set, Esbee signalled that it was time for us to leave. Obediently, under cover of the relative obscurity of dimmed house-lights, we followed him to the adjoining bar where Patsy was waiting. She'd changed from the clothes she'd undressed in to a more modest blouse-and-skirt outfit and was lounging on a bar-stool, lazily sipping a glass of what looked like strawberry milkshake.

'You were simply sensational,' said Al Bombat in greeting, although, in his condition, it might have made for clearer communication if he hadn't attempted so many sibilants.

'Thank you, sweetheart,' she said huskily, making his night. 'So, what do you have in store for me?'

Though her question implied the use of a collective pronoun, her eyes were directed at Al Bombat alone. Under her smouldering gaze, he sizzled to silent ash.

'I thought we'd get a breath of fresh air,' interjected Esbee, to rescue us from an uncomfortable silence. 'Take a drive down to the river; get ourselves some ice cream at Gay.'

Patsy pursed her glossy, red lips and gave a whistle of girlish delight. 'I love ice cream,' she said and unhitched her bottom from the bar-stool with an exaggerated swivel of her hips. 'So, what are we waiting for?'

Despite the beer and vodka-tonics, I was still thinking pretty clearly but, somehow, I wasn't making much sense out of what I was thinking. Throughout the evening, I'd been following Esbee's signals blindly; most of them had to do with replenishing drinks, or slipping the waiter enough currency to keep him by our table more or less permanently, or distracting Al Bombat whenever he leaned too far into Esbee's personal space. Now, when he motioned that I should get the car, I went to do his bidding automatically, although I couldn't help thinking that, if this was his idea of an end-game, I couldn't even tell whether it had begun, leave aside know where it was heading, or how it would end. Of course, in later re-telling, I'd always maintain that I had had his full confidence from the very start.

Thankfully, the rain had slackened to a soft drizzle and my Standard Herald, temperamental at the best of times, growled to life at the first turn of the ignition. I cruised to a halt on the side street next to Trinca's. Within minutes, Esbee emerged, followed closely by Al Bombat and Patsy, his arm around her waist proprietarily, either because he needed her close support to steady his steps, or she was too tall for him to be able to reach her shoulders or, probably, both.

I flipped the front seat forward and Patsy climbed in with a flash of leg and an indulgent cry of 'Naughty boy', as a straying Al Bombat hand nudged her derriere, propelling her in at a speed faster than she'd intended. Bombat followed and collapsed next to her, the proprietary arm around the waist replaced by an equally-possessive beard on her chest.

'Drive,' commanded Esbee, climbing in.

I did.

The tyres whispered on wet, empty streets. The rain fell like a veil of thin, diaphanous mist and the windshield wipers danced to the cadence of its soft, unhurried beat. Despite my best intentions, my eyes kept getting inexorably pulled to the rear-view mirror. Beside me, Esbee maintained a stoic silence, chain-smoking, and letting the smoke out in an unending trail through an intentional gap in the window.

We'd almost reached the riverside when a playful shriek of 'Very, very naughty' came from behind. Al Bombat, unable to restrain himself any longer, had made his move. In the rear-view mirror, I caught a flurry of limbs as, with the single-minded focus that comes, sometimes, from drinking too much whiskey, Al Bombat drew himself up, as straight as he could in the confines of a Standard Herald, and planted a long, wet kiss on Patsy's lips. Seeing little resistance coming from her and, on the contrary, reading encouragement in the sea of giggles she drowned him in, he clambered on top of her, as comprehensively as the constricted space allowed, and let his hands roam, like carefree roustabouts, all over her while continuing to suck, hungrily, at any exposed body part that his undiscriminating mouth happened to meet during its travels.

I glanced apprehensively at Esbee. His rigid profile instructed me to concentrate on my driving.

As I was pulling the car to the side of the road next to the Hooghly river, a high-pitched wail, an amalgam of shock, despair and disgust, rent the silent air, sending shivers down my spine. My first thought was that Al Bombat, in the throes of unbridled passion, had done Patsy some grave, irreversible damage. Then, in a millisecond, I realised, it wasn't so: it was Al-my-pal who was doing all the screaming, not Patsy.

'Saala, bahinchhod,' he howled. 'Yeh lauda kahan se aaya!'

Which, loosely translated, meant that Al Bombat, suddenly shorn of all his drunkenness, was demanding to know what bastardly, sister-fucking concatenation of unholy circumstances had given Patsy a penis.

The next moment, he was drumming desperately on the back of Esbee's seat, wanting to get out, and Patsy was slapping him across the face and on the side of his perspiring, bald head, screaming epithets that cast serious doubt on the legitimacy of his birth and the potency of his manhood.

Amidst all this confusion, a flashlight suddenly switched on, flooding the interior of the car with bright, naked, all-revealing light and a grim voice that I recognised to be Police Sergeant Mann's, hollered from the shadows:

'What's this? What's going on?'

Al Bombat cowered. Patsy hurried to straighten her blouse, and her features. Then, she tugged at her skirt in a show of modesty that was, sadly, a little too late in coming for Bombat, who cowered some more, the light from P S Mann's torch washing his face, but not quite able to wash away his shame.

I got out of the car and took P S Mann aside, in an apparent attempt to appease his deeply-disturbed sensibilities. Esbee joined me and we all stood around in the misty rain for a while. It was a beautiful time of night. Calcutta was fast asleep, though the Hooghly river wasn't, lapping at its shores with quiet persistence. We were pretty wide awake, too.

Esbee and I returned to the car.

'There's nothing I can do,' Esbee told Al Bombat, regretfully. 'He wants to arrest both of you. Indecent behaviour and, possibly, violation of every Obscenity Act in the book.'

'Please...,' said Al Bombat, plaintively. 'Do something.'

'Bastard,' muttered Patsy, delivering a final slap to Bombat's unresisting, defeated back.

We returned to where P S Mann bestrode his trusty mechanical steed. We stood around some more, listened to the river and felt the rain-mist on our faces. Then, we thanked him for his unstinting cooperation and bade him a very good night, promising to take good care of the Police Club and hoping to share a drink, or two, with him there, in the imminent future.

'We've managed to hold him off from pressing charges for another twenty-four hours,' said Esbee, mopping his brow as if he'd just won a hard-fought battle, although it was only the rain that he was wiping away. 'Maybe we'll get him to drop charges, I really can't say.'

'Thank you,' said Al Bombat, packing more emotion into two words than I'd have believed possible. I'm sure that he would have paid more elaborate obeisance if the confines of my Standard Herald had permitted it. For him, Esbee was a saviour descended from heaven although, in the light of recent events and P S Harold Mann's torch, it was a different heaven from the one that he'd thought he'd been in when he first laid lips on Miss Patsy.

We readied for the journey home. Al Bombat expressed a strong resistance, bordering on extreme paranoia, to sitting next to Miss Patsy which, in the circumstances, was hardly surprising. We accommodated him. We thought it was the least we could do.

Miss Patsy took the front seat next to me as we started back. She said something about not having got the ice cream that she'd been promised. I told her that no one served ice cream at one-thirty in the morning and that it shouldn't really matter since we'd all, certainly, got more than we'd bargained for tonight. I didn't hear anything from my passengers, not then, or for the rest of our journey, but if silence also means consent, then, I guess, they must have agreed.

At a hurriedly-convened meeting of the Sales team the next day, Ramaswami, the executive director, with Raj Singh standing, importantly, by his side, informed us that he'd given the matter of outside consultants advising us on how to run our business, a great deal of thought. His investigation had led him to conclude that there existed enough talent and skill within TGEPC to address the sternest of problems, and the toughest of challenges; on second thoughts, which often were so much better than the first (*ha ha*), he was of the view that the company could well do without external consultants who, besides costing an arm and a leg (*ha ha*), would never quite understand, or internalise, the unique way we ran our business. Therefore, he proposed to cancel the BBC study (*mild applause*); instead, a Task Force (*initial caps intended*), comprising officers from Sales and Works, would be set up soon, which, under the able stewardship of Mr Samar Bose, Esbee to most (*thunderous clapping*), would investigate all aspects of our business and formulate a plan to meet the competitive challenges ahead, for the approval of the Board of Directors. And, in case any of us were wondering whether the company would lose money cancelling BBC's contract mid-way, it wouldn't: a thorough professional, Mr Aloke Bombat fully appreciated our concerns and had already volunteered to refund the retainer we'd advanced his firm (*appreciative applause for Al-my-pal Bombat*).

After Ramaswami excused himself from the customary round of tea and biscuits, pleading that he was late for another appointment, a thoroughly pleased, but completely confused, Raj

Singh informed Esbee that, earlier in the morning, a very subdued-looking Anil Pratap had arrived at his doorstep carrying a copy of a personal letter from Al Bombat for Ramaswami. In it, Bombat had written, in somewhat ambiguous prose, that an unexpected conflict of interests had arisen, which militated against BBC continuing with the TGEPC study. Regretfully, therefore, he was resigning the commission; a refund cheque for the fifty percent retainer fee advanced to BBC was enclosed. He hoped that this would, in no way, affect the cordial relationship that existed between BBC and the Management of TGEPC, nor stand in the way of their doing business in the future. Yours sincerely, Al.

'What interests are conflicting?' asked Raj Singh, ingenuously.

Esbee deftly evaded the question suggesting, instead, that it could be one of the issues the proposed Task Force was asked to investigate when it was eventually set up.

'Is it important?' asked Raj Singh and heaved a sigh of relief when Esbee assured him that it was not.

Later in the evening, with the rain beginning to pelt again, I suggested to Rita that the way things had panned out recently, not the least of which was getting back our spare bedroom after many weeks of siege, a celebratory Bloody Mary, or two, might not be out of order.

'So, what happened last night?' she asked. I hadn't yet had a chance to tell her about the final patsy. I was intending to, but not until I'd consumed my first BM.

'We won,' I told her.

'Good for the good guys,' she said in a congratulatory tone, getting up to watch the rain.

'I'm not so sure anymore,' I said.

EPILOGUE

After the Storm and Before the Next

T he glory of our victory over the wicked forces of external management consultants was short-lived. What the unholy alliance of Ramaswami and Big Brother failed to achieve by its rather rough, ready and obtrusive methods, a change in TGEPC's shareholding did, less than a year later, with insidious inevitability. It breached our defences, as if none had ever existed, leaving even The Oracle nonplussed and floundering, as much a helpless spectator as any of us lesser mortals. In a deal done in some remote tax haven, one shareholder sold out to another and, with one stroke of a Mont Blanc, abdicated its responsibility to the company, and the management team that it had once installed. Cut adrift in an uncharted sea, Emem and Raj Singh, the torchbearers of the Old Order, who weren't the best of navigators even when all their compasses were functioning correctly, soon started losing their bearings, and their way. As their boat started wheeling around in endless circles, and taking in copious amounts of water, all that someone had to do was to throw them a rope which, in their frenzy to save themselves from drowning, they'd have readily strangled themselves with.

Someone did, enough to set the stage for a double hanging, although Emem did try to delay his own by making one last attempt to disassociate himself from Raj Singh, blaming him, entirely, for the deficiencies of the Sales division. In this, he was only partly successful because no one could quite believe that Raj Singh had the ability to achieve so much, even *failure*, all on his own.

One of my last, onerous responsibilities in TGEPC was to draft Raj Singh's resignation. After spending some months doing nothing, except staying out of everyone's way in the limbo where senior executives who've outlived their usefulness, are sent, Raj Singh told me, in the confidence of the Management toilet, which we all now had freer access to, as part of the New Order's philosophy of equality, that he'd had enough of this humility (I guessed he meant 'humiliation', but I was not about to correct him in the state of humbleness that I found him in, both figuratively and, with his pants down, literally. I was happy that Chaks was not around to keep count on someone who had, sadly, counted himself out altogether).

I promised him a humdinger which, I think, he believed was something you did when you didn't know the words to a song, or something you ordered when you wanted a quick bite, because he gave me a very strange look before he collected his composure, and his trousers, and quit the toilet.

In retrospect, Raj Singh's resignation letter was one of my more memorable achievements in TGEPC; I truly believe that it got him the farewell dinner that he'd given up on completely. (After all, Emem didn't get his, a month later.) Its success may also have had a little bit to do with the fact that, for once, something that I'd written for Raj Singh was delivered exactly in the fashion it was meant to be, since he didn't have to speak it.

While Emem and Raj Singh were floundering in a sea of misery, mostly of their own making, Ramaswami was trying to ingratiate himself with the New Order by singing like a canary, mostly the same song—about a miserable management and the myopia that it wouldn't correct, despite his sincerest persuasions. He even tried to drag in Al Bombat to provide backing vocals; for some reason that he was never quite able to fathom, Al ceased to be his pal, and refused. For his troubles, Ramaswami was given a posting to another Group company where he personally prospered, although the enterprise he headed, didn't, as a consequence of which, he was soon shown the door.

Rajesh Mehra became very popular with the New Order, to start with. He was seen as a bridge between the old and the new, his caustic irreverence, a criticism of the way things had been run, his inherent capabilities, the way they could be made to. Unfortunately, he became so enamoured of his role of amusing chronicler of other people's tales, and its attendant adulation, that he stopped wanting to write any stories of his own. So, when he'd been drained of all the tales that he had to tell, he was relegated to a marginal position, where he continues to this day, sans his humour, sadly.

The New Order was ideal for the method and diligence of a Chaks, just as it was *not*, for the intelligence, and individualism of a Rajesh Mehra. Within months, Chaks had been identified as a rising star and was being treated as such, rotated between functions and given added responsibilities, all of which he executed with competence, if without brilliance. The last I heard, he was tipped to head the company that Ramaswami had almost run to the ground, before fleeing for a job that offered an even bigger salary and perquisites and, possibly, greater opportunities to amass personal wealth. I am sure that Chaks will be a huge success in whatever corporate assignment he takes up, although his mathematical abilities might get a little blunted, without the practice of keeping count of Raj Singh's malapropisms.

The saddest for me was the fall of The Oracle. Despite being wooed vigorously by the New Order to take over the charge that Raj Singh was about to surrender, he refused to play ball, either out of some archaic and, possibly, misplaced sense of honour, or an unfortunate ego that would not permit him to pay even the slightest respect to some unknown and untested Turk who'd replace Emem. In constantly rejecting its advances, Esbee played himself into a tight corner with the New Order from which the only escape was his own resignation. Thankfully, I didn't have to write it.

But I did have to write my own, not that there was no place for me in the new scheme of things, but because I had suddenly been seized by a wanderlust that wanted to take me in directions that I'd never been in, and paths that I hadn't known existed, let alone travelled. For some reason, the business of pipes had lost its charm, not that it had had a great deal to start with. But what it had had were colleagues who'd become intimates, bosses who'd become friends and events that would remain the happiest of memories. I wasn't about to let any of that change. Under the New Order, I knew that they must.

Just as they had, with Dirty Harry Mann after our shared adventure, at midnight, by the river Hooghly. And with Surjo Sengupta, whom we never heard from ever again, not even a card from Paris on Bastille Day, after the dead Dipen incident and the party to which no one whom he'd invited, came, except Mrs Uma Talukdar, whom he hadn't.

So, when I stepped into the bar of Calcutta Club for my interview with a respected elder of the advertising fraternity, exactly a year to the day that Ramaswami had called off the hounds of BBC (or so he thought), my resignation from TGEPC was already composed in my mind. When I stepped out, many vodka-tonics later, with an appointment letter that had been handwritten in the middle of our discussions and the gaps in our drinks, my resolve was doubly strengthened. Sure, it had something to do with my now having a job to fall back upon; but, truth be told, it had a great deal more to do with the fact that the doyen, in parting, had confided to me that the single-most important factor in my appointment was the fact that I had a round face similar to his. If ever I had heard an argument to sway me, it was this.

In the foyer, there was someone waiting, nervously. He, too, had a round face. The round-faced ones seemed to be taking over, if not the world, at least Calcutta Club.

In the mood of bonhomie that several vodkas, and a comforting appointment letter, impart, I approached him and introduced myself.

'Waiting to see the Old Man?' I asked.

'Yes,' he said a trifle edgily. It was apparent that he'd been waiting a long time.

'Don't worry, I've left him in a good mood,' I assured him. 'By the way, I didn't quite catch your name.'

'Rahul. Rahul Banerjee,' he said.

Then, wishing him loads of luck, I took my first steps towards a new beginning.